Return to Sender

Return to Sender

A Novel

Ann Slegman (signature)

Ann Slegman

HELICON NINE EDITIONS
KANSAS CITY, MISSOURI

All rights reserved under International and Pan-American Copyright
Conventions. Published by the Midwest Center for the Literary Arts, Inc.,
P. O. Box 22412, Kansas City, Missouri, 64113.

Excerpts of this book have been published in
Helicon Nine, The Journal of Women's Arts and Letters.

Partial funding for this project has been provided by the
National Endowment for the Arts, a federal agency, the Missouri Arts
Council and the Kansas Arts Commission,
state agencies, and by the N. W. Dible Foundation.

Cover and Book Design by Tim Barnhart

Library of Congress Cataloging-in-Publication Data

Slegman, Ann, 1954-
    Return to sender / by Ann Slegman. -- 1st ed.
        p.   cm.
    ISBN 1-884235-10-7 (paper : acid-free)
    I. Title.
PS3569.L358R47   1995
813' .54--dc20   94-46360
                                                                      CIP

First Edition
Printed in the United States of America
HELICON NINE EDITIONS

To my parents
To Tom, Kate and David
and
To Gloria, who always knew

Love is dead in us
if we forget
the virtues of an amulet
and quick surprise.

—Robert Creeley

Contents

Prologue

The Stockbroker & the Mardi Gras Queen

Roxanne couldn't believe that everything had come to this. She had always had a deep and abiding belief that her life would someday be normal. In her grade school classes, she would watch all the Susies and Kimberlys sitting up in class, raising their hands when they knew the right answers, writing large, neatly-shaped letters in their Indian Chief tablets. Roxanne would vow to herself: *Someday I will be like them. I will not fall asleep during a spelling bee. I will not throw up on my desk. I will not sneeze on myself. I will not do all the things that I do to make me stick out. I will blend in and drink milk out of a carton like everyone else.* More than anything else, Roxanne wanted what she called a swim team nose—the kind that scooped up at the end like the nose of a Santa's elf from doing all those racing dives. Her own nose hung like an unhinged shower nozzle, hovering too close to her mouth so that when she took big bites of a hamburger, she had to breathe out so that she wouldn't inhale pieces of bun. Since her parents didn't belong to a country club—they were indifferent to all activities that involved sunshine and balance—Roxanne would spend hours in her bathtub, smacking her nose again and again in water to make it turn up. Besides, Roxanne felt that her parents didn't need to belong to a country club to relax or relieve tension; both of their bodies seemed to just float around the house anyway. Sometimes Roxanne imagined that if their house ever did fill up with water—like in one of those huge fish aquariums she once saw in Florida—that life would go on as it always had.

Throughout her childhood, Roxanne remembered her mother doing one of two things—vacuuming or napping. Roxanne loved to watch her mother nap on the sofa—her feet would curl around the arm cushions, and her mouth and nostrils would flare out in tiny, hushed snores. In kindergarten, Roxanne was asked by her teacher what her parents did for a living. Roxanne said that her father was a businessman, and her mother napped. The following day, her mother got a phone call from the principal of Roxanne's school, asking her if everything was all right. Roxanne remembered the long, sad look her mother gave her after she hung up the phone. For two weeks, Roxanne saw her mother awake more than at any other time in her life.

When Roxanne's mother vacuumed, she would simply stand in the middle of a room, stare glassy-eyed in front of her and move the sweeper back and forth. It was as if vacuuming were some form of meditation, or that it gave her X-ray vision so that her eyes could penetrate the living room walls, allowing her to spy on the next door neighbors. Sometimes Roxanne's younger brother, Gus, would emerge from his bedroom, wave his hand in front of his mother's frozen face and then, without breaking his pace, head for the kitchen to get a handful of potato chips. Only Gramma could make Roxanne's mother aware of the fact that there were dust balls accumulating in spots other than the one she was vacuuming.

It was Gramma who gave Roxanne's mother a semblance of stability. Gramma's husband, who had had his own copper wire company near New Orleans, died shortly after their daughter, Emma, was born and left Gramma a sizable income that would keep her comfortable for the rest of her life. Gramma's one wish in life was to make sure that Emma never had a day of suffering. (Roxanne's mother always seemed to be suffering from some unknown cause, so Gramma's one wish was never fulfilled.)

Emma was a Southern beauty in every sense of the word, tall and reed thin with naturally blonde hair that she parted on the side. She also had a fragile kind of grace that people instinctively responded to and that also made them want to protect her.

When Emma was a teen-ager, Gramma wanted to get her elected queen of their small town so that she could ride on one of the floats in the Mardi Gras. Gramma liked telling Roxanne how she made Emma walk around with an almanac balanced on her head and taught her how to wave with her hand cupped. Then Gramma would pull from a high shelf in her closet a box filled with plastic bracelets and coins, bits of rotting elastic, and yellow snap shots of her daughter in a white satin dress riding on a float of white gardenias. Roxanne was fascinated, but at the same time, repulsed by how beautiful her mother was and how indifferent she was to everything around her. Even in the photographs, she had the same glazed look that she had when she vacuumed, as if she were capable of counting all the molecules in the air around her.

After Emma's high school graduation, Gramma developed acute asthma and was determined to move up north where she thought she could breathe more easily. She liked the idea of Kansas City because she had read somewhere that some developer in the twenties had built the first shopping center in America there called the Plaza. She had seen a picture of it in a magazine, and it looked Spanish because it was modeled after the city of Seville. And even though the Plaza wasn't the French Quarter, it seemed as though it had an air of worldliness, and that was good enough for Gramma. When they moved to Kansas City in 1950, Emma had just turned eighteen. They rented a two-bedroom bungalow off Ward Parkway—a short drive from the Plaza, which Gramma considered to be the Midwestern Mecca of sophisticated living. Gramma wanted the best for Emma and wanted her to marry well. She enrolled Emma in the Kansas City Secretarial School, hoping she would capture the heart of whomever she worked for. Emma never learned to type well or take dictation or short hand (she had always been indifferent to any form of work), but the teachers were so entranced with this other-worldly creature that they sent her to interview at a prestigious stock brokerage firm called Stern Brothers.

At that time, James Freedman was a hard-working stock broker at Stern Brothers, trying to make a name for himself in the business and to get promoted to vice-president. The minute he was introduced to Emma, he knew that she was not cut out to be a secretary, but for some reason, he wanted to hire her anyway. He remembered telling a fellow broker that her beauty and her extraordinary incompetence were a deadly combination for him. James was what some would call a perpetual bachelor, settled in his ways, but not necessarily the womanizing type. Yes, he did have dates—everyone seemed to fix him up with all the eligible Jewish women in town—but rarely would he bother to call them again. All those women seemed too brash, too sure of themselves, and he felt as if they were going to eat him up alive. Emma was the only woman he had ever met who made him feel strong and less like the shy bachelor who went home alone every night and heated up cans of vegetable soup in the one pan he owned.

Day after day, James watched Emma turn out misspelled memos and inaccurate sales orders, and his passion quietly grew for her. A few weeks before Christmas of 1951, he went out during his lunch hour to The Peanut, a bar near the Plaza, and downed a couple of scotches on the rocks. He ordinarily never drank during lunch hour, but he knew that he had to be a little tipsy to get up the courage to do what he had to do. He then drove down to Tivol jewelry store and picked out a one-and-a-half carat diamond engagement ring. When five o'clock rolled around, he pulled Emma aside and told her gently that he had to let her go but would she consider marrying him. Emma said yes, and then proceeded to cry the entire way home in James's car. James was never quite sure whether she was crying from happiness or because she felt humiliated about being fired.

At first James's parents were not thrilled with the idea of his marrying a non-Jewish girl, but like everyone else they were very much taken with this graceful and soft-spoken young woman. They arranged for a city judge to marry Emma and James in a simple ceremony in their elegant Tudor home. Gramma liked James (she would have liked anyone Emma married as long as he was a decent sort and able to support her properly), and James respected Gramma, knowing that somehow she understood Emma better than anyone else, better than he ever hoped to understand her. He knew that by marrying Emma he was committing himself to Gramma, too, so when he looked for a house to buy, he bought one with a third floor so that Gramma could move in with them. After Emma and James had been married a year, he was promoted to vice-president of Stern Brothers. The night of his promotion, Roxanne was conceived.

Part I
1966-68

1

Elvis & Aspirin

By the time Roxanne was in eighth grade, she knew that she was homely but not pathetically so. Yes, it was true that her hair was blah brown—the exact color of her pet hamster's coat. Her arms and legs were thin and pale. She bit her nails down to the quick. And she was still *especially* embarrassed about her nose.

But she realized that there were kids who were much worse off than she was—like Lisa Labinovitz who pulled her eyelashes one at a time and would eat them during class, or Eugene Peterson who always smelled of hand lotion and spoiled meat. And Gramma always said that looks weren't everything. Gramma herself was a tall, bony woman with white hair that framed her pink, unlined face. She was well put together except for a bad leg that she got from a childhood bout with polio.

"I'm telling you, you've got it way over all those creeps and goody-two-shoes in your class," Gramma said to Roxanne one night while sitting on her bed. "You've got personality. Take your nose, for instance. It has personality, too. Personality goes a long way in this world, believe me. Now, just look at your mother. No personality, whatsoever. She's like a zombie. Always been that way. I've had to be her personality all her life. But you, you're chock full of it. Personality, I mean."

"Do you really think so, Gramma?"

"Of course, I do. I wouldn't say so if I didn't believe it."

"Gramma, why do I have a personality and Mom doesn't? Why is she . . . you know, like a zombie?"

"Somehow, that's just the way some things work in this world. I think we're the lucky ones, though."

17

"Does Daddy have a personality? Does Gus?"

"Your father, well, yes, your father has a personality there somewhere, but he's so busy and tired all the time, he just doesn't have time to work on his personality. Your brother, Gus, well, that's hard to say. Only time will tell as to whether he has a real, true personality."

"Tell me about the stars, Gramma. What did they do this week?"

"Well, let me tell you, I'm getting plenty disgusted with Frank Sinatra. He's practically chasing after boys. I mean, that new wife of his, that Mia Farrow, who starred in "Peyton Place." Well, some may call her a girl, but I say she's a boy in disguise. No breasts and short hair and she's this thin." Gramma put her fingers together in a circle.

"What about Ava, Gramma? Will Frank ever get back with Ava?"

"Ava's too good for him, I think. Too much of a real woman. Frank may have the voice and enough charm and style to stop that silver ball from falling off the Times Square clock on New Year's Eve. But when it comes to women, that man has no common sense. None. All those movie stars, they're like children. No patience, whatsoever. They have one itty bitty fight about who left the sprinkler system on all night, and, bam, the next thing you know, they're marching off to the divorce lawyer's office. You know what their problem is. They're spoiled. They think that just because the public adores them, their mates have to adore them in the same way. Well, that behavior just doesn't cut it. Your grampa and I, we had some rough times. He once hit me with a garden rake. I still have the scar somewhere, but we stayed together."

"Lemme see the scar, Gramma. Where is it?"

"I'll show it to you another time. It's somewhere on me, I just can't remember exactly where."

"What about Elvis, Gramma? Tell me about Elvis."

"Listen, lambchop, just a few more minutes, you have school in the morning. Elvis, well, I think he just has to marry little Priscilla real soon. *The Enquirer* had some photos of them lounging around his Graceland pool. She's looking more and more like him every day. Her hair is all poofed up and dyed real dark.

That girl's pretty, but she's beginning to look like Dracula's daughter. I don't see how she can be happy, all alone in that big mansion while he's off making movies. Well, you get to sleep right now. That Elvis, he's a good boy through and through. Ed Sullivan was right about him, I know he was. Good night."

After Gramma turned out Roxanne's light, she then crept downstairs as quietly as she possibly could and started to do what she did at the end of every month: She gathered all of her tabloids and fan magazines—*National Enquirers*, *Globes*, her few *Tiger Beats* (she felt that today's bubble gum crooners and teeny-bop heart throbs might be tomorrow's super stars, and she didn't want to get left behind in the excitement). She then bound them all in twine and marked them October 1966 with a grease pencil. She carried them down to the basement and put them among all the other stacks of tabloids and magazines that she had saved throughout the years. When she came back upstairs, she noticed that James was sitting in the den in front of the television, chuckling to himself and hitting the palm of his hand against the side of his favorite easy chair. But what worried her about all this was when she looked at the TV, she noticed that he was chuckling at absolutely nothing except airwaves that flickered a deep blue on the screen.

Early that next morning, Roxanne had a brief dream about Elvis. She dreamed she was like one of those girls in all of his movies. She had a long, blonde pony tail and wore a white bikini. She was frugging around a swimming pool while Elvis stood on the diving board singing something fast. He suddenly stopped singing and proceeded to do a swan dive in slow motion with all of his clothes on. In the pool were a thousand heads of Priscilla with ratted hair and barracuda teeth, waiting to tear into Elvis. Roxanne remembered screaming "stop, stop" in the dream and when she woke up, she was whispering "stop." She had to get up and tell Gramma about her dream, that she had had this terrible premonition about Elvis and Priscilla, and that they should never, ever get married. She would consume him and dominate him, and there would be nothing left for his fans to hold onto. Roxanne put on her terry cloth robe and ran downstairs to tell Gramma, quick, to get out her blue, scented stationery, and they would both write Elvis a long, cautionary letter.

Gramma was standing by the kitchen door, looking outside and shaking her head as she dabbed her eyes with a dish towel.

"Gramma, Gramma, Elvis and Priscilla can't get married, they just can't. I had this dream, I saw it, she'll ruin him, she'll eat him up like a piece of tuna fish. She's no good for him, I know it. Let's write him and tell him everything in my dream."

"Be quiet, hush up, this is no time for such talk," Gramma said. "I should have known he was acting funny last night, laughing at that TV, and there was nothing on it 'cept a bunch of fuzz."

In front of the house was an ambulance with its red lights still spinning. Two men in white coats were taking someone from the house on a stretcher.

"Gramma, what are you talking about. What's wrong?"

"Your father. He swallowed a bottle of aspirin. I found him this morning. Those men are taking him to the hospital to pump his stomach. He'll be all right, I guess."

"Why did he do it? Why?" Roxanne asked, close to tears. "Isn't that how Marilyn Monroe killed herself? With pills?"

"Now listen, Roxanne. Marilyn was much more serious about putting herself under. Your father, well, I think he was just worn out. Or maybe he didn't want to go to work today. Or maybe he needs some reassurance from us that he counts for something, somehow. Now, I have to drive to the hospital and give them some information on your daddy. I'll be back in an hour or so to make some breakfast and drive everyone to the hospital."

"Don't bother about breakfast. If you put food in front of me, I'll throw up, I just know it. Why didn't he say anything to anybody? I feel terrible." Roxanne sat down at the breakfast table and buried her head in her robe. "Poor Daddy," she mumbled. "Poor Mom, poor Gus, poor you, poor me."

"Stop that now," Gramma said softly, putting her arms around Roxanne and holding her dish towel to her nose. "And just remember one thing. Everyone else's life may look good from the outside, but once you see it up close, it isn't always so gosh darn terrific."

"Gramma, what would Elvis do if his daddy took a bunch of aspirins?"

"I think Elvis would eat some breakfast like a good boy and then maybe he would go off and practice a new song. Or he would sit down and write another letter to somebody he loves, even if he knew the letter would be sent back. Remember, we all have to keep busy during bad times."

"Okay, okay. You can fix French toast if you need to," Roxanne said. "But I probably won't eat a bite."

"And I'll call your school nurse and say that you and your brother have the stomach flu. And where's that brother of yours? I swear, I've never heard of a seventh grade drop-out, but he just might be the first."

"I dunno. I guess he's still in bed," Roxanne said, pushing her hands against the table and tilting her chair back on its hind legs.

"Stop that, Roxanne. That chair's gonna fall over some day, and you'll be paralyzed from the neck down. Now how would you like that?"

"I guess I wouldn't," Roxanne said, as her chair landed on the two front legs with a loud clunk.

"Now go in there and give your brother a good shake on the shoulder. I've got to follow that ambulance."

Roxanne dreaded the mere thought of walking into her brother's room. It wasn't just the dissected frogs, spiders and various bugs that were pinned and labeled in showcases around his room. Or his poster collection of Gila monsters ripping apart human limbs and automobiles. Or that one of her dolls was hanging by her neck from the light cord. Or Gus's newest hobby of building make-shift coffins out of the cardboard from their dad's laundry shirts. It was really the smell of his room that Roxanne hated the most—a combination of dirty socks and formaldehyde—a strange and disturbing smell to come from the room of someone so young. Roxanne didn't know how Gus would react to their dad's trying to do himself in; he was so unpredictable. But Gramma once told her that he had taken some test in school, and that he was supposedly a real brain. But that stuff didn't matter much to Roxanne; he was still weird in her book. Gus was crumpled up on one side of his bed, his blonde bangs hanging in his eyes, a large rubber Frankenstein doll looming over his night table.

"Get up, stupid," Roxanne said, pinching his big toe and wiggling it back and forth.

"Stop that. You're stupid yourself," Gus said, groggily. "Tell Gramma I don't feel good. Tell her I can't go to school, okay?"

"Shut up and guess what?"

"What?" Gus asked.

"Dad's in the hospital."

"Why?" Gus asked, with sleep still in his voice.

"Because he swallowed some aspirin, and they're gonna have to pump the insides of his stomach out."

"Did he mean to take 'em?" Gus asked, a little more alert.

"Yeah, he meant to, dumbbell." Roxanne started to get choked up again.

"Shut up, yourself, dumbbell," Gus said, covering his head with his blanket. "Boy, but it's Dad who's the *real* dumbbell."

"Why is Dad the *real* dumbbell?" Roxanne asked.

"Because," Gus said, uncovering his head. "Because if he was gonna kill himself, he should've swallowed rat poison or Clorox. But aspirin. How dumb can you get."

"You're gross and disgusting and sick, and I'm gonna tell Gramma what you just said. You'll get grounded for a week, I know it," Roxanne said with her teeth clenched, hitting his thighs with her fists.

"Don't tell her, don't, cross my heart I didn't mean it, I was just kidding," Gus said, trying to block her fists with his hands. "Here's your doll back," he said, reaching up and grabbing the hanging doll's feet and snapping the string from the light fixture.

"I don't want it back, ever. And we should be glad Dad's breathing or whatever, JUST REMEMBER THAT!" Roxanne said, giving his thigh one last sock.

She ran back into the kitchen, sat down at the breakfast table and proceeded to twist her bangs into a row of tiny, tight knots, waiting for Gramma to get home. Maybe if she concentrated hard enough, things would return to how they had always been in the morning—Daddy clomping down the stairs, warming his hands on a cup of coffee, folding his newspaper into thirds so he could read it next to his juice glass; Mother looking out the back window and taking sips of hot tea; Gus spinning his toast around his plate, looking bored; Roxanne helping Gramma cook eggs and pour milk into cereal bowls. It was now up to Roxanne and Gramma to try to get the family back in order. At least make the family appear that way. If her teachers or neighbors asked, she would tell them that her family was fine. Not just fine, perfect. She would tell them that her father was on a long vacation. No, not a vacation, a business trip. A very important business trip. Because her father—her smart, confident, stable father—had a very important job, and important people went on important business trips. She really needed to discuss all of this with Gramma as soon as she came home from the hospital.

When Gramma finally did return, she immediately took out four eggs from the refrigerator and cracked them into a bowl.

"Well?" Roxanne asked.

"Well, what?" Gramma said, stirring the eggs with a fork. She was being unusually quiet, and this scared Roxanne.

"How is he?"

"He looks pale and terrible, but he'll be all right." Roxanne noticed that she was snuffling into the bowl of eggs.

"What's going on around here?" Emma asked, as she walked into the kitchen. One side of her hair stood straight up, and her purple, lilac-pattern bathrobe was buttoned crooked. "Where's James? I thought I saw whirling red lights. I thought I heard noise. Where's James?"

"Come here, sugar pea, come here in the living room, and I'll tell you all about it," Gramma said in a cooing voice. "Now, Roxanne, you just sit tight. Here's your orange juice," Gramma said, slamming it on the table, a couple of drops sloshing over the side of the glass.

Roxanne could hear Gramma speaking in soft tones to Emma, and she heard little squirrel squeaks coming from her mother. Then there was silence. Gramma walked back into the kitchen rubbing her hands together.

"My hands get so dry in the fall. Roxanne, honey, have you seen my bottle of Nivea?"

"Gramma, what are we going to tell people if they ask about Daddy?"

"Ask? Who's going to ask? And if they do, tell them nothing.

You hear me? Nothing. Remember, discretion is next to godliness—or however that saying goes."

"How is Mom feeling?" Roxanne asked, still confused about what to say to people about her father.

"How is who? Oh, your mother. She took the news just fine. She cried a bit. Then she leaned her head against the back of the couch and just conked out. When she gets up, we'll all eat French toast and then get a move on."

Early that afternoon, the Freedman family piled into their 1965 blue Cutlass to go visit James in the hospital. Gramma drove and at one point shook her fist at another driver on Ward Parkway who almost swerved into the side of their car. No one spoke. Emma let out a few heavy sighs and played with a button on her coat. Gus reached out over the front seat and tried to turn the radio on. Gramma grabbed his hand to stop him from doing so.

Roxanne had always hated the smell of hospitals. She remembered being in Menorah Hospital once to get her tonsils out and throwing up her scoop of ice cream all over her bed because she hated the way her room smelled.

After Gramma parked the car, they stopped in the gift shop to buy a get-well card and a plastic statuette of a man holding an ice pack to his head. They all went up to the second floor and sat in the waiting room of the Intensive Care Unit. Roxanne watched a pretty young mother read the Dr. Seuss book, *Green Eggs and Ham*, to her five-year-old daughter. She wondered if this pretty woman's husband had also just attempted suicide. Gus counted the cracks in the ceiling, and Emma cleaned out the pockets of her coat, ripping up pieces of paper and stuffing them into the stand-up ashtray.

Finally, a doctor peeked around a corner and motioned Emma to come this way. Emma froze in her seat, so Gramma got up and went over to confer with the doctor. They spoke in quiet, serious tones, and after a few minutes, Gramma came over to the family.

"They've pumped his stomach, but there's a danger of it bleeding or something like that because aspirin can eat through the stomach lining. Anyway, they're going to watch him for a few days, but we shouldn't worry about him, he'll be fine. We can all go see him now for a little while. He's sleeping, and he'll probably have tubes and wires attached to him, but we shouldn't be afraid, we should all stand by him and be strong. Do you think we should go to church this afternoon? Should we pray for Daddy?"

"We don't belong to a church," Gus said, watching an orderly wheel a patient down the hall. "And Daddy's Jewish. Why should we pray for him in a church?"

"Gramma, Gus is saying something stupid again," Roxanne whined. "Just shut up, SHUT UP for once in your stupid life," she said pinching Gus's upper arm.

"I think we should all go see Daddy now," Emma said, wadding up a gum wrapper from her pocket and dropping it on the floor. "Which direction is his bed?"

It was true—James did have tubes and wires running from his nose and body. He looked like a used-up heap of a man. Roxanne wondered what made him do it, and if someday he would ever tell her the awful secret he had kept from everyone. Emma set the statuette down on his night table and fished a pen out of her pocketbook.

"Let's all sign the card before he wakes up," she said. "He'll be glad to see it. It'll cheer him up."

There was an old woman lying in the partitioned-off bed beside James who was coughing in her sleep. There were machines with digits and blinking lines everywhere, and Roxanne started thinking about when Elvis heard about his mama's death while he was still in the army, and how Gramma said he was never the same after that. Everything in Intensive Care was so quiet. Roxanne thought that this was what death must sound like. A few blips from a few machines and nurses rustling by in their clean, white uniforms and rubber-soled shoes. Roxanne caught a glimpse of her profile in one of the heart monitor screens, and she turned quickly away. Even during the most anxious times, she never quite forgot how self-conscious she was about her nose. In the meantime, Emma was staring at James and had turned very pale. It was as if the tragedy of it had hit her all at once.

"He hasn't woken up yet," she said, her voice shaking as she walked backwards toward the door. "I think we should leave and come back sometime soon. I didn't think...I just didn't realize," Emma said, starting to push the door open with her back.

"Whoa, girl. Just whoa," Gramma said, running over to her and grabbing her arm. "We've got to stick this out together. You. Me. The kids. We can't leave, at least not right now. Who knows? He might wake up. And he should see all of us."

"I don't think he will wake up. He looks so tired. Did I make him so tired? Watching him makes me tired." Gramma's expression changed from exasperation to worry. She quickly realized that this might be too much for Emma to take.

"Let's not leave, Mom," Gus said, running his hand over the bed rail. "I think it's fun here."

"You would, you little perverted creep," Roxanne hissed at him.

"Now you two watch your dad and see if he starts to turn over or flutter his eyelids and then come and get me if he does," Gramma said. "I'm going to take your mom out to the lounge and maybe we'll read some magazines or get some shut-eye. Now you just watch. Don't take your eyes off of him until the nurse tells you to go." Gramma then took Emma's arm and escorted her out of the Intensive Care Unit while Emma asked a nurse whether James would be able to read his get-well card soon.

Roxanne kept her eyes on her father until she couldn't stand it any longer. He hadn't moved anything in five minutes, and she was starting to get bored. It was as if her father had been stripped of all familiarity, and he was just another sleeping, sick person like everyone else in Intensive Care. Behind another partition, Gus was leaning down and watching an old man's lips pucker as he exhaled. A nurse tapped him on the shoulder, shook her head no and motioned toward the door. She then looked at Roxanne and pointed at her watch, indicating that visiting time was over.

Roxanne was relieved to get out of Intensive Care. She couldn't remember exactly where the waiting room was, and she wandered down a hallway, uncertain where she was going. As she started to turn a corner, she saw a blonde orderly in his mid-twenties facing the wall, pulling at the crotch of his draw-string pants while holding a plastic water pitcher below him. His eyes rolled up toward the back of his head as faint grunts sounded from his throat. As he started to ejaculate into the pitcher, he looked up and saw Roxanne standing there. He quickly wiped himself off with a tissue and put the lid back on the pitcher. He then walked over to the nurse's station and placed the pitcher alongside the others. Roxanne was too surprised to move or utter a sound, and when she finally turned around to run away, she slammed headlong into Gus, who had also been watching the orderly with quiet intensity.

2

The Make-Out Closet

T he following year, something good happened to Roxanne. The most popular girls in her class started passing her notes and asking her to be in their cliques. (Roxanne refused all of these offers because she felt joining a clique would make her an instant snob.) The most popular boys started throwing paper airplanes at her during study hall, and after school they would steal her notebook and play keep-away with it. This all occurred because her new best friend was a popular girl named Vicki, whom everyone considered to be very wild. She had straw-blonde hair, overlapping teeth and bowlegs, but nonetheless, the boys were crazy about her.

Every time Roxanne went over to Vicki's house, her father would be drinking martinis with a pal named Marvin and watching *Three Stooges* reruns on TV. They would always bellow at Roxanne, "There's Barbra Streisand. Hiya, Barbra. Sing us a tune, Barbra. Sing 'People' or somethin' from *Funny Girl*, Barbra." Naturally, this teasing would upset Roxanne to no end: unlike Gramma, she didn't feel that Barbra Streisand was any kind of exotic beauty, and that these men only compared her to Streisand because of her nose.

Vicki's mother was always in the kitchen, smoking cigarettes and doing nothing. She didn't like to cook and would only serve her family Swanson's TV dinners and hash brown potatoes. Vicki's mother would always ask them about the various boys in their class: Who was the best kisser? Who slow-danced the best? Did Mike Falstaff really have good muscles? Did any of the boys know how to French yet? Vicki would answer her in a nonchalant manner, as if she were responding to questions about cheerleading practice or history class. Roxanne was fascinated by Vicki's openness with her mother and wished she could talk to her own mother about all these neat things. She couldn't even imagine having anyone over to her house to meet her mother. Roxanne could just see her, trying to make awkward conversation, then settling into a fidgety silence and Roxanne's friends whispering to each other, "Is she for real?" Roxanne would be so embarrassed, she would have to go hide in the upstairs bathroom and pretend she had stomach cramps.

But the reason why Roxanne enjoyed going over to Vicki's house was for the activities that revolved around the make-out closet in Vicki's basement rumpus room. It had been a storage closet before Vicki's mother cleaned it out, expressly for making out purposes. Soon, Vicki's parties became the big hit among the "cool" junior high students, and even among some high school kids. Vicki would have a whole crowd over, and if a boy and a girl happened to like each other, they locked themselves in the closet and smooched. Roxanne usually played the role of hostess, running upstairs to fetch bowls of popcorn and bottles of soda while Vicki and the other girls were busy in the closet with their boyfriends-of-the-week. One time, Vicki and some of the other kids threw Roxanne in the closet with Bob Folsom, a tall, tough boy who smoked Lucky Strikes and had once been arrested for setting off cherry bombs in front of a drug store. In the closet, Roxanne and Bob merely looked at each other, shrugged and kept quiet so that everyone would think they were making out. Roxanne felt humiliated by this but not altogether surprised; her role at these parties was not to partake in the actual hanky-panky, but to make sure that everything around her ran smoothly in order to facilitate these closet romances. Roxanne also felt that her presence was important for another reason. These parties somehow needed a voyeur, someone who sat on the sidelines and quietly watched all of this teen passion. Everyone at these parties needed to be reassured that they *were* the fastest and the coolest kids at school. Roxanne never had to say anything; her eyes just took in everything and expressed total support and approval. And besides, she felt so good about being included in these parties, she would do anything to ensure she would be invited again.

On a spring Saturday—perhaps one of Roxanne's most memorable days—she followed Vicki around to see her various boyfriends. It was like a neighborhood odyssey, during which Vicki wandered from house to house, making out with all the boys who lived in them. They made out in laundry rooms, attics, bathrooms, porches, anywhere that had some privacy. And, of course, Roxanne was the silent witness to all of this, taking it all in for (what she hoped to be) future reference.

Roxanne's home life, though, was anything but stable. Her father had pulled out of his suicide attempt in good physical shape and was deeply involved in psychoanalysis. He saw his analyst five times a week and instead of discussing the Dow Jones at the dinner table, he would describe what he and his shrink, Irving, had talked about that day. James was compelled to discuss these private thoughts because he still felt terrible about all the pain he had caused his family. He wanted them to be aware of the fact that he *was* recovering from his depression.

During the first few months that he was in analysis, the family tried to listen to him with interest and compassion. They were relieved that he was functioning somewhat normally and had returned to work. Even Gus tried every once in a while to make small talk with him. But now they were growing impatient with how self-centered and out of touch he had become due to all of his extensive therapy.

"Irving thinks that I deeply resent my parents," James said one night while carving pot roast for his family. "I mean, the way they tried to rule my life for so many years, demanding this, demanding that. Those Sunday dinners, those horrible dinners, filled with guilt and responsibility. I always had to be the good son, the perfect, loving son. You have to be superhuman in order to withstand that kind of pressure."

"Please pass the salt," Emma said, pushing her hair back and snapping her barrette in place.

"My relationship with my mother was definitely Oedipal. I worshiped her beyond belief, I thought she could do no wrong. And then at her funeral, that man standing there in the overcoat, supposedly her lover for the last twenty-five years. Everyone, I mean *everyone* in town knew about them, except me and my father. I swear it broke him. Until he died, he just sat around all day in the Jewish Home, cursing her photograph thumbtacked to his bulletin board."

"James, couldn't we talk about something more pleasant," Gramma snapped. "You're not the only one in this world with problems. Take your daughter, for instance."

"What about her?" James asked, dumfounded.

"Yeah, what about me?" Roxanne asked.

"I don't like who you've been hanging around with," Gramma said, shaking her fork at Roxanne. "That Vicki and her parents. They're cheap people. They're what we Southerners call poor white trash."

"What's wrong with Vicki?" Roxanne asked, on the verge of tears. "She's fun. I have a ton more fun in their house than I do here. Her folks act like kids. And they let her do anything she wants. You're just jealous because I spend more time over there than I do here."

"You are wrong, young lady, that's not the point at all. We all know the kind of parties that Vicki and her no-good parents have. It's practically a child pornography ring over there."

"How do you know anything?" Roxanne asked. "You're just a gramma. Grammas don't know anything at all."

"Oh yes I do. I know about *everything* and don't you forget it."

"I'm thinking about going to California this summer," James said. "There's something called the Esalen Institute up north where you can do therapy all day long by the ocean and take baths in hot springs."

"What are you talking about, James?" Emma asked, holding her napkin up to her mouth. "What's he talking about, Mother?"

"I read about Esalen in *Time* magazine. It sounds interesting, doesn't it? Now, I've always worked for this family, haven't I? I've always put food on the table. Well, for once in my life, I should be able to do what I want. Shouldn't I? *Shouldn't I?* Irving thinks it's a good idea for me to go to Esalen."

"Well, then go," Gramma said, throwing her hands up in the air. "Become a flower child for all I care. And as for you, young lady, you watch your step with your little friend, Vicki. She's nothing but trouble, mark my words."

Roxanne threw her napkin under the table and stormed up

to her room.

"She's your daughter, Emma. Do something for her. Talk to her."

"What should I say? What should I do? You tell me, Mother."

"I don't care what you say to her, just go to her. GO."

Emma pushed her chair away from the table and dropped her napkin in the middle of her plate. She then got up and started the long, slow climb up the staircase to Roxanne's bedroom.

Gus sat silently at the table, thinking about the tough chord change at the beginning of Jimi Hendrix's "Foxy Lady." Yeah, it was so tough it made the hair on his arms stand on end. He was teaching himself how to play guitar by listening to records and moving his fingers up and down a broom stick. He had to think of a way to make money—and plenty of it—for a guitar and amp. Maybe he could sell his dissected frog and insect collection. He didn't even like that kid stuff anymore.

"Gus, I need to ask you a question," James said.

"Huh?" Gus said, still thinking about frogs and Jimi Hendrix.

"I need to ask you a question," James said, more emphatically.

"Yeah?"

"You're a bright boy. An extremely bright boy."

"Now, James, he's just a child," Gramma said. "Don't say anything you're going to regret later."

"As a matter of fact, you're brighter than I ever was or ever will be. Now, how come you don't like school? Are you bored with it? Do you know more than the teachers?"

"Nah. I don't know nothin'."

"Say 'anything', Gus. Say, 'I don't know anything.'"

"I don't know anything."

"There, that's better. You can't get ahead in life if you don't learn to speak properly."

"I'm excusing myself," Gramma said with disgust. "I've got some catch-up star reading to do." James hardly noticed Gramma's abrupt departure from the table.

"So, son. You didn't answer my question."

"What question?"

"About school! Why don't you like school? For a bright boy, you don't listen well, either."

"School's okay," Gus said, slumping into his chair, his long, blonde bangs hanging into his eyes. "But school's not that important. I've got...hmmmm...other things going, you know." He paused.

"No, I don't know. I don't know what you're talking about at all. Just remember, there's nothing, I mean *nothing*, more important than school. Your teachers say you have an attitude problem."

"Yeah?" Gus said.

"And your grades..." James said.

"Yeah, they're bad."

"So what's your problem?" James asked, loosening his tie.

"I guess I'm not as smart as you think."

"Now, Gus, help me a little bit. Irving thinks it's a good idea for me to take more of an interest in my family's problems, but as you know, this is all very hard for me."

"Dad?"

"Yes, son."

"Who's Irving?"

"Irving's my doctor. Where have you been? I talk about Irving all the time," James said, getting red in the face.

"Dad?"

"Yes?"

"Can I be excused?"

"Sure. Go right ahead." Gus got up while James stared at the remains of the cold pot roast in the bright, silver platter.

Emma stood outside Roxanne's room for several minutes, too nervous to make a move. She finally tapped with her two fingernails on Roxanne's door and smoothed down her dress and hair as if she were back in high school waiting for a prom date to pick her up in his new car.

"I don't wanna talk to you, Gramma," Roxanne said. "Go away."

"It's not Gramma," Emma said softly, "It's me. Mother."

"Mother?" Roxanne was surprised that she had bothered to come upstairs with the intention of being motherly. But Roxanne didn't have anything to say to her mother, who was so caught up in her own private universe that she could never understand what Roxanne was feeling. So, why should Roxanne even try to explain herself? And she couldn't bear the thought of her mother coming into her room and making some feeble attempt to comfort her.

"Yes, Roxanne. It's me." Emma kept standing outside Roxanne's closed door, not knowing what to do or say next. "Would you like a glass of cold water?" Emma finally asked. "I'll go down to the kitchen, fill up a glass with ice and get you some. Would you like that? Would you think that was nice?"

"No thank you, Mother. Really, I don't think so."

"I can bring you dessert. Some vanilla ice cream?"

"No, Mother. Please."

"Isn't there anything you want? Anything at all."

"No, there isn't." Roxanne knew she was being insensitive to her mother—who was really *trying* to be attentive and sympathetic—and that made her feel even worse. She wished she could go live at Vicki's house for a week. At least Vicki's parents seemed to know what it was like being young and miserable.

Emma became tongue tied once again and reached for the door knob, hoping that some outside force would give her the strength to turn it and march right in there and be able to talk to her daughter about school and boys like the mothers did on "As the World Turns" and "Days of Our Lives." She would like to be able to talk to Roxanne in the same, straight-forward way that Gramma did—but she simply didn't know how. Emma felt weak and upset by all of this and decided that maybe she, herself, wanted that dish of vanilla ice cream. Walking down the staircase one slow step at a time, she wondered—as she frequently did—how everything had come to this.

James was still sitting at the table by the time Emma reached the dining room. He had his head in his hands and was slowly shaking it back and forth. As he looked up from a spot of gravy on the table cloth, his eyes were a blur of blue.

"I've been thinking about something, Emma. Something serious."

"What's that?"

"I've been thinking about the fact that when I die, I have no great legacy to leave behind. There will be absolutely nothing that people will remember me by."

"James, don't be silly. And don't talk like that. It scares me, you know that."

"No, I mean it. What I'm trying to say is, Where's my EMC^2?

My Guernica? My Empire State Building? Where's my greatness, my one lasting achievement that generations will be able to point to and say, 'That was done by James Freedman, you know, that great, brilliant man from the Midwest.' I don't have that. And it bothers me, it really does."

"Really, James," Emma said, taking a dessert spoon out of the kitchen drawer, scooping out a lump of Borden's vanilla and putting it in her mouth to melt. "You have the children. A part of you will always be a part of the children. And if they have children, why there you go. That's your legacy." She took another jab at the ice cream, proud of what she had just said.

"Oh, there's no trick to having children. Any idiot can have children. That's not saying my kids aren't great. They *are* great. But it doesn't take any real talent. Having kids, that is."

"I don't know what to tell you, James. I just don't know anymore," Emma said, shaking her head and snapping the lid back on the ice cream.

"Maybe this is just a phase or something. I'll have to discuss this more with Irving tomorrow."

"Maybe Irving will know what to say. I don't know, but maybe he will."

"I'm fine. Really I am. I'm just thinking out loud."

"I'll clear off all these dishes, okay?"

James was so absorbed in his own failure that he didn't even hear Emma leave the dining room.

3

White Slicker

At school, Roxanne was starting to hear an awful lot of whispering in the hallways and in the cafeteria lunch line, by the gym lockers, in study hall, everywhere she turned. It seemed as though the whole school was whispering about something, and she was the only one who had not been let in on this grand secret. She knew it had something to do with Vicki who hadn't been at school for a couple of days. When she tried to call Vicki at home, her half-crocked father would answer the phone, pretending he was the owner of a fictitious pizzeria and would hang up on Roxanne when she would try to identify him. Then finally she heard something from Sheryl Morris. What she heard didn't surprise her, but she wanted to talk to Vicki about it, anyway.

When Vicki did show up at school the following week, she kept avoiding Roxanne by pretending to rush off to some class or by ducking into the bathroom to apply another layer of Yardley White Slicker to her lips. This was strange behavior for Vicki. Roxanne had assumed that they would always be friends. And now Vicki was treating her like a nothing, a nobody. Roxanne felt hurt and insulted. After all the work she had done for her parties. For an entire week she even delivered an I.D. bracelet and ring back and forth between Vicki and Mike Falstaff. And now this. Roxanne had had it with friends. She had just had it.

Two weeks went by and still no word from Vicki. It was a Thursday at lunchtime, and Roxanne was getting seconds on chocolate cake. The woman at the cash register was punching her meal ticket, and there was Vicki standing in front of her staring at Roxanne's chocolate cake. (Vicki had a complexion problem and never went out of her way to get a chocolate dessert, but she always managed to eat half of whatever anybody else got.) Roxanne just had to laugh. It was as if she were unintentionally using the chocolate cake as bait to win back Vicki's friendship. Vicki ran up to the lunch line to snatch a clean fork from the metal silverware container and then plopped herself down next to Roxanne. Even before Vicki sat down, her fork was in mid-air, ready to swoop down on the icing.

"I don't know what I did to you," Roxanne said. "You tell me why you won't talk to me."

"You didn't do a thing. It's all me. But I don't know if you'll want to talk to me if I tell you what happened."

"I did hear something. Is it true?"

"Well," Vicki said, mashing a few crumbs between the prongs of her fork. "This is hard to get out. Hmmmmm. Yeah... yeah... you heard right. I went out of town somewhere in Kansas and had it done there. It hurt like crazy afterwards. I had cramps, I was doubled over for an hour. I felt really gross. Dad found the doctor, probably some quack who made me sterile."

"Gosh, I'm sorry. Does Mike Falstaff know about this?"

"Yeah. He broke up with me. I hate all boys. I'll never go steady again."

"He broke up with you?"

"Yeah, that asshole creep. You know, I didn't want you to know 'bout this."

"Why? Why couldn't I know?"

"'Cause, well, I thought you wouldn't like me anymore and your family is nice and has all sorts of money, and they would think things about me. I know what people say 'bout me, calling me a whore and all. I'm not dumb, believe me, I'm not."

"So, what do you want me to do?"

"I dunno," Vicki said, standing up and licking her fork. "I dunno 'bout much anymore."

Roxanne just sat there as she watched Vicki toss her fork into the dish bin and walk out of the cafeteria. She felt funny about admitting this to herself, but she also wasn't sure how she felt about anything anymore. Except for Vicki, she had never been able to talk to anyone her own age. Yet the more she thought about it, the only person she had ever really talked to was Gramma. And it was only because Gramma demanded to be talked to, demanded some kind of response. The rest of her family demanded very little, except of course for her father. Because he was going to a shrink, he tried to arouse some kind of reaction from his family by asking them a lot of questions. But the minute any one of them put up a fight, refusing to answer his probing (and sometimes stupid) questions, he backed down immediately. It was as if he were merely going through the motions so he could go into therapy the following day and have something to complain about—like his inability to talk to his family.

And as for Vicki—all she demanded was for Roxanne to be her very own one-person cheering section. While sitting in Vicki's rumpus room or in strange boys' living rooms, Roxanne was unknowingly cheering Vicki on to go further and faster sexually. Perhaps Vicki would have preferred Roxanne to have stopped her from getting into this pregnancy mess. Or maybe she was pointing her finger at Roxanne for not having warned her about the real consequences and dangers of sex. (How was Roxanne supposed to know about these sort of things? She had never even kissed a boy.)

And what about Vicki's parents? Weren't they the ones who were supposed to be watching out for her, telling her to be careful and not to go too far? Weren't they the ones who were supposed to lecture her about saving herself for her honeymoon with Tom Terrific? (Roxanne didn't know what a mother was supposed to tell a daughter about sex since her own didn't have a clue. She even sensed that her mother was physically afraid of her father since she once saw her flinch when her father kissed her.) She was feeling more and more confused; for the last year, she had thought that Vicki's family was ideal compared to her own. All that laughing and gossiping about boys in the kitchen with Mrs. Smith; Vicki talking back to her folks and leaving the house whenever she pleased. Roxanne felt such exhilaration walking through their front door even when Mr. Smith teased her about looking like Barbra Streisand. Two weeks ago, if there had been any remote possibility, she would have been happy to pack up her belongings and move into the Smith guest bedroom. After a few years, maybe the Smiths would adopt her. She liked the idea of being Roxanne Smith instead of Roxanne Freedman. Now, she didn't know what to think about Vicki's parents. Were they the low-rent types like Gramma thought? Or were they just fun-loving and open-minded? Roxanne wanted some explanations. She wanted to tie things up into nice big bundles instead of having to deal with all of these questions, these loose ends. As she put her head down on the cafeteria table, she didn't know what to think about anything anymore.

4

The Sahara

Gus was starting to think about music all the time. He was starting to worry about how to wear his hair. Should he grease it back or let it shag down like the Stones? Only hillbilly musicians greased their hair. And Elvis. He would go with the Stones look. After all, he had to start thinking about image. Image was important to musicians. He knew he was young. Too young to do anything important yet. But he had to start thinking about these things. Look at Beethoven, Mozart, Stevie Wonder, all those guys started young. Much younger than he was. Yeah, just look at those guys.

It was a Wednesday afternoon, and Gus went downstairs to grab something to eat since he hadn't had much at school. He was not sure what he felt like putting in his mouth, so he opened the refrigerator door and stared at what was inside: two cans of Coke, a head of iceberg lettuce, a package of bologna, pickles, French's mustard, A-1 Steak Sauce, a plastic red pitcher full of orange juice. In the freezer there were baggies of frozen hamburger patties, vanilla ice cream, cans of frozen grape juice, a Tupperware container of something disgusting. There wasn't much for Gus to eat. Even musicians had to eat something.

Gus finally decided on bologna. He pulled out a loaf of Wonder bread from the pantry and slapped some mayonnaise on two slices. He liked coating the bread with mayonnaise so that it oozed out the sides. He had a way of eating a bologna sandwich. He would roll it up oblong until it resembled a hot dog. Then he would take his thumbs and flatten the bread. He could still see his thumbprints while he ate the sandwich, and for some reason, that gave him a great deal of satisfaction. He felt as though he were eating something with his very own signature on it.

Now he felt almost human again. And he started thinking about something else—clothes. What did musicians wear anyway? In the poster on his bedroom wall, Hendrix wore a big flowery shirt with billowy sleeves, hip-hugger bell bottoms and a headband. But that didn't seem to be Gus's style—the San-Francisco-flower-child-Carnaby-Street look. Maybe he should dress like The Who or The Kinks, bad boys but smart bad boys. Bad but not bad enough to wind up in jail for killing their old ladies.

Gus went upstairs and looked in the full-length mirror in his mother's dressing room. He just didn't look tough enough. He looked, well, wimpy, like the kind of guy whose tongue and teeth always had flecks of cookies coated on them. Blonde. Round. Near-sighted. He hated his glasses. He couldn't think of any really cool guys who wore them. Maybe Buddy Holly, but was he ever considered cool? Maybe nice—like a debate club president or a science fair winner—but not really cool.

Gus looked at himself in the mirror for a few more minutes. He took one of his mother's black eyeliner pencils and drew whisker-like lines about his upper lip. It looked like dirt. Forget it. He then took his mother's metal comb that was in the shape of a goldfish and smelled like bath powder. He combed his hair straight back with it. Then straight forward into his eyes. That looked better. Now he was getting somewhere.

He looked in the mirror again. How should he stand? How did musicians stand anyway? With their knees bent, butts pulled in, stomachs and crotches pointing over the audience's heads, guitars strapped to their shoulders, microphones clenched in passionate fists. (He guessed that that stance was part of what people were paying for when they bought all those records and attended all those concerts.)

Gus practiced standing like a rock star for a few minutes. He held his mother's hair brush like a microphone and mouthed Door's lyrics into the bristles. He played many riffs of air guitar. He felt he was almost ready to go out and hear some music. He just needed to change his clothes.

He decided on a green T-shirt with a small hole near the pocket, a faded blue work shirt over it and Levi's that had a knee patch of a hand giving the finger. It felt good wearing that

41

patch. Yeah.

He knew of a place in Westport called the Sahara Cafe that only served hot cider and foreign coffees. It was dark and had ugly psychedelic paintings on the walls of nude girls and flowers and a huge bulletin board near the door advertising vans for sale, yoga teachers, apartments, rock bands looking for musicians, rides or riders needed to go to California, Shaklee vitamins, astrology charts, and dance therapy groups. A big black guy named Klemmer was the regular talent there, and he usually played songs by Donovan, early Dylan, John Sebastian, and Richie Havens on his acoustic guitar. Those tunes seemed just a little staid for Gus. He liked stronger stuff—more noise, more electricity.

A guy at Gus's school said that Wednesday nights were talent night at the Sahara. Sometimes the club attracted musicians as far away as Lawrence and St. Jo. That was the time to go to the Sahara, when things were really cooking.

Gus told Gramma he was going to Tony Molina's for dinner. He didn't want anyone in his family to know where he was really going so he figured he would have to walk to the Sahara—down Ward Parkway, through the Plaza and up Broadway a few blocks. It would take him around an hour or so to get there. Not too bad, he thought.

He also considered hitchhiking, but decided against it. He was a little paranoid that someone Gramma knew would see him and tell her about it. And she might get mad and do something weird, like the one time he was in trouble for not cleaning up his room, she hid his chemistry set. Days later he finally found it in a big box in the attic along with a Mixmaster with no plug, five dirty button-down sweaters and a crumpled W. C. Fields poster. Kansas City was just getting too small for someone like Gus. He was already feeling as though everyone knew his business, everyone was spying on him and on each other. What a cowtown. Moo.

Even Gus couldn't deny that it was a beautiful May evening in Kansas City, one of those evenings when the sky was turning pink and purple, and the insects were buzzing around his head, and tulips and daffodils were springing up along the median strip in the middle of Ward Parkway. A bra-less girl carrying a knapsack was walking toward him. He decided he would try giving her a very hip greeting, like the longhairs gave each other during outdoor concerts at Volker Park. It was a sort of bobbing of the head sideways and a soft 'hey.' "Hey," Gus said to the bra-less girl. "Hey," she said back to Gus, but her eyes and enlarged pupils conveyed absolutely nothing behind that 'hey.' Gus turned around and watched her walk her rather stoned, lilting walk, hoping she would not get hit by a bus on her way home.

The Plaza was pretty empty except for some people standing in line to see a Pink Panther movie. All the women with their fancy dresses and done-up hair must have already gone home with their Woolf Brothers and Harzfeld bags loaded into the back seats of their Cadillacs. Right now, they were probably in their kitchens, watching their maids wash the dishes and telling them what to cook for dinner the next night. Sometimes when Gus saw these women having salads for lunch or sniffing around the cosmetic counters of various stores, he would feel a mixture of envy and disgust. He thought that shopping was completely boring, and anyone who spent much time doing it must be a moron. How he hated the idea of Gramma dragging him into Jones or Macys for a new dress shirt or for a pair of penny loafers (he would much rather go to the head shops in Westport or to the army-navy surplus store where the clothes were definitely more his taste). On the other hand, he compared these women to his own mother in her ragamuffin clothes and with her strag-gly hair, and he felt jealous of these women's sons who had such beautiful, sophisticated, presentable mothers. These thoughts made him stop dead in his tracks in front of the J. C. Nichols fountain, which had huge stone horses rearing on their hind legs and water squirting out of fish's mouths. For a few minutes he watched the water cascading down into the cement pool below and imagined if perhaps a few seconds worth of that water was how much saliva came out of a person's mouth in a lifetime, especially if that person tended to drool a lot or was prone to colds or allergies. Really gross but fun to imagine. He then thought about his mother wandering around the house sniffling into the countless wet hankies she kept in the pockets of her dresses and sweaters, his mother crying and blowing her nose for no reason that he could understand except that some-thing out there made her miserable. Then after every crying jag she would always fall asleep wherever she happened to be. Gus had seen his mother asleep on the bathroom tiles and draped over the kitchen sink. Once he came home and saw her in front of the house bent over, her head resting on a clump of dirt (she was in the middle of planting a row of begonias). Gus was sure that none of the Plaza women did anything that strange, that their homes and lives ran like neat and elegant pieces of machinery. Thinking about his mother and the things she did made Gus blush and dig his hands deeper into his pockets. It was getting darker, and a middle-aged man wearing a John Deere hat, his pants nearly falling off his emaciated hips, was panhandling around the fountain. Gus didn't think bums were allowed around the Plaza area, and he would have liked to hang around until the cops showed up and told this guy to scat. But he decided he'd better get going if he wanted to get a seat at the club.

The Sahara smelled of cinnamon coffee, cigarettes, and patchouli oil, an unforgettable smell that Gus would try to conjure up during periods throughout his life that would be even less happy than this one. On a small stage in front, two guys wearing bolo ties and cowboy boots were sitting on high stools singing something about trains and nighttime, which sounded remotely like a campfire song. Gus had a feeling that the song was written by one of those clowns. Nothing like a little hootenanny b.s. to put a damper on a potentially righteous evening.

Gus sat down at a table with a couple and ordered a hot cider which came in a clay mug. "What's the story with the music?" Gus said, leaning over to the guy. "Are these Raytown cowboys gonna stop soon or what?"

"You call this music? I dunno 'bout you, but I'm headin' over to Klemmer's."

"Klemmer's?" Gus said.

"You know the black dude who plays here."

"Sure, yeah. I'm goin' over there myself."

"Yeah?"

"Yeah." Gus didn't know why he had said that. He knew he had to get home soon, or Gramma would wonder where he was.

"Come on," the guy said. "Let's get outta here." He motioned his head to his girlfriend, who was wearing a tasseled Davy Crockett leather jacket and a red and orange tie-dye bandanna around her head. Gus gulped down the remains of his cider and walked out of the club with them.

"Klemmer's house is just a few blocks away," the guy said as soon as they stepped into the cool night air.

"Yeah," Gus said. "Someone once pointed out his house to me once." He blushed because he knew that his comment sounded really stupid.

"Do we have to go to Klemmer's?" the girl said in a whiney voice. "He's such a lech. The minute you leave the room, he's all over me."

"You wish, baby, you wish," the guy said, his face turning red and hostile. "Hey, Klemmer's a friend of mine. Don't say stuff like that about a friend."

"Oh, yeah?"

"Yeah."

"You're full of shit."

"No, baby, you are."

"Fuck you."

Gus felt so bad he simply wanted to disappear from this scene entirely; the vibes between this guy and his girlfriend were thick and ugly. Thank God they soon found themselves climbing up some crumbling cement steps to Klemmer's house. There was a hammock hanging from the ceiling of the porch, and the front door was open. The furniture in the tiny house all looked like garage sale rejects, except for a fluted rattan chair where Klemmer, a black guy in his early thirties, was sitting, strumming an acoustic guitar.

"Hi, Carla. Hi, Brian." Klemmer's velvety voice sounded like it had years of practice of sounding mellow.

"Hi, Klemmer," they said.

"And who are you?" Klemmer asked, pointing the bottom of his guitar at Gus. "A Mission Hills runaway?"

"Nope," Gus said. He was proud of the fact that he sounded fairly composed.

"Well, do you have a name?"

"Yeah. It's Gus," he said, shoving his hands into his pockets.

"Well, howdy do, Gus. Have a seat." Gus sat down on the tattered couch across from Klemmer, and he felt a spring coming through the worn upholstery.

"Listen," Klemmer said, pointing his finger at Gus. "You shouldn't be ashamed of having money. Money's a wonderful thing, it's a real privilege to have it. Did you know I went to a private school? The finest private school in Cincinnati. And my brother, he's one of the finest insurance agents in Hartford, Connecticut. Has his very own company. And I bet you go to a private school. Am I right?"

"No, I go to public school."

"Is that right? Well, have some pretzels," Klemmer said, handing a bag to Gus, his eyebrows arching in disbelief. Gus wanted to devour the entire bag of pretzels, he was feeling pretty hungry. He reached in and took a handful and started popping them into his mouth one at a time.

"Hey, Brian, where's that fine weed you been talkin' about?" Klemmer asked. Brian reached into his flannel shirt, pulled out a joint, lit it, took a long, slow drag and passed it to Gus. Gus had only smoked pot twice before—some kid had handed him joints while waiting for the school bus—but he wanted everyone to think he was cool. He tried to imitate the way Brian smoked, and he started to cough uncontrollably.

"Just a beginner, huh?" Brian said, smirking.

"No, man," Gus said, beating his chest lightly with his fist. "Allergies. You know, asthma." He then took a small hit off the joint—careful not to take in so much smoke—and passed it on to Klemmer. A diapered, light-skinned baby holding a stuffed rabbit came tottering into the living room. He dropped the bunny on the floor and started rubbing his eyes.

"Oh, Klemmer, he's so adorable. Hiya, doll baby. Hiya." Carla said, waving her hand at the baby, her eyes and mouth wide open.

"You remember Viola, the woman I lived with for two years," Klemmer said to Brian, blowing smoke out of his mouth. "This is our kid, Grigor. You know, she wanted a kid real bad and I said to her, 'Okay, fine, but I don't want to get married,' and she said, 'I don't care if we get married, I just want you to be the father of my child,' and I said, 'Fine, I love babies, I love being a daddy when they're little. It's just when they grow up. Phew, forget it.'"

"Yeah, I know what you mean," Carla said, nodding. "I've got seven younger brothers and sisters."

"Then Viola moved out of here about six months ago. And

about a month ago, she dropped Grigor by here for me to baby-sit and then went to some outdoor jazz concert. And do you know she never came back to pick Grigor up. I called her, and she didn't answer her phone. I went by her apartment a few times, and she was just gone. Vanished. But Grigor's here now. He's here to stay. Viola's a sick person, I feel real sorry for her. Anyway, he's better off with me, and I guess she knows that."

"Man, what a drag," Brian said, watching Grigor stick the bunny rabbit's ear into his mouth.

"I'm gonna teach him to play drums. He likes to bang on this little tin xylophone I got him for his birthday. He'll be the best damn drummer this town has ever seen. Better than Ginger Baker and Buddy Rich combined. When he grows up, he'll be the drummer for my band."

"Hi Grigor, hi honey doll, come on over and say, 'hi'," Carla said, patting her thighs with the palms of her hands.

Gus watched Grigor waddle toward Carla, and he couldn't help feeling sorry for him. He sure wouldn't want to have Klemmer for a father. Yeah, Klemmer was nice enough to take care of the kid, but that didn't mean he wasn't an asshole. Klemmer even made Gus's father look like Mr. Goddamn Normal—Robert Young, Fred MacMurray, and Ward Cleaver all rolled into one. What a laugh. But his pity for the kid didn't last long. All that Gus really wanted to do was to go home. His evening had been a waste. He hadn't found any good music. His throat felt sore and dry from the pot and the pretzels. And he needed to use the bathroom.

"Uh, where's the john?" Gus asked, standing up.

"Straight back and to your first left," Klemmer said, pointing straight ahead of him.

Gus was glad to escape into the bathroom. He felt trapped in this dump. He knew that the pot was doing weird things to his head, making him confused, and most of all, sleepy. He started staring at the piece of soap on the side of the tub. It had flecks of sparkles throughout it, and he couldn't stop staring at it. It was as if the soap were starting to absorb his eyes and would soon absorb his brain. Maybe this soap was from an alien planet. Maybe Klemmer was an alien trying to take over everyone's brains in Kansas City. Yeah, anything was possible.

He left the bathroom and decided to check out the rest of the house. One of the rooms had been converted into a practice room and had guitars on stands along with mikes, amplifiers, a drum set, and scattered drum sticks. Gus could see that Klemmer had an excellent stereo system with a reel to reel tape player and a huge record collection. Gus couldn't help himself; he just had to see what kind of records Klemmer had.

Gus turned on a floor lamp and started looking. Lots of folkies like Joan Baez, Woody Guthrie, Pete Seeger, Peter, Paul and Mary, The We Five. And Beatles. Every Beatles record imaginable. A few Rolling Stones, Byrds, Buffalo Springfield, Cream, Jefferson Airplane, Janis, Mozart, Bach, Charlie Parker, Miles Davis, The Temptations, Marvin Gaye and Tammi Terrell, Smokey Robinson. Not bad. Not bad at all. Gus could hardly keep his eyes open. There was a mattress in the corner of the room with an India print spread on it. Gus figured he would take a little snooze on it—just for ten or fifteen minutes—and then try to figure out a way to get home.

Gus closed his eyes, and everything was spinning. He saw flashes of colors, and he had a glimpse of a dream: he was running from someone who was swinging a guitar at his feet. The person had a head like the stuffed bunny that Grigor was holding. Gus awoke with a jolt, and his shirt felt sticky around his neck. He also felt hands. Two hands undoing his belt buckle, unzipping his pants and trying to pull them over his shoes.

"Stop right there," Gus said, pulling his pants back up.

"Hey, I was just trying to make you more comfortable, I wasn't trying to *do* anything. I've got a son close to your age, living in Alaska with his mother. . . . "

"I've gotta go," Gus said, standing up suddenly. Where's Brian and Carla?"

"They left," Klemmer said. "You've been asleep for a couple of hours."

"Oh, shit. What time is it?"

"'Bout one o'clock."

"Oh, shit." Gus imagined the hell Gramma would give him for coming in so late on a school night.

"Do you need a ride home?" Klemmer asked.

"Yeah, I guess so," Gus said, wishing he were older and able to drive himself places.

Klemmer went into Grigor's room to make sure he was asleep. Then they headed out to the driveway where they got into Klemmer's Falcon. At a red light, Klemmer pulled out a joint and lit it with a disposable lighter.

"You want a hit?" Klemmer asked, handing it to Gus.

"No. No, thanks." Gus couldn't imagine anybody smoking so much pot. They were silent until they were a few blocks from his house.

"You can pull over here," Gus said.

"Nice houses. Someday when I'm famous, I'll have a house in this neighborhood."

"Ummmm."

"Come and see me at the Sahara. I play there on weekends."

"Sure. And thanks," Gus said, knowing he would never make it to one of Klemmer's gigs. Not if he could help it. As Gus walked down the grassy median of Ward Parkway, he started to feel ashamed. Not for smoking pot or hanging out or anything like that. But because he had actually wanted Klemmer to do something, to lie on top of him, to touch his penis. And because he was covering up with the front of his work shirt a hard-on that was growing larger by the minute during his short walk home.

The same night that Gus went to the Sahara, Roxanne and Gramma were clearing the table and having a discussion about celebrities. Emma and James were sitting in front of the TV, watching "Get Smart" and leafing through J.C. Penney catalogues.

"Elvis Presley. Now there's the greatest male celebrity of this century," Gramma said, putting the dishes in the dishwasher. "Greater than Rudolf Valentino or Clark Gable or James Dean. I mean it now, I really do. Frank Sinatra happens to be a classier act in my opinion, but there's no one who stirs the heart like Elvis, except maybe Jack Kennedy. But he was a president, which is a celebrity but not a true celebrity. Politicians don't qualify as pure celebrities."

"Why not, Gramma?" Roxanne asked.

"Well, I just can't explain it, dear, it's just a feeling I've got about politicians. They don't say what they're really thinking, they just say what people want them to say. Now, creative people always speak from their gut, they simply don't have any choice in the matter. They would do the same song or whatever if they were performing in front of four or four thousand people. There's something inside of them that drives them to express themselves in a certain way. But that same drive sometimes kills them if they don't watch out. Celebrities can be like those brush fires that burn up the hills and swimming pools all over southern California."

"Gosh, Gramma," Roxanne said, wiping off the table.

"Gosh what, child?"

"I don't know. Just gosh."

"Well, say something intelligent when we're discussing celebrities. This is important information I'm telling you, information you may one day want to pass on to your grandchildren."

"Yes, Gramma," Roxanne said sullenly.

"That's better."

"Gramma?"

"What is it?"

"We always talk about the same celebrities. Elvis and Frank Sinatra. Frank Sinatra and Elvis. Can't we talk about somebody else?"

"Who else is there to talk about?"

"Well, how about Paul Newman?"

"He's a good one, no doubt about it, but he's too pretty for my taste. And besides, he's a family man. What's so fun about a man who loves his wife?"

"How about Sean Connery? You know, James Bond."

"Oh, him. He's sexy. Uh-hmmmmmm."

"And..."

"And what?"

"And what else about Sean Connery?"

"I DON'T KNOW ANYTHING ABOUT HIM. Sometimes, I mean, really, you expect me to know EVERYTHING!"

"What about Liz Taylor?"

"What about her?"

"What do you think about her."

"Oh, she's a hell of a gal, always fun to read about, always up to no good, whether she's getting married for the umpteenth time or ending up flat on her back in the hospital from some catastrophe. She knows how to live it up, that's for sure."

"And..."

"And what?"

"And what else about her?"

"I don't know what you want from me, child. Everyone has their passions. Some people love cribbage, others love bird watching, others love to putter around in their garage and fix their lawn mowers. I love celebrities. It's my pastime, my passion. And I'll read about every celebrity there is to read about, but I only like to talk about a few. Do you understand?"

"Yes, Gramma."

"Listen, I'm sorry to get sharp with you. You're my favorite of this crazy bunch."

"I know."

"I don't know what makes me so cranky. These days, it's the little, silly stuff that seems to wear on my nerves. During the Depression, I could stand in bread lines for hours, endure the most humiliating things without getting the least bit ruffled. Now someone says something just a little bit off, and I blow to pieces."

"I know. And don't worry. I still love Elvis. And I still love you."

"Thanks, child. That's always good for me to hear."

Gramma and Roxanne looked at each other in one of those rare moments when one of them was not flustered or angry, and for that moment, they knew how glad they were to have each other. It was Gramma who turned away first; moments like these were too much for her to take for long.

As Roxanne headed upstairs, something occurred to her that had been going around in her head for a while. What would make Gramma proud of her? What would give her the most pleasure? Somehow Roxanne felt that it was her responsibility to make Gramma happy since no one else in the family cared to. And unlike most adults, Gramma was indifferent to adolescent achievements such as good grades and clean hair. As she passed the long bathroom mirror, it suddenly hit her. Having Elvis in the family. Of course. Roxanne could see the whole thing. Elvis would be sick of Priscilla in a few years. (According to Gramma, celebrity wives didn't have much lasting power.) By that time, Roxanne would be eighteen or nineteen. She would get a nose job, even a jaw job if she had to. She would even bring Elvis's picture to the plastic surgeon. Roxanne would be a younger version of Priscilla with a good, solid personality. Yes, that was it. Absolutely it. It was as tidy and nice as layers of a wedding cake. Roxanne was so pleased with herself that she did eight sloppy pirouettes down the hallway into her yellow and white bedroom.

5

I Ching Coin

That summer, James signed up to go to Esalen. When Gramma found out about his decision, she was so disgusted with the idea of him romping around California with a bunch of lunatics wearing nothing but love beads, that she refused to drive him to the airport.

On the morning of his departure, Emma finally convinced Gramma to at least drop him off at a hotel where he could catch an airport bus. Roxanne stood in the driveway waving goodbye to her father, chewing on the ends of her fingers (she had bitten all her nails off), feeling nauseated from nerves. She wished that he were going on a regular vacation—to somewhere like Miami or Honolulu—like other fathers did. Why did he choose to vacation at this place in California? Did he *really* want to meditate all day long? What was the purpose of it? Why couldn't he be a suburban dad who played golf on Saturdays, watched sports on television and had two drinks before dinner every night?

On the flight to San Francisco, he sat next to a middle-aged woman who had a doped-up poodle in a box shoved under the seat in front of her. James was afraid that the dog was going to make a mess and smell up the plane. The woman was a palm reader from Lawrence, Kansas, who was on her way to a psychic fair. She had a purple, wool poncho draped over her shoulders, a large silver medallion engraved with Chinese characters around her neck, and heavy hoop earrings that made her ear lobes droop. James wondered why women bothered to pierce their ears; it looked, well, barbaric, and he vowed he would never let Roxanne pierce her ears—not over his dead body.

"So, tell me about palm reading," James said, stirring his

Ginger Ale with his finger. He wondered what all the stock brokers at Stern Brothers would think of this conversation, and he had to concentrate on his ice cubes to keep from smiling.

"Well, I make a lot of money in a town like Lawrence," the woman answered cheerfully. "All the students come to me and ask whether they're going to pass their economics classes or break up with their boyfriends."

"Well, aren't the faculty or school psychologists supposed to help them with those kinds of things?"

"You know young people these days. They don't take the Establishment's word for it. They're *very* distrustful."

"I see," James replied, unconvinced. "What about those campus protests that have been on the news?" he asked, trying to change the subject.

"Well, yesterday they burned a papier-mâché Uncle Sam near the Student Union. I'll be glad when this is all over because all that chanting gives me terrible headaches. This anti-war business is just *awful* when you're trying to keep in the flow of universal consciousness. Have you ever had your palm read?"

"Uh, no," James said, shifting in his seat.

"Well, let me look at your right hand. Hmmm, I see. You have very sensitive fingertips, the hands of an artist. I'd say you're an architect."

"Wrong."

"An art director for an advertising agency."

"Guess again."

"I know. A curator at the Nelson Art Gallery."

"Way off base."

"You mean to tell me that you're not in the arts?"

"Not even remotely."

"Then you're a businessman."

"Right."

"No, wrong. That's all wrong for you. You should be an artist. Your hands say so."

"Really now," James said, feeling somewhat irritated by this woman.

"Now, be honest with me. Are you happy in your work?"

"Well, uh, let me ask you. Are you happy with what you do?"

"Of course I am. I've been a palm reader for many lifetimes," she said, dramatically brushing her hair back. "I was the court palm reader for King Fernando and Queen Isabella. I was the one who told them that Christopher Columbus was the genuine article."

"The genuine article?"

"You don't believe me, do you? Well, the history books don't know everything. Look at what they said about the Indians."

"I suppose," James said with a sigh. He was getting tired of this woman and her silly talk, and he wanted, more than anything else, to close his eyes and take a short nap.

"Let me see your palm again," she demanded. James gave her his right hand and rubbed his eyes with his left one. "You've got a hard road ahead, I can see that. Look at all those broken lines. Lots of change, lots of upheaval. You've got two children."

"Now, how did you know that?"

"That's easy. Any palm reading novice knows how to tell that. See those lines right there?"

"Uh-huh."

"Well, that's how you can tell. And you've got two."

"That's really amazing. What else?"

"You've also got a very deep and long sex line. Most men who have that are real playboy types."

"Not me. That isn't to say that I haven't *thought* about running around. I have. Any man gets tempted. I can't believe I'm telling you all this."

"You're not the first one who's said that. I was a priest in a past life, so people tend to tell me their secrets."

"Uh, right. By the way, my name is James Freedman."

"And I'm Miriam. You're Jewish, aren't you?"

"Well, I was brought up Jewish. I'm no longer a practicing Jew, though."

"I knew it, I just knew it."

"You knew what?"

"I knew you were Jewish. I've got a nose for Jewish men, a sixth sense if you will. I can tell if a man is Jewish, without even knowing his last name or whether he's from New York."

"Do you happen to be Jewish?"

"Of course I'm Jewish. I'm originally from Newton, Massachusetts. My ex-husband was a mathematics professor at

K.U. and, like a fool, I followed him to the Midwest even though the Tarot cards said it would be a big, big mistake. He ran off with some female revolutionary who planted a bomb in the laundry room of an all-girl dormitory. It never went off, but I suppose she impressed my husband enough for him to give up his job and grow rutabaga with her in Idaho."

"Well, why don't you move back to Massachusetts and be with your family?"

"God, I hate Boston. It's so stuffy and crowded. I hated Radcliffe so much it makes me sick even to think about it."

"You went to Radcliffe?" James asked, trying not to sound too surprised.

"Uh-huh. But if I move anywhere, it will definitely be the West Coast. It's easier to reinvent yourself there."

"Reinvent yourself?"

"Sure. You know, take on a new identity, a new occupation, new hang-ups, you name it. I've been thinking about becoming a CPA since I'm so excellent with numbers. I could become the accountant for all the psychics in California. That's why I'm going to this fair. To check out employment possibilities."

"Sounds ambitious," James said, again trying not to smile.

"Doesn't it, though."

"Do you have any children."

"No, we never had any. And I'm sorry for this, I really am. I could have passed down my psychic gifts to them. But perhaps it's just as well. Getting divorced can do terrible things to kids' heads."

James was relieved when she started reading a copy of *The Wall Street Journal* that she had taken out of her macramé bag. He was starting to believe that a lot of people like Miriam all over America had gone plain haywire. All of this media hoopla over these student radicals and drugged-out rock stars. It was as if society were permitting people to go crazy, yes, encouraging it, as a matter of fact.

But what was he himself doing? Running off to some God-forsaken place in California where people spent hours screaming at each other about bad breath and feeling unloved. Yet when he made his decision to go to Esalen, it had made perfect sense, considering how much time he spent talking about himself to Irving.

But most of all, he wanted to be well and strong for his family. They needed him—every single one of them needed a father figure to lean on. A father they could count on. Not a father who was going to crack up at the drop of a hat. Irving said that the more you knew about yourself, the stronger you became. That was what James wanted. Inner strength and wisdom.

James's Uncle Max had been strong. A tornado once flattened his farmhouse out in western Kansas, and it didn't even faze him. He simply finished mowing his pasture before it got too dark. Yet Max had to be strong. Being the only Jew in a farming community was tough in those days—or at any time, for that matter. James wanted to keep his uncle in mind as a model of strength and integrity. He also wanted to think that he came from that kind of sturdy stock, like the prospectors who panned for gold in the 1800s. That was how he would see this California adventure. As a way of searching for his own brand of riches. Peace of mind at the end of the rainbow. Psychological pay dirt.

Now Miriam, the palm reader, had dozed off, and James was wide awake. James noticed that she snored. The dog was snoring, too. The few Jewish women James had slept with before he married Emma also snored. Even the most attractive ones. What was wrong with them? Did they all have deviated septums? Roxanne probably thought so. She was constantly whining about breathing problems and wanting a nose job when she turned seventeen. He thought her nose looked just fine. But young girls were so peculiar. So worried about their appearance. Why would anyone bother with such nonsense? All of the nose jobs James had ever seen looked like mass-produced pig snouts. Now, take Emma, for instance. She had never given one damn about her looks, and she always looked breathtaking. Some women were lucky to be so effortlessly beautiful.

The pilot announced that they were flying over Nevada. James had a fantasy about Emma. He imagined her in one of those legalized prostitution ranches, dressed in a see-through teddy, wearing a garter with black stockings and stiletto high heels. The fantasy didn't arouse him; no, he was more amused than aroused. It was so out of character with the disheveled reality of Emma that he couldn't help chuckling to himself.

"An I Ching coin for your thoughts," Miriam said in a low, sleepy voice, blinking her eyes in an exaggerated manner. "I'm glad you're finding something to amuse yourself with."

"Oh, you couldn't pay me any amount of money to tell you what is on my mind."

"That bad, huh? Did I tell you that I find Jewish men very attractive. Especially married Jewish men," she said, touching his arm lightly.

"Why married? You're just asking for trouble if you involve yourself with married men."

"You must be speaking from experience. Now tell me—how many hearts have you broken?"

"None, none. I've been amazingly faithful," James said, scratching his head as if puzzled by his own fidelity. "I just know from talking to, say, some of the men I work with who have mistresses on the side; but when push comes to shove, they wouldn't ever divorce their wives. They just don't want to be financially burdened with alimony and with keeping some young gal in high style." James folded his arms firmly like he always did when he felt as if he had made a good point.

"That makes sense, but let me back up and answer your question," Miriam said. "The reason why I like married men is that I want cuddling and kissing and sex, but I don't want all the hassles of a relationship. At least not right now. Married men are a safe bet because I don't want anyone falling in love with me. Say, I never asked you why you're going to California."

"I'm going to attend workshops at the Esalen Institute."

"No kidding. That's very enlightened. I wouldn't expect that from a conservative businessman from Kansas City."

"Thank you. We conservative businessmen can be full of surprises." At this point, he wished he were at an office party during which he could excuse himself and go to the hors d'oeuvre table and dip into the punch bowl or grab a carrot stick. He always liked good exit lines. Two things his mother taught him: always leave a conversation on a good note. And always leave a party when you're having a good time. He was almost enjoying himself with this Miriam person, but he knew that twenty more minutes with this woman was going to send him over the edge. He might say something rude, and James did not like being rude, even to a mildly obnoxious person like Miriam.

"So, what do you think?" Miriam asked.

"About what?" James asked.

"About us," Miriam said.

"What about us?"

"Would you like to get together in San Francisco? We could get a bite to eat or a drink somewhere in between my palm reading sessions and your encounter sessions," Miriam said, trying to sound enthusiastic.

"I hate to say this, Miriam, but I really don't indulge in extramarital affairs. I know it sounds corny, but I just don't think I could live with myself if I were always running around with other women."

"That's too bad. I thought we could have some fun."

Miriam sat there with her arms folded, not looking out the window or at James, her jaw set in a rigid line. He couldn't believe it. She was actually sulking. Maybe this was why her husband left her for the nubile revolutionary. Maybe he couldn't stand watching her sulk whenever he didn't feel like having sex or when he didn't want to have his palm read. James also realized that even though it made him feel like a hypocrite, he was much more open to having an affair than he was willing to admit. But he didn't want to have one with Miriam. He was not attracted to her—not in the least.

James turned his back slightly to Miriam—as much as the seat belt would allow—and pretended to nap the rest of the flight. Every time she crossed her legs or made any sort of move, he jumped slightly. He was a little afraid of her because of all her connections with the occult. She might put some kind of hex on him and make him impotent. He remembered reading about that very thing in one of Gramma's crazy magazines, that some poor sucker traveled all over the world digging up witches' graves, looking for a charm to cure him of his impotence. James tried to remember who exactly put the curse on the poor guy—his wife or his girlfriend or his mother—but for the life of him he couldn't remember who it was. And even though he knew all those stories in the tabloids were a bunch of crap, the idea of impotence still made him nervous.

After the plane landed, James and Miriam stood up at the

same time, yet she refused to acknowledge his presence. Without even a goodbye, she picked up her poodle and her macramé purse and got in line to get off the plane. So that was how women dealt with rejection, James thought to himself. They all had better get used to it if they were going to be so aggressive in this world.

6

Esalen

James decided to rent a car and drive it down the coast. He figured driving was a big part of the California experience—and that was why he was there, wasn't it? To have some new experiences. To change, to grow, as the Esalen catalogue had said. Perhaps Miriam was right. Perhaps he could reinvent himself. Shed his old self, like the way cicadas shed their dry, translucent skins all over the pine trees in his front yard. And he would return to Kansas City, feeling refreshed and ready to go about his business.

At the car rental booth in the airport, James couldn't decide between a Camaro or a Cutlass. He had always driven a Cutlass, and even his own father drove a series of dilapidated Oldsmobiles. Hell, but a Camaro was fresher looking. It reminded him of those girls with the big white teeth, playing volleyball on the orange juice (or was it milk?) commercials. Yes, he would definitely choose a Camaro, one with a convertible top.

Once he got past the Bay Area, James was amazed by the California coastline. It was lush and green with endless, undeveloped hills sloping down into the brightest and bluest ocean he could remember. The Pacific seemed much happier than its East Coast counterpart. In comparison, the Atlantic was dark and moody and whenever he thought of it, he always envisioned that photograph of Robert Kennedy wearing chinos, running on the Cape Cod beach with his big dog. But now that Kennedy was dead, James couldn't help associating death with the Atlantic, even though he knew that Kennedy had been shot in California just last month.

In the distance, he saw an oil tanker, and he remembered

that he recently told a client not to invest in a particular oil stock because there was all this controversy about off-shore drilling, and that the environmentalists were up in arms about oil spills and dead fish floating belly-up among the surfers and sunbathers.

James drove past the town of Carmel. He had read some-where that real estate was more expensive there than in New York City, and that it was packed with rich artsy types and celebrities. Gramma would love Carmel. Maybe on his way back, he would stop there and buy her a postcard or a knick-nack.

James saw the sign for Esalen off Route 1. Nestled on a hill-side, it could pass for any of the modern-looking, liberal arts col-leges that seemed to be springing up all over America. Though when *his* kids were ready to apply to school, they were going to apply somewhere substantial like Harvard or Smith or the University of Kansas, depending on their grades and SAT scores, of course. They weren't going to some flaky, unaccredit-ed, experimental school that had barefoot commencement cere-monies and co-ed roommates. No siree.

Wait a minute, James thought to himself. He was in California. He shouldn't be thinking like such a fuddy-duddy. He should practice keeping an open mind. Why, a few years ago, he never would have dreamed that he would be in analysis. And look how far he had come with Irving.

James parked his Camaro in the lot and opened the trunk to get his luggage. On the grounds, there were about ten people shouting and making animal sounds and doing their own little dances while a slim, young girl in a leotard cried out, "Stay in the flow. Keep in time with the rhythm of your body. Do what feels good. Let it all happen NOW."

James thought that these people, who were all shapes and sizes, looked hilarious. They were trying so hard to act free and spontaneous. Damn it. There he was, being judgmental and cynical again. He had to stifle these thoughts if he were going to get anything out of this experience.

Watching these young people jumping and shaking their bodies suddenly made James feel old. They all looked like teen-agers. What was a forty-eight-year-old man like himself doing here anyway? If he hadn't already sent in his money, he would have jumped back into his rental car and dashed up the coast.

James also noticed that everyone at Esalen was overly friendly. The guy who handed him his room key gave him such a big smile, James thought his face was going to crack in half. Could people possibly be this blissful? It was almost spooky. They looked like happy robots. Press this lever and smile brother smile.

He was relieved when he walked into his room, and his roommate was slumped over on his bed, smoking a cigarette. He was on the short side with thick, blonde hair and a pock-marked complexion, wearing an untucked Hawaiian shirt. God, he looked normally depressed. And he looked over thirty. James liked him immediately.

"Hi, I'm James Freedman," James said, sticking out his hand.

"And I'm Russ. You just got here?"

"Yeah. How is it so far?"

"I don't know," Russ shrugged. "My wife thought this place would loosen me up."

"Well, has it?"

"Nah, not really. I've been here three days, and I haven't gotten upset. I haven't gotten excited. As a matter of fact, I haven't gotten anything except real bored. I'm not sure why I even bothered to come."

"Oh. So, where you from?"

"Fresno. And you?"

"Kansas City."

"Phew, you've come a long way to this gorgeous nut house. You know what I wouldn't mind? I wouldn't mind a drink."

"Me, either," James said enthusiastically.

"Well, where to?"

"I don't know," James said taking his clothes out of his suitcase and putting them into the bottom drawer. "I'm not from here."

"Neither am I, really."

"Is it against the rules of this place to drink?"

"Well, they don't encourage it, but at the same time, they don't discourage it. You get my drift?"

"Yeah . . . well, where should we go?"

"I don't know. Maybe it's not such a good idea to go after all."

"Yeah. Maybe not. I'm a little bushed from that long drive anyway."

"Where did you land?"

"San Francisco."

"You know, there's an airport closer than that, in Monterey."

"You're kidding. My secretary, she's the one who made the arrangements. You know something? I think maybe she's slipping."

"Maybe so."

"Hey, look what I found. I forgot I even packed it." James lifted up a fifth of scotch from the bottom of his carry-on bag.

"Smart thinking, man. I'll get the glasses," Russ said, walking to the bathroom. "Do you take water in yours?"

"Nah."

"Neither do I," Russ said, walking out of the bathroom with two glasses in his hand.

"Let's make a toast," James said, pouring the scotch.

"Here's to, uh, what? Being here? We're crazy to be here."

"Yeah, that sounds right. Here's to being crazy."

"And being here."

"Cheers."

"Cheers."

The next morning, James woke up with a substantial headache. He then remembered that he and Russ had pretty much drunk their dinner. James hated the idea of starting out these workshops with a hangover. Russ was already in the shower, humming a show tune. How could anyone feel like humming after all they had to drink last night? The guy must be some kind of alcoholic. Or maybe he just knew how to hold his liquor.

"I feel great," Russ said, wiping his face off with a towel. "The best I've felt since I've been here."

"Jesus, I feel like hell."

"I'm going to have to give you drinking lessons to toughen you up."

"Ugh, don't mention drinking. And what makes you the resident expert, anyway?"

"Well, for one, I grew up in an Irish Catholic family, and two,

I was posted in Germany for a couple of years. I would say I've had plenty of practice."

"I guess so," James said, slowly sitting up on the edge of his bed. "Did I say anything strange last night? I vaguely remember babbling about something, but I can't remember what."

"Well, at one point I asked you if you were married, and you said yes, but then all you wanted to talk about was some gal named Kathryn, and how the two of you might have had a beautiful life together."

"Oh. I said that?" James said, rubbing his forehead.

"Yup. I'm afraid so. Who is she?"

"Who is who?"

"This Kathryn."

"Oh, she's someone from my high school days who's been on my mind lately. She was a knockout except for this mangled hand she had. She was missing two fingers from some kind of childhood boating accident. She always wore clean white gloves, even in the hottest weather. Every boy at Southwest High School was in love with her. She had beautiful teeth. And she was president of the class. I saw her recently at a shopping mall. She smiled at me as if she remembered me from somewhere. My wife kept asking who that woman was who gave me that special smile in front of Woolworth. But don't you go through periods in your life when people from your past keep going through your head like some late night TV commercial being repeated over and over until that person's as much a part of your life as, say, your receptionist or your youngest kid?"

"Yeah, I felt like that a lot with my first wife, except she was like the late night programs that feature movies like *Bride of Frankenstein*. She would always call me up at two or three in the morning and threaten to swallow pills if I didn't send her more money for chiropractic school. Can you imagine? A chiropractor killing herself with pills? That's just how crazy she was. No wonder I couldn't live with her. I think she got a big charge out of scaring the daylights out of me."

James's face suddenly turned from hangover pale to red. The mention of pills and suicide hit a nerve, and he quickly turned away from Russ.

"Hey, you don't look so good," Russ said.

"I guess I'm not feeling so hot. But what you've been saying has made me think about something. Have you ever been in analysis?"

"No way. Have you?"

"Yeah. And you know what? It's helped me see myself for what I really am. And my wife, too. When I married her, I thought she was this beautiful helpless thing like Walt Disney's Bambi. Now I know better. Now I know she's truly helpless for a reason. It's because she's a little off-center. Anyone who sleeps all the time and vacuums compulsively and is terrified of driving is a little off-center. But the difference is that I don't fool myself anymore. I see everything clearer now. My mother, she was a woman who could make up her mind in an instant. She knew what she wanted the day she was born. Whatever she asked for, my father got her. A new car? No problem. Redecorate the house? Sure, why not. Irving says that I married someone like Emma as a reaction to my mother. It was a very rebellious thing to do. But after seeing Irving, I now want to find out more. About myself. That's why I'm here, you see. To find out more."

"Why do you want to do that to yourself?" Russ asked. "Isn't it painful to find out so much?"

"Sure. But isn't everything?"

"Well, no. Not everything."

"Name one thing that isn't painful," James said.

"Baseball. Watching baseball isn't painful, even if my team is losing. Did you happen to hear how the A's did yesterday?"

"I'm a Dodgers fan myself, but I think the A's might have won," James said.

"Good, I'm glad. I'm really glad."

James was somewhat relieved that Russ managed to change the subject. All this talk was making his headache worse. "Well, I'm going to jump in the shower and then let's get breakfast. How's the food here?"

"It stinks," Russ said.

"Sounds great."

"It isn't."

"I know that," James said. He hated it when people took his sarcasm seriously. In the meantime, Russ was putting on a pair of heavy wool socks and handmade leather sandals. James could not understand the reasoning behind wearing sandals *and* socks. It reminded him of what priests wore when they traveled on Greyhound buses across the United States.

"My second wife, though, she's real different from my first," Russ told James on their way to the dining room. "She's very normal, very stable. She likes to garden and sew her own clothes. She's recently gotten interested in, you know, stuff like touchy-feely dance at the Unitarian Church, and she thought that this Esalen place would be good for me."

"In what way?"

"Well, I guess you could say I'm a little hot-tempered. I've put holes in my living room wall to prove it. But I've never hit her, I've never hit my kids. Any man who hits his family is really sick in my opinion."

James had an irresistible urge to grab Russ by the shoulder just to let him know that he thought everything Russ did or said was all right. In fact, James thought that Russ was one of the most genuine people he had met in a long time. He couldn't remember when he was able to feel so much like himself in front of another male. Perhaps it was years ago during a vacation in Colorado when he met a boy named Ernie Stieffel from Philadelphia. They spent the entire three weeks skinny dipping in cold mountain lakes and playing baseball. After James returned to Kansas City, he kept thinking about Ernie's intelligence and his natural athletic ability, and some of his feelings toward Ernie frightened him. After writing him two brief postcards, James decided not to be Ernie's pen pal anymore.

While James was eating his eggs and wheat toast, he thought it was amazing that he was thinking so much about people from his past. Maybe this was related to what he had been discussing with Irving the other day. He remembered saying that he was going to use this trip to California to re-evaluate his life so far.

"You've gotten awfully quiet," Russ said, pushing eggs into his mouth.

"I guess I'm doing a lot of thinking."

"About what?"

"Oh, I don't know. People. The past. You name it."

"Yeah, this place sort of reminds me of a camp for adults. It brings back memories of summers in Minnesota," Russ said.

"I can see that. Or even like elementary school. I haven't had a meal ticket punched in I don't know how long," James said.

"Yeah. It makes me feel like a kid...."

"Me too."

"May I sit down?" asked a thin, dark-haired woman, who was wearing a purple paisley cocktail dress. She also had scars across her upper lip and nose, where she had had a hare lip.

"Why sure," Russ said.

"You know I could just hit myself," the woman said.

"Why?" James asked, looking down at his eggs.

"I brought *all* the wrong clothes. I simply don't know what I was thinking. I told everyone at the office I was going on a cruise down to Mexico and while I was packing, I kept thinking cruise instead of this place. Have you ever done that?"

"I can't say that I ever have," James said, rolling his eyes at Russ.

"It's too early in the morning to be really talking about this sort of thing," the woman said. "My name is Amy. What's yours?" she said, looking at Russ.

"Toulouse Lautrec."

"Naah, I don't believe it. What's your real name?"

"My real name's Toulouse Lautrec."

"Come on, what is it really?"

"It's Russ," he said, snickering.

"And yours," Amy asked James.

"Sigmund Freud."

"Come on. You guys are putting me on."

James started laughing so hard that he had to put his napkin up to his mouth so he wouldn't spit his eggs across the table.

"You guys are a bunch of clowns."

By this time, Russ and James were guffawing and wiping their eyes.

"I haven't seen such immature behavior since high school," Amy said in mock disgust. This comment made Russ and James laugh even louder. Amy then let out one tiny, high-pitched giggle, and she daintily put her hand across her mouth. James thought that she looked charming when she did this, like a

Japanese geisha girl. Russ attempted to speak a couple of times, but he kept laughing and gasping for breath.

"So . . . so," Russ said, hoarsely. "What's on the agenda for you all today?"

"Well, I don't know about *you*, but I'm getting one of those massages that everyone's been talking about," Amy said. "It only costs eleven dollars, and the best masseur is some hippie named Norman who used to be a junkie in New York City, and he supposedly tells the weirdest stories about shooting up in bombed-out buildings and being so stoned he would play fetch with rats. And he's telling you all of this while he's giving the most incredible massage."

"Hmmmm. I think I might pass up ole Norman," James said to Russ with a wink. "He sounds rather unsavory."

"No, no, he's supposed to be *wonderful*," Amy said, waving her arms. "He says that when he gives massages, his fingers feel like pulled taffy."

"Pulled taffy?" Russ asked, mockingly. "Now, James, would you trust your body to a guy who says his fingers feel like pulled taffy?"

"No way," James said.

"I'm glad you agree with me, ole chap."

"Righto," James said.

"I'm leaving," Amy said brusquely while standing up. "You boys have fun together, you hear?"

"Do you suppose she was pissed off?" Russ said to James as they were getting up from the table.

"Do you care?" James asked.

"Nah, I guess I don't. But we were sort of shitty to her. And don't you think she would be cute if it weren't for those scars on her face?"

"Hmmmm, I suppose so. There's something sweet about her. But she's not my type so it's hard to say."

"So who is your type? That Kathryn gal?"

"Kathryn's fantastic, there's no doubt about it. She's ideal fantasy material."

"Yeah, the well-groomed hostess, the perfect mother, and a tigress in bed, even if her hand is . . . ." Russ said.

"You've got it. But I'm sure she wouldn't live up to my fantasy. She's probably frigid."

"Probably."

"But let's hope not," James said, laughing.

"Yeah, right...so where you off to?" Russ asked.

"Some encounter workshop. Where you going?"

"I'm going to give Gestalt with Perls one more try and then I'm giving up on it. He and guys like Maslow and William Schultz are the big shots here, you know. But the things that people say in there are so wild, you just wouldn't believe it."

"Like what?" James asked.

"Like one guy who was in the hot seat yesterday dreamed that he saw himself as a bottle of Pepto-Bismol because his stomach gives him so much trouble. And the other day, a woman dreamed about a giant vagina swallowing her mobile home. I don't know what all this crap means. If I caught my kids talking like that, I'd wash their mouths out with soap and water. Besides, I don't remember my dreams. Do you?" Russ asked.

"Nah, I never have. And I agree with you one hundred percent about the soap and water business. I think our society is *way* too lenient about obscenity."

"You know, it's nice to meet someone who actually makes sense," Russ said, giving James a pat on the back.

"I guess I'll see you at lunch."

"I'll look for you," Russ said.

James arrived at the workshop entitled "Unlocking Your Inner Door," something he had registered for a month earlier. The room was stultifyingly quiet. Some couples were standing in front of each other, not saying a word, looking puzzled and self-conscious. Others were holding hands and touching each other's faces. One couple was lightly punching each other in the arms. Another was hugging, and the woman was crying on her partner's shirt sleeve.

All of a sudden, James started to miss Irving—the neat, white walls of his office, his soft, leather furniture and his clock hidden from view. The blatant emotionalism at Esalen seemed messy and uncomfortable compared to the fifty minute discussions he had with Irving on a daily basis. The group leader, who was a small man dressed in Levis and a Mexican shirt, took James by the arm and placed him in front of an attractive woman in her mid-thirties with dark, shoulder-length hair and rich, brown eyes. She was sitting on a large pillow.

"I want you two to stand in opposite corners of the room, look into each other's eyes and approach each other very slowly without saying a word," the group leader said in a quiet voice. "Then I want you to express whatever you're feeling toward each other, but don't plan what you're going to do. Just let your feelings take over at the moment you come together. But no talking. Do you understand?" Both James and the woman nodded. "Good," he said, rubbing his hands together and walking away.

James shrugged at the woman in an aw shucks manner. In the meantime, the woman was looking down at the floor with a serious expression on her face. Then she started to walk quickly toward James and bumped him hard with her shoulder.

"Ow," James said, rubbing his arm.

"No words, just feelings," the group leader said.

"But she—" James protested.

"Shhh...." the group leader said.

James looked around the room in exasperation, but no one seemed to sympathize or care about this particular psychodrama. Many of them were veterans of the Human Potential Movement, and they had seen and felt it all.

For the next fifteen minutes, James and the woman stood at opposite ends of the room, not looking at each other. Then the group leader quietly called all of the couples over, and they sat down in a circle.

"I think you two need to have a dyad," he said turning to James and the woman.

"What's that?" James asked.

"It's a discussion. You two need to find out what kind of subconscious messages you were giving each other. He must have been sending off something very intense, Lydia, for you to react that way."

"He was," Lydia said.

"Well, work through it. Get down to the bare bones of the matter."

"Well...well," Lydia said, her lips trembling a bit. "He reminds me of so many men I know, he makes me angry just to look at him."

"What else, Lydia," the group leader said in a gentle voice.

"He makes me want to scream," Lydia said.

"Well then go right ahead. Scream," the group leader said.

"AHHHHH," Lydia screamed, pounding her fists into her lap. "AHHHHHH."

"How do you feel now?" the group leader asked.

"Much better. Much, much better."

"How do you feel about the feedback you're getting from Lydia...I'm sorry, I didn't catch your name," the group leader said to James.

"It's James. I don't know what I'm feeling. I guess somewhat confused that...I don't know, I just got here, and this is all new to me."

"Let's get back to you, Lydia. Let's get specific about what it is about James that makes you angry."

"He seems, I don't know, arrogant, like all the men in New York City."

"What is it about him that makes you feel that way?"

"His looks, his confident manner. It all spells successful and spoiled, and I can have anyone and anything I want."

"How does that make you feel, James?"

"It makes me want to laugh," James said.

"Why?"

"Because it's so far from the truth. I mean, I've done all right professionally. But confident? Spoiled? I don't think I would be here if I felt so on top of the world."

"What do you think about what James just said, Lydia?" the group leader asked.

"Maybe I jumped to conclusions," she said, eyeing James closely for the first time. "Maybe I'm projecting my own feelings about men onto him."

"I was just going to say that," a young woman said, who wore an embroidered peasant shirt and frayed bell bottoms. "I think James seems like an okay guy, not like the kind of guy you were talking about."

"But he does share some of those same qualities that Lydia is all hung up about," a bearded man said who was sitting in a modified lotus position. "He admits to being successful. I think that's what she was picking up on."

"So what if he's successful. Just because you're successful doesn't mean you're not a nice guy. My father made a million dollars, and you couldn't find a nicer man if you tried," the woman said with tension in her voice.

"That's not what I'm saying at all," the man answered loudly.

"Then what are you trying to say? You always put down everything that comes out of my mouth."

"I think we've come to a communication impasse here," the group leader said. "I want you two to stand up and continue to communicate but without words this time."

The man released his lotus position and jumped to his feet. The young woman reluctantly pushed herself from the floor and hung her head as if she had done something wrong. The man crouched down on one knee, pulled her on his other knee and bounced her up and down like a proud parent would do to a toddler. The young woman hid her face in her hands. They stayed like this for a few minutes until the group leader told them to stop. Then they both stood up and grinned at each other.

"So, what happened between you two?" the group leader asked.

"I'm not sure," the man said. "But I think we might be putting each other in a family context, if you know what I mean. I think we're treating each other like a father and a daughter would."

"That's it. That's what makes me so mad at you. You're always treating me like a child, and I'm not a child at all," the woman said.

"I'm sorry, I really am," the man said in a remorseful voice. "Other women have accused me of doing the same thing."

The young woman reached for the man's hand and kissed it and held it for about twenty seconds. Then they both sat down, and James swore that her face had an ethereal glow to it.

"Lydia, I feel we've gotten a little sidetracked from what was going on with you," the group leader said softly. "And what I think you need to work on is building your trust level. We're going to do an exercise called Roll-and-Rock. Now, Lydia, stand up and close your eyes, and I want everyone to form a tight circle around her. We're going to pass her around as if she were a sack of potatoes. And Lydia, you should try to relax all of your muscles and give yourself over to the energy of the group."

At first, Lydia was very stiff as if she were expecting someone not to catch her, and she was bracing herself for a fall. But after being passed around a few times, she felt secure and allowed her body to go limp. She was literally rolling from person to person. Then the group, on the urging of the leader, picked her up parallel to the floor and gently rocked her back and forth. Then they lowered her to the floor. Lydia lay still for a few minutes and covered her eyes with her arm. Tears were coming down her face. Slowly she stood up and looked around the circle until her eyes fell on James. She then threw her arms around his neck and gave him a long, wet kiss on the mouth. From that moment on, James knew they were going to end up in bed.

7

A Bed of Leaves

For the next two days, James and Lydia were inseparable. James had a heart-to-heart talk with Russ, and after Russ discovered that Lydia had a very attractive roommate, he agreed to trade rooms. On those mornings, Lydia and James went to yoga class together even though James could hardly squat with any comfort or flexibility. After yoga, they bathed in a hot tub and quietly engaged in underwater foreplay.

They went on long walks and made love on a bed of leaves. All these new experiences made James vacillate between feeling very free and feeling very self-conscious.

Yet James had never made love with such sensuality or abandon. While he was having sex with Emma, he would handle her with the utmost delicacy, as if her fragile limbs would shatter like the Baccarat vase that he had once knocked off an end table in the living room. But Lydia was a strapping, passionate woman, a woman he could gently wrestle with and kiss on the neck.

Lydia had lived alone in New York for about fourteen years. Her life was both sophisticated and difficult—from regularly attending off-off-Broadway theatre and concerts at Carnegie Hall to being mugged at knife point in front of her apartment. Due to these accumulated experiences, she seemed at first appearance to be a tough know-it-all who was impatient and unwilling to let anyone get to know her. But after James spent some time with her, he realized that Lydia had a warm, vulnerable side. James liked the idea of being involved with such an independent woman, who was quite a shining light in the advertising field. As a matter of fact, Lydia had worked on the popular Alka-Seltzer TV campaign, and James remembered the stomachs of the go-go dancer and the boxer along with the slogan, "No matter what shape your stomach is in," and how clever he always thought those commercials were. But what James especially liked about Lydia was the fact that she was the first Jewish woman he had ever cared for. He was beginning to believe that by caring for her, he was learning to like his own Jewishness a little more.

By the third day of their affair, James and Lydia had stopped going to workshops altogether and were growing tired of people whispering about them and giving them knowing smiles. So they decided to drive up to Carmel and check into a quaint place called The Pine Inn that looked as though it should have been in New Hampshire.

During one of their long walks along the beach, James found out why Lydia was so angry towards men and why she had come to Esalen in the first place. A few months before, the man she had been dating had shot himself in the head after she had broken up with him. And it was Lydia who had found his skull shattered all over his bathroom walls.

Michael had been a brilliant lawyer at Paul Weiss, but he was mercurial and full of contradictions. According to Lydia, he was arrogant but afraid of being alone. He had a child-like dependency on her but would be demeaning towards her in front of his business acquaintances. He was always fretting that she hadn't attended a fancy college and didn't have a trust fund, yet would constantly accuse his colleagues of being spoiled and over-educated. Lydia resented Michael's suicide. She felt as if he had gotten his revenge by making certain she would always be afraid of loving someone else.

"I couldn't stand being with him any longer," Lydia said, digging a hole in the sand with a clam shell. "We had been dating for seven years, and we were no closer to getting married than when we first met. And I'm not getting any younger. I mean, I'm thirty-seven years old. Anyway, I was starting to wonder whether I *wanted* to be married to this type of man. He was getting more and more impossible, and I was having serious doubts about his sanity. I told him he should go to a psychiatrist, and I would even make the appointment. And if he didn't like that psychiatrist, I would find someone else for him to go to. But

Michael wouldn't listen to anyone. No, he thought he had all the answers. One night we were out at a restaurant with some friends, and someone teased him about something so insignificant, you just wouldn't believe it. Something about the color of his tie—I mean, we're talking stupid. Michael got very quiet, and the muscle in his jaw started to pulse. Then our friend asked him if he was all right, and Michael threw a glass of water in his face and walked out of the restaurant. It was a shock, to say the least. I knew right then and there that this man wasn't sane or healthy and that this was the end for us. He begged me not to break up, and he would call me at odd hours at night and in the early morning, saying he didn't see any sense in anything anymore. But you see, I had been hearing this for seven years, so I didn't pay that much attention. He told me things like he didn't see the purpose in life, and I would be filing my nails or washing the dishes, only half-listening to him. He was so self-centered, such a baby. He probably thought I wasn't suffering enough, so he figured he would do something that would really make me suffer. And he did. That bastard...." Lydia began to cry into James's shoulder.

"It's not your fault," James said, putting his arm around her, not really knowing what to say.

"I remember when one of the senior partners at his firm called me at work," she said, wiping her face with a crumpled Kleenex. "I was in a meeting, but he said it was urgent, and that I should check up on Michael. He hadn't shown up at the office, and he hadn't called, and he wasn't answering his phone. That was very unlike Michael. He was an excellent lawyer. Very conscientious. I still had his key, so I went over there, and that's when I found him. I knew he had it all planned out. I knew he wanted me to find him. He really didn't have any other close friends. All the friends we had were my friends. He figured his life was ruined and so he wanted to ruin mine, too. You see, I knew his mind so well. He thought things through. He would often dictate his ideas into his dictaphone, and after the place was cleaned up, I looked for it to see if he had recorded any thoughts before he killed himself."

"And had he?"

"No. Not a thing. And no note. That was the one thing that

was strange about his suicide. Michael was such a verbal person. Very articulate. And not just about law. He could recite Shakespeare and Eliot perfectly. He had that kind of mind. It was like he saw things too clearly. Everything affected him so much."

"He sounds like quite a fellow. . . ." James broke off in mid-sentence and stared off into the water for a few minutes; his face had a completely blank expression.

"James, are you okay?" Lydia asked, her voice sounding frightened. "James, where are you? Come back to earth?"

James shook his head and smiled slightly. "Lydia, I want to tell you something, but I don't want to scare you. There's something about me that maybe you should know. I've never discussed this with anyone except my analyst. Not even with my family. A couple of years ago, I tried to do myself in, too. . . ."

"You're kidding," Lydia said, backing away from James. "I don't believe it."

"But I thought if I told you what was going on with me, it might help you not to feel so bad. My attempt wasn't as serious . . . if I told you how I tried you would probably laugh."

"No I wouldn't. Honestly, I wouldn't at all."

"I took a bottle of aspirin," James said, throwing a small pebble into the waves. "But it was nothing anyone did in particular. I just wanted to escape everything. My family, my job. Suicide seemed easier than walking out and having to explain myself later."

Lydia had a puzzled look on her face and pushed her hands deep into her pockets.

"Can aspirin actually kill a person?" Lydia asked.

"If you take enough of them, sure."

"It sounds as if it were more of a plea for help than anything else."

"Maybe . . . ."

"Well," she said, putting her arms around his neck and smiling wistfully. "I'm glad you made it."

The two days went by so fast that James almost forgot he had a plane reservation to go home the next day. He knew he was falling in love with Lydia, and that scared him. It wasn't Lydia he was afraid of. He thought she was a remarkable woman, someone he could see living with for the rest of his life. In fact, Lydia was a more sensible choice for a partner than Emma ever had been. But by falling in love with Lydia, he was feeling more attached to his family and more afraid to leave them. He wasn't sure if he could ever create a whole new life for himself, especially in a city like New York. But he had to see this affair through with Lydia—at least spend some more time with her.

During their last evening together, Lydia kept begging him to come visit as soon as possible. Despite the fact that she was so independent, James sensed a certain desperation about her since she was going back to such a lonely life. But she did not suggest that he leave his family for her, which was a relief to James. At one point they were looking in some shop windows on Ocean Avenue, and she admitted that she might be falling in love with James, but she wasn't sure if she were capable of devoting herself fully to a relationship. She still had problems to work out concerning Michael's death. When they made love on the morning of their departure, there were some feelings of sadness as well as a sense of anticipation about future possibilities.

On the plane back to Kansas City, James could not get Lydia out of his mind. Every time he turned his head, he swore he could smell the way her hair smelled on the pillow. A woman across the aisle shook her gold bangle bracelets, and it sounded like Lydia putting on her jewelry to go out for dinner. The sound of another woman combing her hair and opening her makeup compact made his throat contract. He hoped that he wouldn't be such an emotional wreck by the time he arrived in Kansas City. Hell, maybe all of these feelings would pass. Maybe he was just going through some crazy, mid-life crisis, like it said in the book that he picked up in the airport newsstand. A man in his forties starts feeling his mortality, and that's when he needs vitality and excitement. In one way this affair made him feel so alive; yet, strangely enough, for the first time in a while, James was starting to think about escaping—and various ways to do himself in.

During the rest of the flight, James leafed through the Esalen catalogue so he would be able to tell his family what he supposedly did at the Institute. Modern Buddhism, Shamanistic Dreams, The Transformation of Self, Developing Clairvoyant

Powers, Holistic Medicine, The Karma of Politics, Intermediate Massage, The Theatre within the Mind, all of these courses sounded too far out for James. He decided that he would tell them that he alternated between the encounter groups and Gestalt therapy, which was the closest to the truth.

Gramma and Emma met him at the airport. On the way home in the car, he talked non-stop about how wonderful Esalen and California were. He described the workshops he attended and dropped the appropriate phrases such as sensory awareness, role playing, and psychic evolution. Emma looked at him as if he had just landed on the wrong planet. Gramma wondered if he were suffering from over-stimulation and heading for another breakdown. Both of them were quiet while James nervously chattered away about things he knew little or nothing about. By looking at Gramma's face, James realized he was in a bind. New ideas always made Gramma suspicious. And when Gramma was suspicious, she always made sure that she carefully scrutinized the object of her suspicion. James would have to be extra careful during these next few weeks. He would only call Lydia from the office, and she must not, under any circumstances, call him at home. Perhaps he was just being paranoid. Here it was, the first time he had taken a vacation by himself, and he had gone and had an affair. Not just an affair of the flesh, but an affair of the heart. Hell, he might truly be in love for the first time in his life. He knew he loved Emma too, but it was more of a protective love, not a love for someone he respected—like Lydia.

When the three of them arrived at home, they found Roxanne and Gus sitting sullenly in their respective rooms. They had had a fight, and James decided to unpack first and then give his daughter a good talking-to about the importance of getting along with her only sibling. Gus was a more difficult case, and he didn't have the energy to try to get him to open up.

"So, what's the problem?" James asked Roxanne who was braiding and unbraiding the fringe on the bottom of her bed spread.

"You don't *really* want to know," Roxanne said. "And anyway, I've got a stomach ache, I don't feel like talking. You should probably go back to California and stay away from your stupid family."

"Don't be silly," James said, fearing that somehow Roxanne had just read his mind. "I care about what's going on with you two."

"Not this time, Dad. You really don't want to know this time."

"Come on, Roxanne. Give your old dad a break."

"All right. You've asked for it."

"Okay. Sock it to me."

Roxanne sighed in disgust. She hated it when her father used media or counterculture lingo.

"Well, Gus was in the bathroom for a long time this afternoon, and I had to go real bad, but he wouldn't come out so I knocked on the door a bunch of times—"

"Now, Roxanne, do you think you were being fair to Gus? After all, there are other bathrooms in the house."

"Dad, you're not listening to me. I mean, God."

"Sorry, sorry. Go on."

"The reason why I wanted to use my bathroom was because I had gotten all this new makeup and I wanted to try it."

"When did you start wearing makeup? Does Gramma know you wear makeup?"

"Dad, you're not listening to me. Forget it, just forget it."

"I'm sorry, honey. I didn't mean—"

"I said FORGET IT!"

"I'M NOT GOING TO LEAVE UNTIL YOU TELL ME WHAT THIS IS ALL ABOUT," he yelled, getting red in the face.

"All right, all right already. Parents. Sheesh," Roxanne said in a resigned voice, flopping back on her pillow. "But don't say one more word until I'm finished. Promise?"

"Promise."

"Well, I'd left all my new makeup on the sink, so finally I just said I was coming in. He hadn't locked the door or anything like that. And he'd opened all my makeup and was putting it on. Lip gloss. Mascara. My aqua blue eye shadow. God, it was so gross. I mean, first of all for a boy to be into my makeup, I mean, how weird, but also it was new and I don't like lending it out 'cause you can get pink eye and stuff like that. I yelled and hit him hard, but he was laughing so I hit him again. I think Gus is a pervert, I really do. Why do I have to be stuck with a pervert brother?"

James was surprised by this story. It would be different if Gus were a little younger, but at his age, it was unusual for a boy to be interested in makeup. Now Roxanne was looking at him, demanding some sort of answer about something that he himself couldn't explain. But he knew he had to come up with something. Anything.

"Well, I think Gus is going through some kind of phase. I'm sure he'll get over it."

"I've never heard of a boy wearing makeup unless he's queer or something. I bet Vicki's brother wouldn't be caught dead in makeup."

"How do you know? Have you ever asked her?"

"Well . . ."

"So, then. How do you know?"

"I just know. He likes boy stuff. Like basketball. And cars. He can name the brand and year of every car that drives through Winstead's—"

"When have you gone to Winstead's with him?" James said, feeling like Roxanne might have gone out on a date behind his back.

"God, Dad, I mean . . . sometimes Vicki's mom takes us to Winstead's for a burger. Now you happy?"

"But does this boy drive?"

"No, he's younger. God, sometimes you're so weird."

"I'm just concerned, that's all . . . you're almost old enough to date."

"Almost! Lots of kids in my class have been dating for a year now."

"Well, that's just too bad. You're my daughter, and what other parents allow is their own business."

"God, you're so mean. I wish I had other parents."

"Don't talk to me like that."

Roxanne grew quiet and hugged her pillow. James was frustrated. It seemed as if every attempt to relate to his children alienated them even more. Nothing had really changed. Maybe he would try something that Gramma frequently did.

"I was reading in a magazine on the plane that that Elvis you like so much was very close to his parents."

"No one my age cares about Elvis," Roxanne said. "He's gotten boring and fat in the face. I like another singer better."

"Who's that?" James asked.

"I'm not gonna tell you."

James had had enough of trying to talk to his daughter. While walking out of her room, he was feeling glad that he had come home to domestic turmoil because he couldn't dwell on Lydia so much. He decided that he would mention something about Gus to Gramma, who was in the downstairs bathroom trying to get the toilet to stop running. She was shaking the handle, and James held up the top while she fiddled around with the chain and some of the pulleys.

"Did you know that Gus and Roxanne had a fight?" James asked her.

"So what? Those two are always fighting."

"But do you happen to know what it was about?"

"No."

"Well, Roxanne caught Gus putting on her makeup."

"She what?"

"You heard me."

"I don't believe it."

"She wasn't lying. Not this time."

"Well, I'll be . . . just like Liberace."

"What did you say?"

"You know, Liberace. He wears makeup and sequins and plays the piano under a fancy candlestick holder. Maybe Gus saw him on TV recently. And remember that Negro singer in the fifties who wore all sorts of goop on his eyes and styled his hair—"

"Stop talking about those damn celebrities. This is serious. This is family we're talking about."

"I know, I know," Gramma said, closing the toilet top with a loud clunk.

"Well, what should we do about it?"

"Talking to that boy won't do a bit of good. I know that," Gramma said.

"Do you think I should take him to Irving?"

"No offense, but I don't think Irving can do a whole lot."

"Well, I happen to think he can. I happen to believe in analysis."

"Well, bully for you. My opinion is to let that boy be. Gus likes music. Maybe he's connecting makeup and music. This is a confusing time . . . and anyway you can't tell the girls from the boys these days. I say he's just confused."

"And I say he's got a problem."

"And I say leave him alone," Gramma said, giving the toilet handle one final shake.

"Gramma?"

"What, James?"

"You're not helping that toilet one bit."

"I'm glad you noticed, son. Welcome home."

The next morning Gramma was sitting at the breakfast table chewing on white toast with the crusts carefully cut off. Emma was filling her tub with mounds of bubble bath because she had read in *Good Housekeeping* that soaking in hot water can sometimes make you feel better. Gus was still asleep since he had stayed up late the previous night, going over sheet music he had stolen from The Toon Shop. Soon, Roxanne shuffled into the kitchen in her bathrobe and fuzzy slippers and started to heat up a cinnamon roll in the toaster oven. While she spread butter on top of the roll with her finger, Gramma gave her the evil eyeball.

"I heard about you two," Gramma said in a menacing voice.

"So?" Roxanne said, trying to sound nonchalant.

"What's going on with you and your brother?"

"He's a weirdo. A queer weirdo at that."

"Don't talk about family like that. Don't you ever."

"When did you start siding with *him*? I thought you liked me best."

"I don't like it when you treat your brother poorly."

"He's a pervert...."

"He's a creative soul trying to make his own way."

"Gramma! How can you think that?"

"I can think any which way I want. That goes for your father, too."

"What about Daddy?"

"Oh, nothing in particular. I've got my eye on him, that's all...."

"I heard him whistling in the bathroom last night. He seems happy."

"That's what makes me think. I've never known your father

to be happy."

"Maybe that place in California worked or something."

"I don't believe in all that head-shrinking hocus pocus. I think it's something else."

"What, Gramma?"

"I'm not going to say."

"Come on," Roxanne pleaded.

"Huh-uh," Gramma said, shaking her head. "It's just a hunch I have, that's all. Nothing else."

Gus was feeling fidgety in bed. He was turning over and over again in a half sleep, and the sheets and blankets were twisting around his legs. He kept remembering the look of surprise on Roxanne's face after she opened the bathroom door and saw him standing there. There was nothing wrong with what he did. A lot of rock stars wore makeup so that they looked better. Even her precious Elvis wore mascara. So there....

And yet...he still wasn't sure why he had done it. All he knew was that he was always looking for ways to get back at Roxanne. Not for any real reason. He just couldn't stand her. That was all. But he understood why Roxanne got pissed off. He wouldn't like it if, say, she had ripped open something of his— like a new package of guitar picks. Jesus, he was actually feeling sorry. This was a new one. He had never felt bad about doing anything shitty to her before. Maybe Gramma was getting to him. She used to lecture him about respect and all that junk, but she had eventually given up...hey, wait a minute. If Mick Jagger had a sister, he wouldn't respect her. No way. To be like Mick, you had to be disrespectful. And nasty. Gus was grooming himself for the big time. Definitely.

And yet...Gus didn't want to go downstairs. He didn't want to face Gramma and her disapproving looks. Maybe he would slip out of the house and go someplace for breakfast. He didn't know where. He figured he would just start walking. Yeah, walking sounded good. That was just what he would do.

Emma got out of the bathtub and wondered how she was going to spend her day. She could sit on the folding chair in the back yard. She could stand around the kitchen, sipping lukewarm Lipton tea. She could plant a few begonias she had bought at Rosehill nursery on Holmes. She could play crazy eights with Gramma. She could vacuum, although she hadn't done that for a long time. She could . . . why, there were many more possibilities than she ever imagined. Maybe that hot bath helped. She was feeling a little better about herself and the world in general.

Emma put on her madras blouse and Bermuda shorts which had faded into a wash of grays and pinks. Finally, she was ready for some sunlight. But something stopped her from opening the bedroom door. It was a feeling she frequently got, a dread that yanked at the bottom of her stomach and worked its way up to her throat. It was a dread she had to fight off, or she would never be able to open that door. There. She did it. That wasn't so bad. It was nine-thirty, and Emma was heading down the stairs on a muggy summer morning to make herself some hot tea. Maybe the air-conditioned kitchen would be a nice place for her to spend the day after all. . . .

Damn it, James thought to himself, swiveling his chair around to look out his office window at the building across the way. He was dreaming about Lydia again when he had a pile of memos to answer and customers to call. What made him think about Lydia for the umpteenth time was that he just remembered a conversation he had overheard in the hall a few weeks before. A New York company was interested in buying some small outfit in Kansas that made plumbing parts. The CEO of this New York firm was looking for people at Stern Brothers to help in the negotiating process. James was more of a straight stock salesman than anything else; perhaps he would express interest in learning how to negotiate and ask if he could accompany whoever was assigned the job. He was certain that the president would give his approval, since he was always telling the vice-presidents that they needed to diversify their expertise. He couldn't believe how smooth this was all going to be. Here was a viable, above-board way to get to New York. It was too good to be true. Easy as pie. It made him nervous. He was actually sweating through his summer suit. He never trusted anything that seemed too easy. He was going to have to play this with a very cool head or everything would fall through. Right. He picked up the phone to call Lydia. Maybe he should wait. He didn't want to seem too eager. Yes, he would wait. A day or so. Maybe....

8

The Floater

On a Saturday morning in September, Roxanne was still lying in bed at ten-thirty. She didn't want to get up yet, since she was having her favorite daydream.

She wanted to believe it was true. She even clasped her hands together and prayed it was true. She wanted to believe that someone in her family had found her in a wicker basket on her parents' doorstep, a pink blanket tucked under her chin with a short, anonymous note pinned to it. She felt as though she didn't belong. Not in her house or to her family. Nowhere. She wanted to believe that a couple from Leawood would some-day step forward and claim her as their long-lost child, and she would move into their ranch house with wall-to-wall carpeting and a good air conditioner. Yet it was Gramma who said that her mother had in fact gone to Menorah Hospital and given birth to her. She was more depressed than ever. No hope of escaping the genetic cord tying her to her weird father, her weird mother, and her weirder than weird brother. No hope.

Roxanne turned over in her bed and tried to forget about her family for a while. She tried to think about something neater. Like boys. There was one boy she was particularly interested in. He didn't hang out with any one clique. He was more like a floater. He seemed to have lots of different friends from lots of different cliques, and Roxanne respected that. He was so well-adjusted for a kid her age. No one else she knew was like that. Everyone's home life was almost as screwed up as hers was. Could he possibly have one of those mothers who always wore an apron and a clean, flowery dress and greeted him after school with a kiss and a plate of freshly-baked cookies? Nah, impossible.

The boy's name was Rick. She liked the way that Rick and Roxanne sounded together, the R's rolling off her tongue. She could just imagine it: Eddie Martin, one of the cool senior jocks, is about to call kids up to invite them over for a last-minute party. He's rubbing his stomach through a hole in his T-shirt and drinking a beer from his folks' refrigerator.

"Hey," he says, "how 'bout inviting Rick and Roxanne? They're a good time."

"Sure," says his buddy, Steve Paxton, crunching a beer can in his hand. "Call 'em up."

At every party she and Rick would be together holding hands and ogling each other. Other kids could hardly stand being around them, they would act so mushy. Wouldn't that be too great?

Rick was cute but not conceited cute. The conceited cute boys always were after the cheerleaders, and she was definitely not the cheerleader type. Rick, on the other hand, was skinny with dark brown hair that waved past his shirt collar. His two front teeth were slightly chipped, and he had a hint of a mustache. He always wore a St. Christopher's medal around his neck, and his bell-bottom jeans were held up with a thick, hand-made leather belt embossed with tiny flowers.

But most important, Rick would be able to see beyond her very average looks—especially beyond her nose that still swooped dangerously close to her upper lip—beyond her nail biting and her bouts with her bad stomach and into her deepest, most secret thoughts. He would know her so well that he could predict her reaction to everything—food, people, movies, clothes. Just think of it. And he would recognize her strength of character and her good personality, like Gramma always said.

Roxanne decided to call Vicki to ask her what to do about Rick. What should be her next move? Vicki was always more aggressive with boys than Roxanne could ever be. Probably too aggressive. Since Vicki had gotten pregnant, she was not as popular as she once was. Some kids stayed away from her because she had a bad reputation, and they didn't want one, too. But Roxanne still liked her, even though they frequently fought and sometimes didn't speak for weeks at a time.

"He's the first boy you've ever really liked. I think you two would look really cute together."

"Really? You think so?" Roxanne asked.

"Sure," Vicki said, blowing on her wet, candy-pink nails. "Do you happen to have the latest *Seventeen*?"

"No."

"Well, there's an article I think you should read called 'Twenty Ways to Make a Boy Like You.'"

"Very funny, Vicki. Very funny."

"I'm serious, Roxanne, you should read it. Anyway, Rick's in my study hall. I'm gonna try to sit close to him to see what he does and where he goes. Then we can go where he goes. Get it? This could be it, the start of who knows?"

"Knowing me, it'll be the start of something stupid and terrible."

"Don't think so much," Vicki said.

"Shut up," Roxanne said, slamming the phone down before Vicki could get in one more word. She then threw her favorite stuffed bear against the bedroom ceiling, and it landed on the floor with a soft thud.

9

Loop-O-Plane

T he following week, Vicki ran up to Roxanne in the hall at school and dropped all of her books on Roxanne's feet. Vicki was wearing a white poor boy with stains on the front, and her bangs were chopped unevenly across her forehead. Before Roxanne had a chance to cry out or kick her in the shin, Vicki told Roxanne that she had overheard Rick making plans with his buddy, Jack Atkinson, to go to the Southwest High School carnival on Saturday night. Roxanne and Vicki agreed to meet in front of the stone Christian Science Church across the street from the high school at seven-thirty on Saturday night.

For twenty minutes, Vicki and Roxanne stood by the ferris wheel outlined with white flashing lights, looking for Jack and Rick. All the waiting and looking made them hungry so they decided to go and get something to eat. Vicki slurped on a grape snow cone, and Roxanne picked at pink cotton candy. After wiping their sticky hands on their jeans, they finally spotted the two boys trying to throw quarters into glass ashtrays in order to win a huge Daffy Duck. After three dollars worth of quarters bounced from glass to floor, the boys gave up and moved on to the target shooting booth. Roxanne and Vicki followed them and pretended to be absorbed in people squeezing different colored oil paint on spinning pieces of paper.

"This is better than the stuff I've seen in art books," Roxanne said. "Better than what's his name."

"Who?"

"You know, the guy who dripped paint on canvasses. You know who I mean."

"Huh-uh," Vicki said, shaking her head.

"I'll think of who he is. I'll wake up tonight saying his name out loud."

"There they go, stupid. Come on."

The girls followed Jack and Rick to the popcorn stand and pretended to be absorbed in the kernels bouncing and exploding in the popper. After the boys threw the last bits of popcorn into their mouths, Roxanne and Vicki followed them to the Loop-O-Plane and watched them pay for tickets to get on.

"I wouldn't go on that for anything," Roxanne said, walking backwards.

"Chicken," Vicki said.

"You go then. I get sick on rides that spin and go upside down."

"All right, chicken. I'll let you know what you're missin'— hey, that rhymes."

"Bye," Roxanne said, waving to Vicki and some other girl as the Loop-O-Plane operator fastened the bar across their laps. She was feeling a little jealous, since Jack and Rick were sitting in the other car. She watched the cars rock forward and backward, then turn and twist upside down for about ten times. Now, she was actually glad she had chosen not to go on the ride. Just looking at it made her stomach feel queasy. When the ride operator opened Rick and Jack's door, they tumbled out of their seats, guffawing and pushing each other forward. Vicki and the other girl were slower to emerge from their car. Vicki looked pale and shaky.

"God, I've got to lie down," Vicki said, collapsing in the grass. "I think I'm gonna barf."

"There's a trash can over there," Roxanne said, pulling her up by the arm.

"Are you okay?" Rick asked, bending over Vicki.

"She's fine," Roxanne said impatiently, trying to get Vicki to stand up.

"She looks shitty," Jack said to Rick. "A good puke would do her good."

"Come on, Vicki, let's go," Roxanne said through clenched teeth. This was not the way she wanted to be introduced to Rick Templeton.

"You're..." Rick said to Roxanne.

"Roxanne Freedman," she said, turning red.

"And I know who you are," Rick said, looking down at Vicki.

"I feel terrible," Vicki moaned.

"Someone was talking 'bout you the other day," Rick said to Roxanne.

"Oh, I can't imagine who," Roxanne replied quickly. She was hoping Vicki hadn't let it slip out that Roxanne was interested in him.

"Let's get this girl to a john before she pukes all over herself," Jack said, pulling Vicki up on her feet. He and Rick draped her arms over their shoulders and carried her over to a portable bathroom.

"I can't go in there. I'll die from the smell," Vicki said, backing away. "I'm going to go behind this building. Don't worry 'bout me."

"So," Roxanne said feeling awkward, "I guess she'll be all right."

"Nothin' like a good puke to set the day straight," Jack said. Roxanne thought that that was the dumbest thing she had ever heard.

"Listen, my folks live just a few blocks from here. After she's finished, let's go over there."

"Sounds good," Roxanne said, trying to sound enthusiastic.

A few minutes later, Vicki came stumbling from behind the building wiping her mouth.

"How do you feel?" Roxanne asked.

"Ugh, don't ask."

"We're headin' to my house," Rick said. "You can lie down there."

"Good," Vicki said. "Lying down is my favorite position."

"We know that," Jack said, nudging Rick in his side.

"That's not funny," Vicki said. Even Roxanne had to stop herself from laughing.

Rick lived in a gray Cape Cod house with a wreath hanging on the red, front door. Rick's parents were sitting on the living room couch, reading. The Beatles' "Sgt. Pepper's Lonely Hearts Club Band" was playing on the stereo. There were large, abstract paintings with slashes of color on every wall. A black and white photograph of Civil Rights protesters marching and linking arms was hanging over the fireplace. The house smelled of spicy pine trees, and Roxanne noticed a cone of incense burning in a dish with Middle Eastern designs on it.

Rick's parents were probably the same age as Roxanne's, but they certainly looked different. Rick's father was wearing jeans and a worn, tweed jacket. He had a salt and pepper beard and was smoking a pipe. His mother's black hair was pulled off her face into a tight bun, and she was wearing a red, embroidered dress from Guatemala and dangle earrings in the shape of birds.

"Rick, this record is remarkable," his mother said, closing her book on her lap. It was *American Dream* by Norman Mailer. "Have you listened to it?"

"Uh-huh."

"And who are your friends?"

"Vicki and Roxanne, my parents, Joan and Dan. And Jack."

"Of course we know Jack. Hi, girls. Do you live around here?" Joan asked.

"Not too far," Roxanne said. She was amazed that Rick introduced his parents by their first names.

"And do call me Joan. I hate for young people to call me Mrs. Templeton."

"Have you girls heard this record? Have you, Jack? It really is remarkable."

"I have it at home, Mrs. Templeton. Can I lie down somewhere?" Vicki asked.

"Of course, dear," Joan said, taking Vicki by the arm. "And don't be shy about calling me Joan."

"So, have a seat," Dan said, tapping his pipe into an ashtray and pulling his chair closer to the couch. "Where were you kids tonight?"

"At the Southwest carnival," Rick said.

"Did you go on many rides?" Dan asked.

"Yeah, some. We, uh, also shot some targets," Jack mumbled.

"Well, let me tell you a story about going to the state fair when I was a boy," Dan said leaning back in his chair and filling his pipe. "Every year they had a freak show and there was the usual assortment that you would expect—the bearded lady, Siamese twins, the Reptile Man, midgets, cretins. Well, I was

94

absolutely fascinated with these people. I would hang around the tent long after the fair was closed and watch them talk and eat supper and walk from trailer to trailer. I lived in a small town in central Missouri, and there wasn't a whole lot to do on summer nights. I remember one night I was crouching behind a small bush watching them drink a bottle of champagne. I wasn't exactly sure what they were celebrating, but they kept patting this one midget on the back and pouring the champagne on his head. Anyway, I suddenly felt this hand on my shoulder, and I turned around and saw one of the ugliest faces I had ever seen. It had bumps and warts and was pasty white. I was terrified, to say the least; I thought he was going to whisk me away from my mother and father and baby brother and put me to work for the circus. But that wasn't his intention at all. All he did was shake his head no. By that, he meant, 'Leave us alone. We're looked at enough as it is. We want our privacy now, away from normal people's eyes.' At least that was how I interpreted it. It was my first real lesson in learning how to respect people who are different. I ran so fast, I think I made it home in record time." Dan let out one loud laugh and reached over to light his pipe.

Roxanne was fascinated by Dan Templeton. She had never met an adult who was so willing to talk to kids in such a cool way. She looked over at Rick, and she bet he was proud to have such interesting parents.

"Let's go up to my room," Rick said to Jack and Roxanne. "See ya later, Dad."

"Nice talking to you both. Come back any time."

Rick's room was on the third floor; his parents had converted the attic into a bedroom suite with pine paneling and blue shag carpeting. Most of the posters on the walls were of motorcycles and race cars, but the one that intrigued Roxanne was for Shakespeare in the Park.

"Mom got that in New York City this summer," Rick said. "She teaches drama at Rockhurst High School."

"What does your dad do?" Roxanne asked.

"He's a shrink."

"He's neat...both of your parents are neat."

"That's what everyone says. They bug me just like normal parents."

95

"About what?"

"Anything, everything, you name it."

"I think your mom is great. If my mom ever said, 'Call me Estelle' to any of my friends, I'd eat a can of dog food," Jack said, picking up a softball and pretending to throw it through the window.

"Uck, gross, Jack," Roxanne said.

"So, what are your parents like?" Rick asked Roxanne.

"They're awful, stupid, crazy."

"Sound like normal parents to me," Jack said.

"You've never met *my* parents, though. They're *really* crazy... no offense, but can we change the subject?"

"How 'bout my sister, She's a senior this year, and she's really bad news, a real nut case," Jack said, rolling a toy car down the middle of his face. "She's almost as crazy as her younger brother."

"I'd say her younger brother has her beat," Roxanne said, throwing a small pillow at his stomach.

"Hey, you two. Let me ask you somethin'. Do either of you get stoned?"

"Sure, yeah, all the time," Jack said, shrugging. Roxanne didn't believe him. She was convinced that he was almost as inexperienced as she was.

"What about you?" Rick asked Roxanne.

"Uh, I've never tried it."

"Do you want to?"

"I don't know—hey, what about your folks? Wouldn't they get mad?"

"They've smoked lots of times. Don't worry 'bout them."

"In front of you?" Roxanne asked.

"What do you mean, in front of me?"

"Have they smoked in front of you?"

"No, but they've told me all about it, and how this painter friend of theirs has turned them on at dinner parties."

"Wow, I can't believe your folks smoke pot," Jack said.

"You mean, yours don't?" Rick said with a grin.

"Sure, yeah, right. My folks getting stoned? That's so funny I forgot to laugh."

"So how 'bout it, you two? I've got a joint all rolled."

"You guys go ahead. I'll just watch."

"What 'bout you, Jack?"

"Sure, why not...maybe we should put something under the door."

"Nah, they won't care. I got this joint from my older brother. He's in college."

Roxanne guessed that perhaps Rick had smoked a few times before this, but that he wasn't all that experienced either. All three of them sat on the floor in a circle with their legs crossed Indian-style and passed the joint around. Roxanne didn't smoke at all but watched Rick and Jack take small drags. After about twenty minutes, they heard heavy steps in the hallway and a loud knock on the door. Rick went to answer it, and he stood outside in the hall, talking to his mother in a low voice. He came back with an embarrassed look on his face.

"I guess you guys better go."

Both Roxanne and Jack knew exactly what had happened, and what was said between them. Rick was in trouble with his mother, just like the two of them would have been if they had tried to smoke marijuana in their bedrooms.

"Is Vicki asleep?" Roxanne asked.

"Yeah, I guess we better wake her up. She's in my brother's old room," Rick said.

"Boy, did she miss all the excitement," Jack said, nudging Roxanne in the ribs. They were both feeling smug about Rick's parents not being so hip after all.

"I can't believe all that stuff happened," Vicki said to Roxanne while they were walking home. "It sounds like a great time. Getting caught smoking pot. I'm a poet and I don't even know it. Did you make out or anything?"

"Come off it, Vicki. I don't even know him. He's a nice guy."

"And what else?"

"Knock it off, Vicki." Roxanne hated it when she teased her like this. "Jackson Pollock. That's who I was trying to think of. It was just on the tip of my tongue."

"Jackson who?"

"Remember at the carnival when we were watching them paint those splotchy pictures—oh, never mind."

"So, do you think you two will be boyfriend and girlfriend?"

"You're stupid and ridiculous. Go away, get lost," Roxanne said, running ahead of Vicki.

"Rick and Roxanne, sitting in a tree, F-U-C-K-I-N-G. First comes love. Then comes marriage. Then comes Roxanne with a baby carriage," Vicki yelled at Roxanne while she was running ahead.

"F-U-C-K YOURSELF, JERKFACE," Roxanne yelled back at Vicki. "FUCK YOU."

When Roxanne walked into the house, she could hear Gramma and James trying to have a discussion in the den. A few weeks earlier, Gramma had held a family meeting and decided they all would try to discuss things instead of argue. What she meant by a discussion was that no one in the family would be allowed to raise his or her voice or get red in the face. No one would be allowed to call each other names, slam doors, go off to his or her room and mope. Granted, this was only an experiment, but so far the success rate was certainly questionable. It was nearly impossible for Gramma to talk to any family member without getting into some sort of argument.

"I don't like it one bit. First you go off to this crackpot place in California. Then you come home and for weeks you're walking around with a dopey smile on your face. Now you say you've got business in New York City."

"Gramma, this certainly isn't the first time I've gone to New York on business. Honestly, I don't know why you're being so suspicious."

Roxanne decided to sit outside the den door and eavesdrop on this discussion between her dad and Gramma. But first she got a throw pillow from the living room so that she could be more comfortable. She had to be extra quiet not to wake up her mother who was napping on the couch. Even Gus had turned down his record player and was peeking outside his room so that he could hear better.

"Where is my daughter? She shouldn't be hearing any of this. Emma! Emma! Where are you, dear?"

"I'm here, Mama," Emma said groggily from the living room.

"Honey, why don't you go upstairs and tuck yourself in bed," Gramma said, walking out of the den. Roxanne quickly stood up and pretended to be doing something in the kitchen. "There, that's a good girl," Gramma said, leading Emma by the elbow to the staircase and then watching her trudge up the stairs. "Nighty night, dear. Sweet dreams. And as for you, Miss Nosy," she said, turning to Roxanne. "I suggest that you also go upstairs to your room. It's past your bedtime, isn't it?"

"Yes, Gramma."

"That's how I like to hear you sound. Sweet and obedient, like a little angel."

"Yes, Gramma."

The minute Gramma shut the den door, Roxanne pulled out the throw pillow and plopped herself down once again.

"I want to be straight with you, James," Gramma said, pacing around the room. "If you've found another woman in your life, I can't really blame you."

"Gramma, how can you even accuse me. . . . "

"Now, listen to me, son. I know this family hasn't been easy to deal with. I know Emma hasn't been the kind of wife every man dreams of. I'm not blind or stupid, you see."

"No, you're neither one of those," James said, chuckling.

"But I am one thing. I am grateful to you. For marrying Emma. For taking me into your home. For trying to talk some sense into those kids' thick skulls. You see, I do understand how hard you've tried with this family, even though a lot of it has come to a lot of nothing."

"Well, I don't know how to take that, Gramma."

"Wait a minute, I'm not finished. What I'm trying to say, and not very well, is that if you're having an affair with some woman in New York, you have my permission."

"Gramma, I've had some crazy conversations with you, but this beats them all hands down."

"I mean it, James. You're a good provider, a good, basic human being. You deserve better than all this. You deserve a little fun. But I want you to make a promise."

"What, just tell me what?"

"I want you to promise that no matter what, you will come back to this family and live out your life with us. You can make your 'business' trips to New York, and you can call your sweetie back East, but you must promise to always come back to us. Is it a deal?"

"This is the most ridiculous—"

"Say it, James. Promise me this one thing. You haven't fooled me for one minute. Ever since your trip to California, I've heard you whistling around the house."

"Gramma, I...."

"Say it. Please. For us. Your family. If you love us, make us this promise."

"All right, Gramma. I promise. But I'm telling you, you're just talking nonsense...."

"Don't say anymore. I'm going to bed. Good night, son. And bless you."

Roxanne couldn't believe how everything had come to this. Her own grandmother had told her own father that it was okay to have an affair. Incredible. Even if he weren't already having an affair, why, he could go out tomorrow and have one with a clear conscience. She felt as though she and Mom and Gus had been betrayed by the one person they loved and trusted the most. All her life, Roxanne felt that Gramma had such a good sense about things. No matter what the circumstance, Gramma could navigate her family through crises and prevent them all from capsizing emotionally. But perhaps circumstances had changed. Perhaps Gramma—like everyone else in her family— had lost her way. Roxanne took the pillow she was sitting on and slammed it back on the living room couch. Then she grabbed it and slammed it down again. And again. And again. Gramma was watching Roxanne in the doorway and shaking her head. Poor dear, Gramma thought. She doesn't know the ways of the world. Gramma had recently read an article in the *Enquirer* that said most celebrity wives knew that their husbands had affairs; but they preferred to ignore them in order to enjoy the prestige of being "Mrs. Somebody" until the day came around when their husbands gave them the boot. But Roxanne will learn about those things. She'll learn about them soon enough. Gramma turned around and crept upstairs while Roxanne buried her face in the arm of the couch.

10

Room Service

That Gramma is an amazing woman, James thought while buckling himself into his airplane seat. *God, she goes right for the guts of a situation. Scary stuff. And that promise she had me make, it's absolute lunacy. But you know what's really scary. She's absolutely right. And she knows that I know that she's absolutely right. Jesus, I'm confused. And Irving doesn't approve of my affair with Lydia at all. Naturally, he doesn't say anything, but I can tell from the looks he gives me. He probably thinks it's some form of escape or rebellion against something. Well, screw that. I think I love Lydia. And everything I do should not have to have the seal of approval from my analyst.*

So, why do I feel so nervous? Maybe it's not nerves. Maybe it's excitement. Maybe there's been so little to get excited about in the last few years that I'm just not used to feeling this way. Maybe that's it . . . wait a minute, who the hell am I kidding? I'm scared out of my wits. That's right. Scared. Here I am having what I thought was a secret affair, and it's like my whole goddamn family is breathing down my neck, watching my every move. They might as well have cameras in my hotel room—what, with all the information they know. I know what I need. I need a drink. Fast. Where's the goddamn stewardess when I need her? Where's the call button? I hate it when the plane starts to shake. Or to dip, so that my face feels like it's being pulled down into my seat. I'm covered with sweat. I'm going to have to shower before I even call Lydia. She's going to see me as some neurotic fool, and she isn't going to want me. This isn't going to work, I just know it. Why can't I turn the plane around like a simple automobile? I wish I were driving to New York, so that by the time I got to St. Louis, I could come to my senses. Here's the stewardess, finally.

101

"I'd like a scotch and water," James said.

"That's a dollar, please," the stewardess said.

"Here you go," James said, handing her a dollar bill and some change.

"We don't accept tips, sir, but thanks all the same."

God, I'm such a stupid jerk, trying to tip a stewardess. Where's my head? That's another reason why I should be turning around. She's going to see me as some yahoo from the Midwest, with no manners or polish like those slick New York guys. I should give up on this whole thing. That's right. Give up while I still have a shred of dignity.

The drink started to make James sleepy, and he dozed fitfully the rest of the flight. Once the plane landed, he got a taxi to the Lancaster Hotel on East 38th Street, which was close to Lydia's apartment on 35th between Park and Madison. He made a phone call to verify the meeting with the vice-president of TBF, Inc., the company that wanted to buy the plumbing outfit in Kansas, and one to Myron Silber at the St. Regis who was the negotiator from Stern Brothers. Then he decided to take a walk downtown toward B. Altman.

The store was like a remembrance of his childhood, especially when his mother used to take him into the old Emery, Bird, Thayer store on the Plaza to buy him back-to-school clothes. The high ceilings, the polished wood floors, even the slightly dusty smell intrigued him, and he wandered around the men's department for an hour, trying to kill time. Already he was feeling calmer and more confident about seeing Lydia. Yet he wanted to savor New York on his own—at least for a little while.

As he was riding up the escalator, James suddenly felt tired. He didn't know whether it was the traffic or the crowds of people or the drink on the plane that caused him to feel this way, so he decided to go back to his hotel to rest for a while.

At the hotel desk, there was a message for him to call Lydia at work. As soon as he got up to his room, he dialed her number.

"Where have you been?" Lydia asked. "I've been waiting for you to call." James sensed a certain anxiousness in her voice. He could also hear a typewriter in the background.

"You sound busy," James said, loosening his tie and stretching out on the bed.

"I am, but that's not the point. When did you get into town?"

"A couple of hours ago. I walked around a bit. Now I'm ready for a nap."

"New York will do that to you. When are your meetings?"

"Tomorrow."

"What do you want to do about dinner? I know a wonderful French restaurant on the East side."

"Maybe we'll get room service up here."

"Hmmmm, that sounds like more fun. I've got to work until at least seven. I'm under deadline for this damn report."

"Great. Then I can nap. Call me when you're done."

"Can't wait to see you. I've missed you."

"Me too. Talk to you soon."

His conversation with Lydia left him feeling flat and dissatisfied. It sounded so predictable, so cliché, as if he were reading a dime novel about a married man embarking on an affair with a career woman from New York City. Perhaps he was just feeling self-conscious about the whole thing, and that was making him all the more sensitive.

James slept a long, dreamless sleep until he was wakened by the hotel telephone. Lydia was downstairs with a magnum of champagne.

"Could you wait a few minutes," James said groggily. "I need to clean up a bit."

"Sorry I didn't call from the office, but it was getting so late. You *do* sound pooped."

"I'll ring you downstairs when I'm more presentable," James said, wiping his face and mouth with his hand.

"Don't take *too* long."

"I won't."

"Bye."

"Bye." James splashed hot water on his face and ran an electric razor over it. He brushed his teeth, straightened the covers on the bed, and zipped up his suitcase. All in all, the place looked decent. James dialed the hotel phone and told the desk clerk that the lady could come up now. Lydia did not disappoint James—she looked pretty in a blue knit suit with her long, brown hair combed off her freshly made-up face.

"Lydia, this is a *lot* of champagne," James said, taking the bottle and her coat from her. "Is it really just the two of us tonight?

Say, you look wonderful," he said, giving her a long hug.

"You silly. Let me see how you look. Not bad, not bad at all. A little more Midwestern than Californian, which suits me just fine."

"Have you had dinner?"

"No, and I'm starved. And the reason for all the champagne, is, well, we may have a double celebration on our hands. First you being here, that's the most important, and then my boss said that I may get promoted to account supervisor."

"That's marvelous, Lydia. Is it definite?"

"Well, the president needs to give his final approval, but I can't see any problems there . . . are you good at opening champagne?"

"Any man worth his salt is. Let me get a hand towel and glasses. Here we go." The bottle opened with a pop and some champagne foam sprayed on the rug.

"Oh boy," James said, pouring champagne into the hotel glasses.

"Here's to a wonderful run of luck," Lydia said, holding up her glass.

"Hear, hear."

"And to a wonderful man visiting from the heart of America."

"Hear, hear."

". . . and to wonderful us."

"HEAR, HEAR," James said, clinking glasses with Lydia a final time and gulping down his champagne.

"Easy, pardner. We've got all night to celebrate."

"Right. Let's order something to eat."

"I'll call up," Lydia said, looking on the dial for room service. The menu sounded like food from a coffee shop. James ordered Salisbury steak and Lydia baked chicken. After she hung up the phone, James patted the bed next to him. Lydia checked her watch and reluctantly lay down. The food was going to be at the room in twenty minutes. James then kissed Lydia on the face and unbuttoned her silk blouse below her bra. He slipped his hand over her breast and nipple while he stroked her thighs, working his way up to her panties. There was a knock on the door.

"Room service."

"Damn. That didn't seem like twenty minutes to me. Hold on," Lydia said, buttoning her blouse. James got up and opened the door. He signed the ticket as the waiter put the silver tray on the small imitation Chippendale table in the corner. Both she and James ate in silence. The food was as bad as it sounded over the phone.

"Where's that champagne? We need something good to help choke this down."

"I'll get it," Lydia said.

As glad as he was to see her, James still wasn't feeling like himself. Everything he said sounded so stilted and boring. He wanted to stop observing his own actions—like some social scientist—and relax and be part of the moment, as all the therapists said at Esalen. But he couldn't stop himself from feeling removed from the situation.

"So, will you get a pay raise with this promotion?"

"Oh, yes, I would say maybe twenty percent or so. I may start looking for another apartment."

"Really. So what's wrong with the apartment you're in now?"

"Well, it's awfully small. I could use some more space."

"Really, now." *Come on, James, think of something witty and interesting to say. You're having an affair with an attractive, successful woman and all you can come up with is this dull question-and-answer-type conversation. Where are the laughs, the Noel Coward repartee, the soul-searching discussions? Maybe this was a signal, that this affair wasn't going to take off after all. Maybe it happened to flourish in California, like a bird of paradise or some other exotic plant. But take it out of its natural environment, and it. . . .*

"James, you look like you're in another world," Lydia said, laughing. "I remember that about you from California."

"Funny thing you should say that. People always say that about my wife."

"Oh," Lydia said. James could tell that the mention of Emma hurt her feelings somehow. "I'll put this tray outside the door," Lydia said, standing up suddenly. She came back into the room and started looking around.

"What are you looking for?" James asked.

"My purse and briefcase. This isn't working, James. I think I'd better go."

"Hey, wait a minute, hold your horses. Why leave so soon?" he asked, grabbing her hands.

"Because I feel uncomfortable. Because I sense you're feeling uncomfortable, too. Because I'm no good at having affairs with married men. Because I had such an incredible time in California...oh, forget it."

"Wait a minute, what do you mean forget it?"

"I don't know, I'm feeling, I guess, disappointed. And confused. I thought it would be, you know, smoother. More romantic. We'd be in each other's arms like in California and pick up where we left off."

"Listen, don't think those same thoughts haven't gone through my head, too."

"See, I was right."

"I've been feeling disappointed, too, like something was missing."

"Exactly."

"Maybe the thrill was gone."

"Right."

"And for one small moment I was willing to let you find your things and leave. But something in me said, 'Wait a minute. Don't give up so soon.' And I was also thinking about why we were attracted to each other in the first place. It was because we could talk so easily, like we're doing *now*."

"Right, I feel the exact same way. So...I guess I'll stay, okay? James, are you feeling all right?"

"Sure, why shouldn't I be?"

"You're perspiring so much."

"I am? Well, what do you know," James said, wiping his forehead. "I guess it must be all the commotion...I mean, how often do I have such a wonderfully intense time, if you know what I mean...excuse me for a moment. Now don't go away."

"Don't worry," Lydia said, sitting on the bed and kicking off her shoes.

James went into the bathroom and looked at his pale, sweaty reflection in the mirror. *An extramarital affair can really take it out of a person. Look at me, I'm a mess. Okay, just keep your cool and wash your face and neck and, damn, my bathrobe's in the other room. I could have changed into my bathrobe and then it would have elimi-*

nated all that awkward fumbling of buttons and zippers and all that nonsense. . . . Well, I'll just take off my clothes anyway. Okay, here goes. What she sees is what she gets. . . . "

"Ta-daaaaaaaaaa," James said, trying to pose like a muscle man in front of the bathroom door.

"Oh James," Lydia said, laughing into the covers of the bed. "You look so . . . so cute."

"Cute? What's so cute? Cute is for puppies and greeting cards."

"James, look at your feet. Black shoes and black socks and the rest of you all stripped down."

"Oh," James said, looking down at himself. He quickly removed his shoes and socks, feeling like someone out of those old-fashioned porno photos from the 1920s. "Is that better?" he asked, crawling into bed.

"I should say so," Lydia said, hugging him around his waist and kissing his ear. "Now let's get to it."

Their love making was passionate and somewhat rushed, since their separation had made them both feel especially needy. It felt good for Lydia to be having sex again; she had had a long, dry spell since California. James remembered why he was so taken with Lydia; she was so sensual in bed, so womanly. Unlike Emma, she was not afraid to take the initiative. And Lydia really enjoyed sex whereas Emma merely saw it as her marital obligation, something unpleasant she had to put up with. The more James thought about it, the angrier he felt. All these years, he had been cheated out of a normal sex life by staying in his marriage to Emma. Gramma's insistence that he promise not to leave the family started making more and more sense. She knew that James had compromised his life for a wife who was unable to offer him the things he really needed—like sex. And he felt he had missed out on so much—such as, well, sex. And a full emotional life. And having a real woman to share his problems and accomplishments with, not some child in a woman's body. And why in the hell had he married Emma in the first place? Because she was so goddamn beautiful? Well, that obviously wasn't enough anymore, was it?

The more he thought about these things, the less he was able to sleep. He tried counting backwards from 1001. He tried reading an Agatha Christie mystery he had bought at the airport. He tried doing some relaxation exercises he had learned in his yoga class at Esalen. He felt more exhausted and more wide awake and more angry than ever. Also, he was nervous about not being alert for his meeting in the morning. How stupid of him to forget his Valium. How could he be so dumb?

At around 5:00 A.M., James awoke with a start. He was achy from his bout of insomnia, yet he had a huge erection. He wanted to make love to Lydia. Why wouldn't she stir or turn over to show that she was surfacing from her sleep? Maybe he would sit up in bed and read for a while. Maybe he could subtly arouse her that way.

Having an affair was such hard work, especially a long distance one. But James remembered what his father had always told him. Nothing in life was ever easy. And nothing that James was doing—shifting about in the bed or loudly turning the pages of his mystery—was causing Lydia to wake up. He was going to have to do something a little more aggressive. Like get up and go to the bathroom. This was all such foolishness. Why did thoughts about women and sex reduce him to a bumbler, a dolt.

When he returned to bed, Lydia was propped up on her elbow.

"How did you sleep?" she asked.

"Uh, okay, I guess. How 'bout you?"

"Not bad."

James got back into bed and pressed himself against her. Lydia didn't resist his advances and welcomed him inside of her.

Sex with Lydia was the greatest thing. He wished he weren't feeling so damn tired so that he could get the most enjoyment out of it. He was going to come quicker than he had expected. His whole body felt as if it were coming, as if a brick had hit his chest.

Lydia felt James collapse on top of her. That was faster than usual. While they were making love, Lydia watched James's face for a while. She frequently enjoyed watching the mouths of her lovers contort and sigh, and she noticed the tiny cracks of worry around his mouth. Lydia knew that this affair was going to be complicated. James had so many misgivings and doubts. Maybe the whole thing just wasn't worth it.

James's body felt so heavy on top of her. She shook him so that at least he would roll over. My God....

It took all of her strength to push him off her. His face was blue-gray. She sat there, not knowing what to do next. This couldn't have happened. It only happened to other people. Or to prostitutes. It couldn't have happened to her. She was from a good family. And had a good career. She was a good person. She was. Seconds went by. She felt his pulse. She pounded on his chest with her fists. Nothing seemed to happen. Somehow, she picked up the phone and dialed the operator. Get an ambulance as quickly as possible. Now what? Get him dressed, make him look respectable. She tried pounding his chest again. She tried something she learned from a lifesaving course she had taken as a teen-ager on Martha's Vineyard. Breathe into his mouth, pinch his nostrils, tilt his head back. She did that for a while. Nothing. Funny, how she felt nothing. She then tried to get him dressed. It was like dressing a heavy sack of flour with arms and legs to struggle with. The worst part about it was trying to zip his pants over his penis. She had heard that hanged men frequently died with an erection. But James wasn't dead, she was sure of that. The ambulance men would revive him. He would be all right, she was certain. Absolutely certain.

When she heard the sirens, she wanted to run down the hall to let them in, but she couldn't. All she could do was open the door and collapse in the hallway. When the men rushed in with their heart shock machines, they were not the least bit startled to see Lydia lying on the hallway floor completely naked. They turned her over to see if she was, in fact, the victim. She pointed toward the open door behind her. Both of the men shook their heads and headed into the room. They had witnessed similar scenes in apartments and hotels all over New York City.

11

Meshugah

When Lydia woke up in the white hospital room, she knew that James was gone. She knew she had not been able to save him and neither had the medics.

"He's gone, isn't he?" Lydia asked the empty hospital room. "He's gone, isn't he?" she asked while pushing the nurse page button frantically.

"Good morning," a nurse said whose hands smelled of strong soap. She pulled the light cover under Lydia's chin.

"So, I was right," Lydia said, sinking down into the covers.

"Right about what, dear?"

"He's gone, isn't he?"

"Who's gone, dear? You'll have to ask the doctor."

"I need to know now. I need to call his family and tell them...oh, God, I don't know what I'd tell them. I also need to call work."

"I'm sure everything's been taken of. I'll get the doctor as soon—"

"Oh, God, it's so terrible. So terrible," Lydia said, shaking her head. "But someone needs to contact them. NOW."

"Who, dear?"

"His family. JAMES FREEDMAN'S FAMILY IN KANSAS CITY."

"Now, let me explain some things to you. If something's happened to a friend of yours, the doctor who took care of him was supposed to contact his family. Now, I know someone who's been very worried about you."

"Please, not my mother...."

"She's been here since they brought you in yesterday. I think she stepped out for a bite to eat."

"I've been here a day?"

"Yes, but I'll let the doctor tell you all about it. Oh, it looks like it's time for your pill."

"What pill?"

"Just something that will help you rest better."

"I've obviously been resting for twenty-four hours. I don't need anymore rest. I do need to talk to the doctor."

"First take this pill, and then I'll make sure the doctor comes around soon."

"Is this a bribe or what?"

"Of course not."

"All right, all right. Doctor knows best, doesn't he? Salut," Lydia said, swallowing the pill and chasing it down with a paper cup of water.

"Lydia, I'm Dr. Weinstein," a tall man said. "How are you feeling?" he said, lightly touching her arm.

"Um, all right. I guess tired," Lydia said, through a blur of sleep.

"I'm afraid you've had a little shock, haven't you?" he said.

"Is he gone? Is James Freedman gone?" Lydia said, trying to sit up in bed.

The doctor put his hand back on her arm.

"Well?"

"I'm afraid . . ."

"Oh my God, I knew it," Lydia said, covering her face.

"There was nothing you or anybody could have done. He died instantly. He suffered no pain."

"Oh my God, I killed him, I can't believe it was because of me."

"Darling, don't say that to the nice doctor."

"Hello, Mother."

"But the most important thing, Lydia, is to try to get some rest," Dr. Weinstein said.

"What about work? Has anybody called the agency?"

"I called and said you were sick. Now, darling, listen to Dr. Weinstein and do everything he says. Right, Doctor?"

"Yes, right, Mrs. Lipschutz."

"It's Lip*shitz*. Like what life dishes out to us sometimes."

"Oh, Mother..."

"Now, Doctor," Mrs. Lipshitz said in a loud whisper, pulling him aside. "Be sure to stop in and see my daughter a few times a day. She's been through so much and she needs special attention. Will you do that for me, Doctor?"

"Mother, I can hear every word you say. I'm sure the doctor has other patients who also need special attention. Like the dying ones."

"Just get some proper rest, Lydia, and you'll be fine. I'll be stopping back in to see you."

"Such an attractive young man," Mrs. Lipshitz whispered to Lydia as soon as Dr. Weinstein left the room. "Do you think he's married?"

"Mother, I'm exhausted and upset and the last thing I want to think about is whether or not my doctor is married."

"Well, he wasn't wearing a wedding ring, and you know something? You should start thinking about these things a little more carefully instead of going after married men with weak hearts." She took out her compact and a tube of bright, red lipstick and started to apply a thick coat to her lips.

"God, you are so incredibly insensitive. Will you please get out of here before I have a complete nervous breakdown? And how in the world did you know James was married?"

"I have my ways."

"You're amazing, Mother. You really are."

"And that meshugah Michael was no better."

"Please don't remind me. It's like I have a curse. Go out with Lydia Lipshitz and die."

"Honey, don't say that."

"It's true," Lydia said, shaking her head. "It's true."

"Listen, it's going to be all right, I just know it," Mrs. Lipshitz said, grasping Lydia's hand. "I've got a good feeling from all this. Remember, everything always happens for the best.... Oh my goodness, it's getting late. I've gotta go home and make lamb chops for your father. Now, get some sleep and I'll see you in the a.m..," she said, leaning over and giving Lydia a light kiss.

Lydia watched her mother gather her pocketbook and wool jacket. How typical, she thought to herself. As soon as a single remark hit uncomfortably close to home, she checked her watch and ran for cover. When Lydia leaned back into her pillow and shut her eyes, all she could see was James's blue-gray face, which was the same color as the eels on bins of crushed ice displayed on the sidewalks of Chinatown.

On the morning of James's death, Gramma answered the phone at eight. Some male voice wanted to speak to Mrs. Freedman. A long-distance voice. Gramma didn't like the sound of it. She knew it had to be trouble.

"This is she," Gramma said. No use getting Emma involved.

"I'm Dr. Steinbach at New York Hospital...."

To Gramma, he sounded like some kid trying to talk like a doctor. He didn't have that sense of authority in his voice that only experience and money and arrogance could develop. Like the doctors on "Ben Casey" or "Dr. Kildare." Imagine, the unfairness of it all, having some hospital flunky tell her bad news over the phone.

...and I have some unfortunate news for you..."

"Well, let's not beat around the bush."

"Uh, your husband..."

"Come on, boy, spill it."

"...expired at 7:04 this morning in his hotel room from a cardiac arrest. We did everything we could to save him, but he had died almost immediately."

Gramma was quiet for a few seconds. She thought it was going to be bad news, but she didn't think it would be this bad. Maybe a broken leg. A bump on the head from being knocked down by a robber or a cab. Amnesia. A temporary coma, maybe. But not this. It was just like what her mother said when her father died. A person is never prepared for a loved one's death even if he has been sick and dying for months.

"Mrs. Freedman."

"Yes, yes. I was just thinking..."

"I just wanted to again extend my condolences...to you and your family. Now, I'm going to switch you over to medical records, and they'll inform you of the proper procedure. Again, I'm sorry."

"I'm sorry, too, for chrissakes. Now, who am I talkin' to?"

113

"The people in medical records."

"All right. Put them through."

"Mrs. Freedman, I'm Mrs. Wellfleet in medical records."

"Yes, yes."

"I'm sorry but we need some information from you. I know it's difficult at a time..."

"So, let's get on with it."

"Okay, fine. Now, is this address current on Mr. Freedman's license?"

"It should be. We've been living here for umpteen years."

"All right, then. Now, was he still being covered by Blue Cross, Blue Shield at the time?"

"How should I know? Call 'em up at Stern Brothers, where he worked. You spell that S-T-E-R-N. And you know how to spell, 'brothers,' don't you?"

There was a pause.

"This is Mrs. Freedman, isn't it?"

"Of course it is. Who else would you expect?"

"Well, you just don't sound, I don't know..."

"Sad enough? Upset enough? Well, my dear, different people express themselves in different ways. How do you know how I'll feel when I hang up this phone? I could burn down this house or kill a neighbor or fill up a creek with tears."

"Please, Mrs. Freedman. I understand and I'm sorry, but please, listen to me carefully. What you'll need to do in the next day or so is come to New York to identify the body. New York University Hospital is on First Avenue and Thirty-third Street, and when you get here, ask for one of us in medical records. After you've properly identified the body and signed the release, we'll send him to the funeral home of your choice. Do you know where you want the body sent? Mrs. Freedman, are you still there?"

"Yes, yes, I'm just thinking. I've never given it much thought...until now, that is. Let me look in the yellow pages. Ah, here's one I know. Stine and McClure...a lovely looking place if I've ever seen one. Brick colonial, mighty dignified. That's S-T-I-N-E, not S-T-E-I-N on Gillham Road. Now do you have everything?"

"Yes, but..."

"We'll be in New York tomorrow or sometime."

Gramma quickly hung up the phone because the tears were starting to come out of her eyes and splash onto her bathrobe. Goddamn that James. Goddamn him. How was she supposed to handle this family without him? She needed him. And already she missed him. Sure, they fought. But that man tried. Yes, indeed, he tried to be the best family man in town. No doubt about it. He failed most of the time. But so did she. And who said that old was supposed to outlive young? She was looking forward to a graceful old age. Now, she was going to have to work hard just trying to keep all the lids screwed on tight.

And my God—how was she going to tell Emma? Gramma didn't know if she could take it. And what about those kids? Something like this could really break them. Recently, Gramma had been waking up in the middle of the night, smelling a mixture of burning wood and spoiled vegetables. She would run around the house, sniffing for fires or a deserted grocery bag, but nothing was ever there. Now she understood that these olfactory hallucinations were a premonition. If failure and heartbreak had a smell, they would smell like burning wood and spoiled vegetables. Gramma began to cry even more. She was tempted to do something unthinkable. She was tempted to walk into the garage, stuff rags under the door and turn on the car. She had read somewhere that it was the most painless way to die. But that was unthinkable. Whether she liked it or not, she was now the sole head of the family. And she couldn't leave until all of them had learned how to survive on their own.

Wait a minute, wait just a gosh darn minute. It was about time for something like this to happen. A crisis was exactly what she needed for Emma's coming of age, for her sudden jolt into adulthood. It was about time for Emma to grow up, to stop being coddled and left to her own helpless devices. For once in her silly life, Emma was going to take on some real responsibilities. She no longer had James to fight the family battles, to help around the household, to be the mother *and* the father to their children. Forcing Emma to stand on her own two feet was for her own good because Gramma was certain that Emma would outlive her, unless God forbid, some other terrible thing happened...no, no, that kind of awful luck only struck a family once unless, of course, it was the Kennedys.

Gramma fussed with her hair in the downstairs bathroom mirror so at least she would look presentable while she was relating the bad news to everyone. She figured that this would be a moment that her grandchildren would remember, and she didn't want them to remember her as looking like a slob.

But first she had to square things away with Emma. She marched up the stairs and started to knock on Emma's door—but something made her stop. She had started out with such a strong resolve to treat Emma like an adult, yet her natural impulse to protect Emma was getting the best of her. No, this was it, the end of Emma's golden era, the end of her comfy cozy dream world, the end of her Camelot in Kansas City. Welcome to the world of pain and failure and heartbreak, Emma. Welcome. Gramma knocked until her knuckles got sore.

"Huh?" Emma finally said.

"We need to talk," Gramma said, opening the door.

"What do you want? I'm too tired to talk."

"I don't care how you feel, missy. I'm not leaving until I finish everything I need to say and that's final," Gramma said, sitting herself down on the edge of the bed. She took a deep breath. "Things have got to change starting right now. You'll understand more after I tell you why, but first—and I know a lot of this is my fault because I've let you get away with so much over the years—but first you've got to promise me that during this terrible time you'll be strong and courageous and help me with the preparations and with the children and be my comrade-in-arms. Now, I know you don't understand what in the world I'm talking about because I haven't told you what has caused this terrible time. Just be patient and indulge me for a while. I know I've let you stay a child throughout the years because that was your natural way, and James accepted it, and the kids, I guess, accepted it, and I had certainly accepted it, so I figured why rock the boat, if you get my meaning. Do you?"

"I think so," Emma replied.

"Anyway, I can't pamper you any more. Something has happened—and I'll get to that in a minute—that will change who we are and what we're supposed to be doing."

"Mother, I don't understand. What are you trying to say?"

"I'll get to that in a minute. But first I want you to take an oath. Hold up your right hand, come on, hold it up like the court witnesses do on 'Perry Mason.' Come on, I don't have all day. Now repeat after me. I, come on, say. 'I.'"

"I."

"Emma Elizabeth Freedman."

"Emma Elizabeth Freedman."

"Promise to be a strong and brave person."

"Promise to be a strong and brave person."

"During this time of adversity."

"During this time of adversity...Mother, what is this all about?"

"Patience, patience, I'll tell you all about it after you take your oath. Now, keep holding up that right hand. And I promise—come on, repeat after me."

"And I promise..."

"To take on more family responsibilities."

"To take on more family responsibilities."

"To help my mother in the rearing of my children."

"To help my mother in the rearing of my children."

"To act my age."

"To act my age...Mother, I'm how old?"

"You're thirty-six. You knew that, didn't you, dear?"

"I guess so, but sometimes...sometimes I can't remember my exact age. Sometimes I can't remember if I'm thirty-four or thirty-seven..."

"Come on, come on, let's get on with this. I don't see your right hand."

"Mother...it's James, isn't it? You wouldn't be talking like this if something hadn't happened to James."

"We will discuss it in a minute. We haven't finished our oath. Now, come on...and I solemnly swear until the day I die to keep this oath because I love my mother very, very much and I know that she loves me, and I would never do anything to disappoint her or make her twilight years full of despair and struggle."

"And I solemnly swear until the day I die to keep this oath...Mother, I can't remember the rest."

"Never mind, you've said enough. Now, sit down...oh,

you're already sitting. Well, anyway, here goes. Your husband...James, that is."

"Yes?" Emma said, hugging her knees.

"He's, uh, well, he won't be coming back home...that is, in any great shape."

"Mother, what are you trying to tell me?"

"Goddamn it, girl, you are making this so damn tough for me. Can't you guess?"

"Well, I know something's wrong."

"Yes," Gramma said, leaning forward and motioning with her hands as if she were coaching a teammate in a game of Charades.

"Something's very, very wrong. And it has something to do with James."

"Go on...."

"But I don't know what else. You haven't told me what else."

"I'VE HAD IT UP TO HERE WITH YOU...Okay, let's take a different tack. Let me calm down a minute." Gramma took a few deep breaths. "What's the worst thing that can possibly happen to a person?"

"The worst?"

Gramma nodded.

"Well, a person can get very hurt. Or very sick. Or die..."

"You guessed it."

"Guessed what? Very hurt? Very sick? Or..."

"The last one."

"You mean he died? You mean James died?"

"I've been trying to tell you that for I don't know how long. Now, sugar pea, don't—whatever you do—don't get hysterical on me. Remember your oath. Remember what I've been saying for the last few minutes. Bravery, keeping a stiff upper lip, all that stuff. I'm gonna need you now, honey. I've gotta stop playing momma, and you've gotta stop playing baby. I know there is sadness in these times. In a year, you'll think back and, sure, you'll miss James. But now there are others to think about. Think about the kids for a minute. I've just told you this. Now we've gotta tell them. You and me. Together. That's how things are gonna be from now on. I can't carry the ball by myself. I didn't have to while James was alive. But now that he's gone…"

"Gone?" Emma said, putting her hand over her mouth.

"Gone. You knew that, didn't you, sugar? He's gone…
for good."

"For good?"

Gramma nodded.

"So…now what?"

"That's the attitude I like. Confused but forward thinking.
Remember what I was just talking about."

"The children?"

"That's right. You're catching onto this suffering business
mighty fast."

"We should tell them…about their daddy?"

"Yes, well, I mean I can do most of the talking, and you can
just stand there and look motherly. Can you handle that?"

Emma nodded.

"Are you okay…I mean, you're so calm. And no tears. I
thought surely this home would float in all your tears."

"I'm okay."

"Well that's a welcome relief. All right, let's go," Gramma
said, grabbing Emma by the wrist. "Oh, and another thing," she
said, stopping in the doorway, her hand still tight around
Emma's wrist.

"What?" Emma asked.

"We're going on a trip together…"

"A trip?"

"Why, yes. And guess where?"

"I don't know. Where?"

"Come on, take a guess."

"The moon…and then heaven. I don't know. I give up,"
Emma said, giggling quietly.

"To New York, silly. I thought you'd guess it lickety-split.
Now, you won't have to do a thing. Just keep me company and
stay out of trouble. Can you do that?"

Emma nodded again.

"That's a good girl. You're being such a good girl," Gramma
cooed, stroking Emma's hair. Gramma had to make herself stop.
It was going to be just as hard to start treating Emma like a
grown-up as it would be for Emma to start acting like one.

* * *

If someone was to come up to me when I was nine or ten and say, 'Roxanne, not only is your dad gonna try to do himself in in a few years, but he's gonna up and die in New York City,' I would have said to that person to go stick it somewhere, or something. I guess it's too easy to say, why me. But I'm gonna say it anyway. Why me? I mean, what have I done? I haven't blown up a bank. I haven't murdered anyone. All I've done is gone to school and gotten okay grades and tried to survive. I mean, that's it. Now I can't even be a normal person anymore. At school, I won't be Roxanne Freedman, a-normal-girl-who-just-wants-a-cute-boyfriend-like-Rick-Templeton; instead, I'll be Roxanne Freedman, an-unnormal-girl-whose-father-just-died-under-strange-circumstances.

When they were telling us, Mom was so pathetic, standing there with her mouth open. She looked all crumpled up like that pillow case over there in the corner. And Gramma looked so worried and pale. I hope this doesn't bring on that dizzy spell she had after watching those Vietnamese peasants being shot on television.

Then Gus ran out of the room and left the house and went who knows where. He sneaks out all the time now, and they're too busy and dumb to even know it. Why do I have to be stuck here by myself with no one to talk to? And why are they both going to New York and making us stay with a neighbor? Why can't we go, too? What's it supposed to feel like when a parent dies? Am I feeling all the right things? Am I sad enough? Whenever I thought about Mom or Dad dying, I always imagined myself in black, filmy clothes, crying constantly at the funeral, but still looking put together with waterproof mascara and a black mesh veil over my tiny, red nose (I would have gotten the perfect nose job a few months earlier). Yet I haven't really cried, and I don't feel like crying. What's wrong with me? Daddy made me so mad...he could be such a jerk. I wonder when I'll start missing him. Will I ever? Yeah, I'm sure I will. He's dead, and it's not like he's on some business trip, he's gone for good, no Daddy slamming the front door, no Daddy whistling some stupid song at the breakfast table, no Daddy with his dumb Irving talk, no Daddy fights, no Daddy, no Daddy ever. When I sit here and really think about it, the whole thing is pretty impossible to believe.

That asshole, he deserved to die, that asshole, I'm glad he's gone, and I'm gonna be gone as soon as I get my chops together and head out to California and record with guys like Jagger and Morrison and Clapton and Lennon. I'll be so famous, everyone will hear and read 'bout me, and they'll be sorry for anything they've ever done 'cause when the magazines ask about 'em, I'm gonna say I've got no family, I was an orphan, someone found me in a trash can wrapped in newspapers like the bums sleeping on park benches downtown. Or maybe I'll say I've got some distant relatives in the Midwest, and maybe they'll trace Gramma down, but by then I'll be so famous it won't matter. I'll be able to say whatever I please whenever I please, and it won't matter 'cause I'll be so famous and so rich no one will touch me, no one ever.

12

An Empire State of Mind

When Gramma saw Emma walk into the kitchen the next morning, she had to look at her twice. Never had she seen Emma look so neat and tidy, her blonde hair smooth instead of tangled and hanging in her face. Her simple gray dress was pressed and spot-free. She had a matching patent leather purse and was wearing a small, round hat. Gramma wondered when Emma had bought a matching purse and hat, and then she remembered that they had gotten them for Emma's honeymoon over sixteen years ago. Gramma thought Emma looked pretty darn good, why almost fashionable, although Gramma knew very little about fashion.

"Honey, you look like a song. Are you nervous?"

"Uh-huh...."

"Well, you don't look it. You look as cool and pretty as can be. Have you packed?"

"Well, sort of...can you check and see if I've put in all the right things?"

"Sure, darlin'. Do you want a little breakfast first? A person shouldn't fly on an empty stomach, and those stewardesses usually don't get around to serving breakfast until the flight is halfway over, and then what they serve is usually awful anyway."

"Uh, Mama, can we wait to eat until you've looked in my suitcase? I mean, I don't think I could eat until I knew I was bringing all the right things...."

It had been a long time since Emma had gone on a big trip, and in the past they had always traveled by car. The last time they went out of town was when they drove down to the Ozarks, and Roxanne was car sick there and back, and Gus was

122

lost in the woods for an entire day. Some vacation. Gramma also wondered how wise it was to book their reservation in the same hotel where James died. She knew it wouldn't bother her any, but it might bother Emma to be sleeping in the same building where a tragedy of such magnitude had taken place. Maybe Emma wouldn't put two and two together, but Gramma didn't know where else to go in New York and besides she already had the phone number and address on the refrigerator.

When Gramma looked through Emma's suitcase, she saw that it was full of a variety of nightgowns and bathrobes—silk, flannel, cotton, terry cloth, light wool ones—and four pairs of Carter's cotton underwear. Nothing else.

"Why darlin'? Why?" Gramma asked, holding up two of the nightgowns.

"Well..."

"Well, what?" Gramma demanded.

"I was watching TV the other morning," Emma said, slowly looking into the suitcase. "And I saw this movie that took place in New York, and there was this beautiful woman starring in the movie and the whole time she only wore nightgowns in her apartment, and she had a pitcher full of drinks that she kept stirring. I figured that that was what people wore when they were in New York...."

"Nightgowns? You think that's all people wear in New York. What about going outside? Did you ever think of that?"

"No, not exactly...but that's why I wanted you to look in my suitcase. To give me some ideas. I knew there might be something wrong."

"Yeah, plenty wrong, young lady," Gramma said, yanking clothes off of hangers and out of drawers and throwing them into the suitcase. "Now, I want you to listen to me and listen good. I may regret taking you to New York...in fact, I probably will regret it 'cause I'm not sure you're ready for all this commotion. But we made a deal and a deal is a deal, and I don't like going back on my word. Now, before we go, I want you to make me one promise. Promise me not to go out of the hotel without me by your side. If you get hungry or thirsty, you can order from the downstairs restaurant. Is that clear? I don't like the idea of you wandering the streets and talking to strangers. Now, there are going to be plenty of ugly things I'm gonna have to do by myself, but you won't have to come with me for any of that. There will be a TV, and I'll get you magazines and one of those hot pretzels off the street. You'll have fun listening to the noise and the traffic and the people in the hall. Do you want to say something?"

"Uh-huh. If I can't go outside, can't I bring my robes and nightgowns?"

"Forget the damn robes and nightgowns. What I packed is much, much better. Now, what about a fall coat?"

"My red one?" Emma asked, hoping for approval.

"Perfect, just perfect, I would've picked that one myself. Oh my gracious, we are late, and we won't have time to eat much except some Wheaties. And we've got to say goodbye to the kids."

"Roxanne," Gramma said, knocking on her bedroom door.

"Yeah?" Roxanne said.

"Remember what I told you 'bout picking up the paper and the mail and making sure there are lights on in the house and watching out for strangers prowlin' in the bushes."

"Yes, Gramma," Roxanne said, opening the door a crack. Lately, she was sleeping without any clothes on, and she was feeling modest, even in front of her mother and grandmother.

"Don't you want to give your gramma and mama a kiss for good luck?"

"I guess so," Roxanne said, screwing up her mouth.

"What do you mean you guess so? I didn't raise my grand-daughter to act so rude. Now, be a good girl and give us a kiss."

Roxanne kissed her grandmother and her mother's cheek through the crack of the door.

"Gramma?"

"What is it, sugar?"

"Gramma, you know, this whole thing with Daddy dying and all. What I want to say is...I mean, what's gonna happen to us? I dunno, this might sound stupid."

"No, go on. Nothing's gonna sound stupid right now. We're all suffering in our own private way."

"Are we gonna have to move? I mean..."

"Honey, don't worry about nothin'. Between me and your

daddy, we've got enough to live on. As a matter of fact, we've got plenty. Take care of yourself and look after that brother of yours. He's hurting more than all of us put together."

Gramma and Roxanne kissed one final time, and Roxanne felt good inside like she used to when she was younger, and she didn't know so much.

Emma and Gramma went across the hall to Gus's room and knocked on the door. A radio was playing faint rock music.

"Gus, we're leaving. Gus, open your door and say goodbye."

"Bye," Gus said in his bedroom.

"Open the door and say goodbye to us in person. NOW."

Gus pulled the door open slowly. His hair was disheveled, and his eyes were two swollen red slits.

"Now be good and polite to the Langworthys. They were nice enough to take you in...and give us a hug." Gus gave his mother and grandmother quick squeezes. "And be a good little man...." Gramma had to turn away because she knew if she looked at Gus for one more second, she would start to bawl.

Since Emma had never been on an airplane before, Gramma didn't know how she would react to flying. Gramma was surprised to see how much Emma enjoyed herself. She read the seat belt instruction card at least five times. She listened attentively to the stewardess who explained how to retrieve an oxygen mask in case the plane started to crash. Emma turned on and off her overhead light, her air blower, and even paged a stewardess with her call button. While the plane took off, she closed her eyes and held onto the sides of her chair as if she were climbing uphill on a steep roller coaster. Emma continued to keep her eyes shut until the plane leveled off into a steady hum. Then she couldn't stop staring at the surrounding sky. Every time the plane passed by cloud formations—especially the ones that looked like swirling parfait desserts—she tugged at Gramma's sleeve and insisted that she look out the window.

After the stewardess handed out Cokes and 7-Ups to the passengers, Emma gazed longingly at a blue swizzle stick in the shape of an airplane that one of them had given a little girl across the aisle. The child noticed Emma's gaze and started to give the swizzle stick to her until Gramma insisted that the little girl keep it. But what convinced Gramma that Emma felt comfortable was how quickly she nodded off into a nice, long nap, even with a half-eaten tray of food folded down on her lap. While Emma was getting off the plane, she shook the stewardesses' hands and thanked them, calling all of them by their first names.

Getting to the Lancaster Hotel was some big effort for Gramma and Emma. Their suitcases were close to the last ones to show up on the conveyer belt. A porter hit the back of Emma's leg with his luggage cart. Gramma asked three people where she could find a cab, and they all ignored her. Then once Gramma and Emma were told where to go, they had to stand in a long line. Trying to carry the suitcases and hold onto Emma was a chore for Gramma. She was taking slow, heavy breaths as they wound their way through the line. By the time they flopped themselves into the back seat of a cab, they were both exhausted. Emma started to sniffle.

"Now what?" Gramma asked.

"I don't know. It's all so...busy," Emma said.

"First time to the city, ladies?" the cab driver asked. He was an olive-skinned, squat man who wore a Yankees cap and jacket and had long, black hairs growing out of his knuckles.

"Why, yes, yes it is," Gramma said, trying to be polite.

"Well, don't let nothin' bother you, 'cause it ain't worth it. I'm a New Yorker born and raised and whenever anybody tries to give me any grief, I just ignore it. Once you get used to the noise and the filth, I swear to God it's no problem."

"Why, thanks for the advice, Mr., Mr. — " Gramma said, straining to read the long, Greek last name on the glove compartment.

"George, the name's George. Where you from?"

"Kansas City..."

"Kansas City, yeah, they had some crazy ball team in them A's, but they're in California now, ain't they? Probably where they belong. And the Chiefs played in the first Superbowl. Yeah, at least it's a decent sports city. I have a cousin, he lives in Des Moines, and they don't have nothin' there, no sports teams, no nothin'. I don't know how he can stand not goin' to the ball game or the fights or the track. But you ladies probably ain't interested in that kind of stuff, am I right?"

"Right," Gramma replied, wishing this uncouth man would keep his mouth shut.

"Look," Emma said, pointing to the tall buildings and bridges in the distance. "Look."

"Yeah, lady. New York. Greatest city in the world. But if you don't mind my saying so, let me give you a piece of advice. I don't mean no offense, really I don't, but you ladies, well, you don't look so, you know, experienced, and I hate to see nice ladies gettin' hurt, if you know what I mean. If someone comes up to you in the city and asks you the time of day, just keep on walkin'. Nine times out of ten they're kids on LSD just waitin' for suckers to take their eyes off their business. Another thing to watch out for: don't, whatever you do, don't give money to the bums. Lots of times they have guns hidden in all them bags they carry around."

"Thank you, Mr. George. We're quite capable of taking care of ourselves," Gramma said. No one—especially some ignorant cab driver—was going to tell her how to handle herself in New York City.

"Okay, lady, okay," he said, holding up both hands from the steering wheel and muttering to himself.

"What did you say?" Gramma asked, leaning forward.

"Nothin', nothin'," George replied.

"Look, Mama," Emma said, pointing her finger upward. "The famous building, the one James liked to talk about."

"You mean the Chrysler?" George asked.

"No, she means the Empire State," Gramma snapped. "Now where you going?" she asked as they approached the Midtown Tunnel.

"It just so happens, lady, I'm treatin' you fair and square. I could have been a real louse and taken you over the Triborough and charged a lot more, but I'm takin' you through the tunnel, and we'll end up just blocks from your hotel. Now, you happy?"

"Well," Gramma said, chagrined that this numskull was right. They all sat in silence while Gramma refused to look out the window; Emma waved at cars passing them by on Thirty-fourth Street and gasped as they went by a gourmet food shop's window display of French, braided, and round breads surrounded by a medley of imported cheeses.

While they were waiting for the light to change on Madison, George pointed down the block and said, "Your building's over there, ladies. Me, I personally like the Chrysler 'cause I love that top part. Don't it look like some old-time jukebox or somethin'. But if I went into a bar and asked a bunch of guys which one they liked, the Empire State or the Chrysler, I swear the bar would be split right down the middle—hey, where's she goin'?"

Emma had opened the car door halfway and was starting to put her foot down on the asphalt.

"Emma, that's dangerous and you know it!" Gramma said slamming the door and locking it. George wondered whether he should forget the hotel and drop off these two loony birds at the next corner.

"I wanted to go to the building," Emma sniffled. "It's just right there, like the man said. I want to see it."

"Later, dear. Not right now. We'll be sure to see it before we leave," Gramma said, untangling Emma's hair with her fingers.

"Promise?" Emma asked.

"Promise," Gramma said.

After Gramma paid the cab fare, George sped off as fast as his cab would take him. No more nuts for today. That younger one was some knock-out, but the old bag was a bitch. He didn't give a shit about work. Let the dispatcher call till his voice got hoarse. He was gonna stop for a quick drink and take a poll at the bar. Which one? The Chrysler or the Empire State?

The Lancaster Hotel lobby was small but decorated in an elegant fashion—cream-colored marble floors, an entire wall of mirrors, fresh-cut flowers in lead crystal vases, Louis XIV furniture with cream and pink satin upholstery. Emma thought she had just arrived in a brand new fairy-land castle. She ran her hand along the smooth satin of the love seat and threw herself down in one of the chairs, crossing and uncrossing her ankles. She would have been content to spend the night on the love seat, all bunched up like a lazy kitten, even though she knew that she and Gramma had a room upstairs with real beds and closets.

After Gramma checked in, she had a bellhop carry their bags into the elevator. Emma had an urge to press some of the buttons to see what the other floors looked like, but she knew that Mama would get angry, so she stopped herself in time.

Emma and Gramma were disappointed with their room. It was small with brown curtains and covers, and the windows faced a brick wall. If they leaned way over, they could get a glimpse of Thirty-eighth Street—that is, if they were standing on a chair and pressing the sides of their noses against the window.

Gramma knew she had a long day's work ahead of her. First, go to the hospital and claim the body. After that, she would arrange for the body to be taken to a funeral home near New York University hospital to be embalmed. She knew she would be exhausted from the entire process, but she wanted to get this over with as soon as possible; it wasn't right to dawdle when there was a body to be buried. Gramma wondered why she kept referring to James as "the body." She figured that calling him that was another way of coping with this mess.

Gramma watched Emma open and shut the dresser drawers, the closet doors, and the bathroom cabinet; she was thoroughly convinced that bringing Emma to New York had been a hare-brained idea. Yet she had done it, anyway, against her own better instincts. She just didn't want to be going through all of this by herself.

"Come on, Emma sweetie, stop that right now," Gramma said, shutting the drawer that Emma was inspecting beside her bed. "We're both tired, aren't we? We could both use a nap. Come on, let's lie down? Now, doesn't that feel better?" Gramma said, holding Emma's hand across the space between the two single beds.

"No, Mama, I'm wide awake, honest I am," Emma said, struggling to free her hand from Gramma's grip.

A thought occurred to Gramma that made her let go of Emma and sit up straight in bed. It was as if she had gotten a glimpse of something that she had no right to be witnessing. She couldn't believe it hadn't been obvious to her before. The other woman, James's sweetie back East. She had been with him when it happened. How else did he get to the hospital so early in the morning? Maids didn't come around to clean rooms until at least eighty-thirty or nine, and sometimes as late as the afternoon. And it would have been a maid who would have found him—that is, if he were alone at the time. Well, there was no sense dwelling on something that was over and done with. She almost felt sorry for her, whoever she was. There was no proper way for a mistress to mourn her dead lover in public. She had to mourn to her pillow at night or on her psychiatrist's couch or on her mother's shoulder. She had to mourn on her way to work or in a grocery store check-out line or in an empty movie theatre or in the woods on a Sunday morning. Gramma had one thing that she was thankful for—that Emma was never a man's "other woman." She knew that the mere notion of it was far fetched, but she had to be grateful for small blessings. She looked at her watch and realized she had wasted enough time.

"I've got to get moving, darlin'," Gramma said, putting on her coat. "Now, remember what I told you. No going outside. I'll come back with plenty of nice things for you, don't you worry. If you really get bored, you can go downstairs for a minute and talk to the nice man behind the desk or to the man who brought up our suitcases. Okay? Here's an extra key and the TV," Gramma said, turning it on to a channel where a man with long sideburns was soundlessly interviewing a woman wearing a black mini-skirt and white boots. "I won't be too terribly long."

After Gramma left, Emma flipped the channel and sat on the bed, staring at the soap opera stars in mute combat. The hotel phone started to ring, and Emma watched the red-headed woman on television pick up her princess phone. Emma thought for a moment the actress could answer the hotel phone for her. After it continued to ring two more times, Emma rolled over on the bed and said hello.

"Is this Mrs. Freedman?" the woman's voice asked. Emma watched the soap opera woman's lips move to see if, perhaps, she was going to tell her some crucial plot twist over the phone.

"Yes," Emma said after a long pause.

"Well, I thought I'd take a chance and call you at the same hotel where James was...anyway, this is a friend of his, and I just want to say how very sorry I am...about his death, that is. He was a very fine man." The woman cleared her voice.

"I didn't know James knew anyone here."

"Well, we worked together."

"Oh...."

"Here, that is. And in Kansas City."

"Oh." Emma couldn't think of anything else to say to this voice. "Well?"

"Yes?"

"Ummm, thanks for calling, I guess."

"Yes, of course, you're welcome." Lydia slammed down the phone because she didn't want Emma to hear her voice break after sounding so calm during the entire conversation. She figured that calling Emma wasn't very smart, and she was probably being selfish and hurtful to James's family. But she needed the emotional release; at this point she didn't care what they thought anymore.

"Goodbye," Emma said to the dial tone, watching the woman on television slam down the phone and light up a cigarette in a long, slender holder. She took out a pencil from the drawer by her bed, put it in her mouth and puffed on it slowly. Was this what some women did to make themselves beautiful? The woman on television was not wearing a nightgown. Perhaps Gramma was right—she didn't need all of those nightgowns after all.

Emma listened to the screeching traffic down below and imagined what it would be like to walk among human beings wearing watches and overcoats and hats, holding scraps of paper with addresses scribbled on them. Busy human beings with deadlines and destinations. Women whose high heels clicked down the sidewalk in a metronome of accuracy, their hair sculpted into stiff bubbles and flips. Yet, Emma had no destination, no scrap of paper telling her where to go. For a moment, Emma longed for a distinct sense of purpose. Perhaps she could have been a help to Mama. Perhaps she could have bought sandwiches or run an errand or made a phone call, anything to seem useful. But duties of that kind always made Emma feel so inadequate, since she could never do them right. She would dial the wrong number or drop the sandwich on the floor, and she would get flustered because she was a failure at even the simplest task.

Emma stood on a chair and pushed the side of her face

against the window to watch the activity down below. She remembered seeing a photograph of the building when she was a little girl in a huge picture book that Mama kept on the shelf. The book's spine was cracked, and she remembered one after-noon how she and Mama were bent over the floor trying to apply glue to the loose pages. She remembered Mama had promised her that someday they would go to the very top and then see a musical on Broadway and afterwards get a dish of peppermint ice cream at a fancy restaurant. Mama had not mentioned ice cream or musicals since they arrived in New York. If she could break those promises, she could certainly break her promise to take Emma to the building. James would have wanted her to see it; he used to talk about it with such awe. Emma peered outside the window again; she tried to pull it open, but it was nailed shut. How different could walking around New York be from walking around her neighborhood in Kansas City? Just a few more cars and taller buildings and more people? And that woman who called—Emma guessed that if she could call her back and ask her if she should go see the building, the woman would say, "Yes, of course, I was a friend of James's, yes for goodness sake, go see the building." See, Mama, the friend of James's would've said yes.

And James once said that the big antenna on top of the building sent out television signals. She wondered if that was for all of America or just for this city. Somehow she couldn't believe that one tall building could bounce signals as far as South Dakota. She shut her eyes for a moment and imagined the television waves streaming across the air, through the glass of her hotel window and directly to her head as if she, herself, were the main antenna for all of New York. She liked that idea. She liked it very much. She could almost feel the good, strong electrical pulses just beneath the surface of her skin. Emma grabbed her red car coat, her gray purse and the hotel key that Gramma left for her and started to rush out the door. She nearly forgot to put on her new pair of Hush Puppies. She tied them up so quickly that her fingers got knotted in the laces. She had an important place to go. She was in a hurry. She had to get to the building while the signals to her head were still coming in clear.

Gramma knew she was on the late side, but after all the

awful stuff she did that day—first at the hospital, and then at the midtown funeral home—she couldn't resist having a little fun, so she took a cab to the Plaza Hotel and stood outside, keeping a look-out for celebrities. She had debated to herself whether the Waldorf was actually the better hotel for celebrity watching, but after thinking about it, she decided that if she were a celebrity and were given a choice where to stay, she would choose the Plaza. Maybe it had more glamour, more of the old New York charm Gramma saw on late night movies. Maybe those Eloise books that she used to read to Roxanne influenced her decision; she kept imagining that little girl with the stringy hair sliding down the hotel banister and drawing mustaches on all of the portraits in the hallway. She couldn't get that spoiled and nasty Eloise out of her mind. What kind of people would bring up a child in a hotel? And what kind of hotel would attract that kind of people? It made her curious about the place. Damn curious.

Gramma noticed a long, gray limousine pulling up to the curb, and she craned her neck to see inside the tinted glass windows. The man who stepped out of the back seat looked just like Jack Lemmon until Gramma realized that the mouth was all wrong, and that the woman he was with was wearing some chintzy-looking white fur. Jack Lemmon would never let his wife go out in public wearing something like that. And when the two opened their mouths, Gramma could hear thick, Southern accents. Gramma hated Southern accents. She couldn't understand how she could have lived in New Orleans for so long, listening to those lazy vowels day in and day out. There should be some law in New York City that only celebrities were allowed to ride around in limousines with tinted windows.

Gramma checked her watch and, gracious, it was late. She hoped that Emma had the sense to get something to eat on her own. Perhaps Emma had ordered food from downstairs or had gone to the corner for a hot dog and a cola.

When she got back to the room, the first thing she saw was Emma's red coat on the floor. So she had gone outside. All right, she could handle that; Emma just needed a good talking to. But why were the lights out? And there was someone in the room—Gramma could hear breathing in the far corner, and she put her hand over her heart to try to slow it down.

"Mama, I saw it. I've been up there," Emma whispered.

"Lord, you scared me so. I thought it was a burglar, waiting to hit me over the head with a lamp—now, what did you say?" Gramma said, switching on the lights.

"You know..."

"No, I don't know."

"Yes, you do. How could you not know?"

"Child, I'm tired, and I'm not in the mood for guessing games. Have you eaten anything?"

"Yes."

"So, what did you have?"

"Sky..."

"Sky? Is that some kind of Popsicle from the street?"

"No, it's just what it is. Sky. Plain old sky. Can't you tell I've been up there? Can't you tell? And Mama, it was wonderful. I can't begin to explain...look what it gave me. All kinds of gifts."

Sure enough, there was a semi-circle of Empire State building memorabilia surrounding Emma's feet: a room thermometer attached to a copper miniature Empire State Building; an Empire State Building plastic paper weight that was filled with water and artificial snow; an Empire State pewter mug; an Empire State ruler and pencil set; a stuffed Empire State with a gorilla hanging off the antenna; a back-to-school Empire State notebook; an Empire State baseball cap and T-shirt; an Empire State ashtray and decorative plate; an Empire State thermos with a matching travel bag.

"Oh, my God...." Gramma said, shaking her head. "My God...."

"I spent all my money..."

"YOU WERE SUPPOSED TO SAVE IT FOR SOMETHING ELSE, SOMETHING MORE SPECIAL."

"This *is* special, Mama. The most special thing possible. The building is in me...it is me. It tells me things about itself. For instance...I'm located at 350 Fifth Avenue between Thirty-third and Thirty-fourth Street. I'm 1,472 feet high. I weigh 365,000 tons. Shreve, Lamb & Associates designed me. I cover about two acres. My basement and lobby go thirty-five feet below the ground. I cost $40,948,900 to build...."

"Wait a minute, wait one damn minute. Darling, listen to me, please. The building isn't telling you a thing. Nothing. Understand? You're reading those facts from some brochure you got from up top. The building can't talk. Honest to God, I would tell you what's right." Gramma was starting to panic. This time, Emma had really done it; she had gone off the deep end.

"I may be reading this, yes, but my voice is echoing what the building says. It's controlling my every move. I have never felt so, so..."

"So what, dear?"

"So..."

Emma was standing very still with her hands pressed together over her head, as if she were praying to the heavens. She reminded Gramma of some Egyptian hieroglyphic she had seen in an old National Geographic of a flat, dancing maiden with black-rimmed eyes pressed sideways against the wall of a Pharaoh's tomb. Her sweaty face was contorted into a grimace in an effort to keep her hands over her head, but her eyes were empty of expression. The muscles in her body were taut, and her legs shook. Gramma had never seen Emma work so hard at anything in her life.

At first Gramma's mind couldn't quite make sense of what was happening. It took a minute of staring to realize that Emma had completely fallen to pieces. There was no denying it. She was certifiably cuckoo. Nuts. Bonkers. And she was standing completely still. With her hands over her head. Like a building. Of all things. Gramma felt hot and cold at the same time and rushed to the bathroom to vomit. Then she crawled out of the bathroom to see if Emma was still crazy. She was, only this time she had sat on the floor with her hands still pointing over her head. Gramma felt sick all over again and grabbed a wastebasket but nothing came out of her mouth. She was too frightened to touch her and felt her own mind shutting down. She couldn't think straight. Maybe she was going cuckoo, too. Like daughter, like mother. Maybe this was just a passing thing with Emma. A phase. What those shrink types call temporary insanity. Maybe if she watched Emma closely the entire night, she would snap out of it. Or if she concentrated hard enough, she could will her to get well like the evangelists did on Sunday morning television. While Emma sat on the floor, Gramma watched her from the bed. And prayed.

Gramma woke up at four in the morning because her cardigan sweater was pulling against her neck. Emma was asleep on the floor, surrounded by her Empire State souvenirs, her legs rigid and pressed together, her hands touching lightly over her head. Gramma couldn't imagine falling asleep in such a bizarre pose. But if Emma believed—really believed—that she was the Empire State, why that was probably how a building, with a huge antenna, slept. Gramma turned over and pushed her face against the mattress. She wanted to push out the words that were in her head. Crazy. Baby. Girl. Emma. Crazy. Gramma always knew that Emma's mind could jog loose at any moment. But why now? Why?

She knew she had fallen short of her duty by going to sleep. If only she had stayed awake, maybe something could have happened. She knew the mind could do things. Special things. Work miracles. She wanted to believe it.

She sat and stared at Emma. She was too upset to move. She was a failure. A big, stupid failure. What next? Call New York University hospital. Get her shot up with something and have her put in a strait jacket. She knew the hospital's number by heart, she had dialed it so many times. She tried to reach for the phone but couldn't do it. How could she possibly get Emma on that plane for the funeral? THE FUNERAL. JAMES. She had forgotten all about James. She was suddenly overwhelmed and felt her face get hot and her stomach tighten. She had to, quick, call that Mrs. Wellfleet, at New York University Hospital. Such a bitchy know-it-all—but efficient. Gramma would certainly give her credit for that.

She dropped the phone a couple of times, she was so nervous. At first she had a hard time speaking, and the person who answered the phone at the hospital almost hung up. Gramma managed to explain some of Emma's symptoms to this person, and she gave Gramma the phone number and name of a Miss Thompkins, the head of psychiatric nursing, at Bellevue. After Gramma muddled through her story, Miss Thompkins asked whether Emma had any history of mental illness (according to

136

Gramma, Emma had always acted peculiar, but Gramma didn't know if that was considered mental illness), and then Miss Thompkins said she wanted to commit Emma to Bellevue right away. But Gramma didn't want to; she didn't want to leave Emma in New York all by herself. This was a big, dangerous city for such a pitiful creature. Now she was starting to come to, feeling a little like her old self again. She was getting good and mad. There was a body to be buried—Emma's husband, for chrissakes. Emma should at least be given the chance to attend the funeral, whether she was crazy or not. Couldn't they understand that? Why did these so-called medical experts want to make everything so difficult?

Miss Thompkins continued to explain to Gramma why it was impossible for Emma to go to Kansas City that day: a person who was in a statue-like pose could not be given one shot of Thorazine and then sent on her way; she needed to be sedated for at least four to seven days so that her blood level was under control and this, in turn, would stop her from assuming the pose. If she were not properly drugged, she could become violent on the plane. Miss Thompkins also informed Gramma that if she didn't want to leave Emma at Bellevue or have her transferred to New York University's psychiatric hospital in Westchester, she had to have Emma escorted on a plane by a mental health technician.

"Topeka, Kansas, happens to have one of the finest psychiatric institutions in the country. Menninger. Are you familiar with it?" Miss Thompkins asked Gramma.

"No, but that doesn't mean a whole heck of a lot."

"Well, I'll check with a referring psychiatrist to see if we can get her flown to Topeka as soon as possible. It depends on whether there's an available bed for her. Now, you'll be in New York how much longer?"

"I ALREADY TOLD YOU, I'M LEAVING TODAY. I'VE GOT THIS BODY TO BURY. EMMA'S HUSBAND, AS A MATTER OF FACT. I THINK HIS DEATH...MAYBE THIS KOOKY CITY BROUGHT ALL THIS POSING STUFF ON."

"Please...you don't have to shout. I understand what you're going through...what you must be feeling...."

"NO ONE ON THIS ENTIRE PLANET COULD POSSI-

BLY UNDERSTAND HOW I'M FEELING. I'VE GOT A DEAD SON-IN-LAW. A CRAZY DAUGHTER. DO YOU REALIZE ALL THE ARRANGEMENTS I'VE GOT TO MAKE? MY NERVES ARE JUST RAW."

"We'll send an ambulance as soon as possible for your daughter. By the way, is she incontinent?"

"Is she what?"

"Is she using the toilet? Some people don't when they're in this condition."

"Well, I haven't noticed if she's gone on herself. Should I ask her?"

"Well, not—"

"—Honey, are you using the little girl's room? I think she's still sleeping," she whispered to Miss Thompkins, realizing how silly it was to ask Emma any kind of question about herself.

"Please, no need to worry about it, Mrs. Sendall. But do me a favor. Don't touch your daughter under any circumstances. She might strike out...even at you."

"At me? Her own mother?"

"Yes. And I know it's tempting to comb her hair or tidy her up for the hospital, but don't...all right?"

"Certainly, Miss Thompkins. You're the loony expert, if I'm not mistaken."

"We'll have an ambulance over to the Lancaster in no time. Just sit tight."

"What choice do I have?" Gramma said.

After all, where in the hell could she go?

As the ambulance drivers and the mental health technician strapped Emma into the stretcher, they spoke to her in soft tones and explained everything they were about to do to her. Emma struggled and looked up at everyone with large, darting eyes, and Gramma was reminded of the time when a baby bird got wedged in a crack in the floor of the upstairs porch and how she carefully scooped it up with a dust pan and placed it on a flower bed in the back yard. While Gramma watched the men carry Emma down the hall, she wondered whether the baby bird survived that unseasonably cold spring.

* * *

138

As Gramma tilted back her airplane seat, she was amazed that she was able to catch the afternoon flight to Kansas City. She decided that the only way she would survive this ordeal was to stop thinking. And feeling. She was numb. And exhausted. She could hardly remember all the events of the day. She had filled out so many papers for Emma's admittance to Bellevue that her hand felt arthritic. She had been nervous about Emma being alone at Bellevue—she remembered hearing horror stories years ago about how dirty it used to be and about the abuse inflicted upon the patients. She envisioned pasty, drooling patients wearing pajamas soaked with urine, strapped to narrow beds. If she saw any evidence of that kind of treatment, she would have yanked Emma out of there so fast. But from what she could observe, the hospital looked clean, and the staff and doctors seemed alert. Even though everything at Bellevue appeared on the up and up, as far as Gramma was concerned, all hospitals were snake pits.

After she had checked Emma in and had consulted with the referring psychiatrist, Dr. Feingold, about what to do next (she had to admit she was confused by all this bureaucracy and trauma), Gramma hailed a cab to the Lancaster Hotel where she threw everything into the two suitcases and checked out as quickly as possible, leaving her home address with the desk clerk in case there were shoes left under the bed. She then got a cab to the funeral home and rode with James's body to the airport. The hearse driver was a good-looking fellow in his late twenties who was studying Method acting with Lee Strasberg. He told Gramma he hoped to draw from some of his experiences in the funeral home when he was analyzing a character's motivation. Even Gramma knew who Lee Strasberg was—Marilyn Monroe had studied with him for a while.

Now, as she stared at the open mouth of the man dozing beside her on the plane, she doubted if the family could endure all these blows. She ordered a scotch on the rocks from the stewardess—she deserved it, damn it—and her tears did not make the drink go down any smoother.

13

Lilies

The funeral for James was a no-nonsense affair, just what would be expected from Gramma. Only a few people attended: the Langworthys, three of James's co-workers at Stern Brothers and a tall man wearing a brown and white pinstripe suit that looked too small. Gramma guessed that this gentleman must be Irving, and she had heard so much about him from James that she felt a funny kinship with him, as if only they and they alone knew what made James tick.

Both Roxanne and Gus thought that the funeral was sickening but for different reasons. Roxanne despised the flower arrangement of Easter lilies and ferns in front of the podium. Why hadn't Gramma selected something like roses and baby's breath, something that wasn't so morbid? Gus was listening to the organ music and wondering why people always got the worst musicians to play at funerals. Why hadn't Gramma hired some guy from over by Linwood or The Paseo, someone who played Motown and jazz by night and churchy stuff by day?

When Gramma was planning the funeral, she felt that someone religious—a priest or a rabbi—should conduct the service because she figured that was what James would have wanted. Since James was, after all, born Jewish, she finally chose a rabbi from Temple B'nai Jehudah, who said repeatedly throughout the eulogy that, even though James was not a religious man and was not a member of The Temple, he was still a child of God. Also, Gramma, Roxanne, and Gus had never heard Hebrew before, and they were puzzled by this strange, guttural language that the rabbi said in prayer. At the grave site, Gramma was absolutely fuming; she had spent an hour and a half, talking to this rabbi about James's prickly personality, his favorite food (Chinese), the fact that he had no hobbies to speak of and his passion for psychoanalysis, and this rabbi had not said one single personal thing about him. She was so peeved that she forgot to get upset, even while the casket was being lowered into the ground. Roxanne and Gus were both rubbing their eyes, like they used to do when they had spent an evening in front of the television watching "Saturday Night at the Movies."

Gramma had not had the guts to tell the children about Emma—at least not before the funeral. All she said was that their mother had been delayed in New York—nothing more. She figured she would tell them later about her, perhaps while they were in the kitchen putting out the cold cuts and rolls on platters for the guests making condolence calls. But then again, there probably wasn't anyone besides those at the funeral who would bother to come around; the Freedmans were not very good at establishing social contacts.

Later that afternoon, the kitchen was quiet, except for the sound of Gramma pulling and ripping Saran Wrap from its cardboard container. Gramma felt terribly hot, and she struggled to open the window above the sink.

Gramma noticed that Roxanne and Gus were unusually quiet—no arguments, no poking or teasing, no "he did this" or "she did that." They were acting too good to be teen-agers, certainly too good for Roxanne and Gus. Gramma felt that teenagers should be allowed to be obnoxious, even if their behavior did get on her nerves. After all, if they didn't get those impulses out of their system by the time they were adults, they would be hated by everyone and never offered a proper job. Perhaps they even sensed she had something to tell them.

Gramma, however, did not know what to say to Gus and Roxanne. She felt as though she had the most difficult job in the United States, much more difficult than President Johnson had with his Vietnam War. Should she start out being light-hearted, perhaps even optimistic? Or should she be honest and just come right out and say, "Not only is your father dead, but your mother thinks she's a building." The more she thought about it, the more she realized that telling them all at once would probably hurt the least—like pulling off a Band-Aid quickly instead of tugging at it bit by bit.

"Okay, kids, time to quit what you're doing and sit down for a spell," Gramma said, pulling out two chairs from the breakfast table.

Gus and Roxanne looked at each other and smirked. They weren't doing anything they even had to stop; what mattered was knowing how to look busy.

Gramma hated being in this position once again, being the one to tell the children more bad news; she should probably just change her name from Edna Sendall to Edna Gloom-and-Doom.

"Now, you know your mother—" Gramma started to say.

"Boy, do we ever," Gus said, rolling his eyes.

"How could she not come to Daddy's funeral," Roxanne cried. "How could she?"

"Roxanne, Gus, stop your disrespectful talk THIS INSTANT. I'll tell you exactly why... she would have loved to come... well, love isn't the right word, but I know she would have felt it was her wifely duty to attend her own husband's funeral... that is, if she could have...."

"What do you mean? What's wrong? Has Mom flipped out, or somethin'?" Roxanne asked, spinning one of the serving forks on the table with her finger.

"ROXANNE FREEDMAN, STOP PLAYING WITH THAT UTENSIL."

"Well? Has she flipped out?" Gus asked.

"Tell me what you mean by 'flipped out,'" Gramma said, trying to be evasive for as long as possible. Forget the Band-Aid idea—she didn't know how to tell bad news quickly.

"You know, gone wacko," Gus said.

"Oh, that," Gramma replied. She took a deep breath before she spoke. "Well, uh, yes, your mother has, in fact, flipped out. Gone wacko. So... what do you think of that?"

"See, I told you, smarty pants," Roxanne said, taking Gus's face in her hand and squeezing his mouth until it pooched out like cartoon fish lips.

"Jesus," Gus said, pulling his face away from Roxanne's grip.

"Gus thought something real stupid happened to Mom. He thought that—"

"Shut up, shut up, SHUT UP!"

"He thought that one of those alligators that were flushed down toilets came up through a manhole and tore off her legs."

"I DID NOT!"

"YOU DID SO!"

"DID NOT!"

"DID SO!"

"I HATE YOU!"

"I HATE YOU MORE!"

"WHEN I'M GONE, YOU'LL BE SORRY," Gus shouted.

"NO WAY. I WON'T CARE FOR ONE SECOND—"

"Kids, kids, KIDS. Stop your bickering right now and help me set the food on the dining room table."

"Can't we go outside?" Roxanne said, twisting her hair into knots. "I'm going crazy in this place...."

"Like mother, like daughter," Gus snickered.

"SHUT UP, ASSHOLE," Roxanne said.

"You sit your fannies down on that couch for fifteen minutes and wait for people to come around and pay their respects. Then if you must... if you have to... you may leave."

Both Roxanne and Gus sat on the couch with their hands wedged between their knees. Gus started shaking one of his legs.

"Stop that," Roxanne said, hitting his thigh with her fist.

"You stop it," Gus said, punching her on her thigh.

"GRAMMA, HE HIT ME," Roxanne said, faking a sob in her voice.

"How old are we supposed to be? You're close to adults and I want you to start behaving that way," Gramma said, smoothing the table cloth.

Fifteen minutes went by, and no one came to pay a condolence call. Gramma looked agitated. She would have assumed that at least the Langworthys would have come over. It would have been the right thing to do, being neighbors and all.

"All right, all right already. You may go. But change first. I don't want you messing up your nice clothes."

Both Roxanne and Gus raced to the staircase; Gus pushed Roxanne out of the way, so that he could get to his bedroom first.

"GRAMMA, HE PUSHED ME."

"I don't want to hear another word from you two. Remember, you're almost grown up ... both of you."

Both Gus and Roxanne emerged from their bedrooms at the same time, wearing identical bell-bottom jeans, black turtle necks and blue jean jackets, except that Gus had a suitcase in his hand.

"Where do you think you're going with that?" Roxanne hissed, pointing at his suitcase. The Langworthys had finally arrived, and Gramma was offering them cold cuts and rolls.

"I told you before. I told you I'd be gone."

"You did not. I mean you did, but you didn't sound like you really would be...."

"I've got everything in here," Gus said, holding up his suitcase. "I've got my guitar, and when I've made it, I won't be calling you about it."

"Well, thanks. Thanks a lot," Roxanne said, turning away. "So where do you think you're going?"

"To be a rock star in California."

"A ROCK STAR! MY DUMB FOURTEEN-YEAR-OLD BROTHER IS GOING TO BE A ROCK STAR? IN CALIFORNIA?"

"Shhhhh.... Not so loud," Gus said, pointing downstairs to Gramma.

"Wait a minute—"

"Don't try to stop me. I've been planning this a long, long time, and nothing's gonna stop me, even if you tied me down or locked me in a closet for the next five years."

"You can't just leave me with all this," Roxanne said, waving her arms around. "You just can't—"

"Watch me," Gus said, starting to go down the stairs.

"So, Mr.-Big-Shot-Rock-Star, where did you get the money for a bus or plane ticket?"

"From Dad's money drawer."

"You stole money? From Dad? You asshole.... I'm telling Gramma right now."

"Hey, wait a minute. Don't. Let me explain, okay? All right?"

"Okay," Roxanne said, unconvinced that she could be talked out of tattling on him.

"So, uh, I don't know ... you see, I guess it goes like this. You hate me, and Gramma hates me, and now that Dad's dead, and Mom's gone nuts, and I know some stuff about myself..."

"Like what?"

"Like none of your business...anyway, I know...I know some stuff...I have, uh, too many...too many things in my head...I don't know, it's hard to explain...."

"You can't leave me and Gramma...you just can't," Roxanne whined.

"Maybe when I'm famous, I'll send you a postcard."

"GRAMMA, GRRRRRRRAAAAAAAAAAMMMM-MMMMMMMAAAAAAA!!!!!"

"By this time, Gus had grabbed his suitcase, run down the staircase and was out the kitchen door.

"GRRRRRRRRAAAAAAAAAAAMMMMMMMMMM-MAAAAAAA!!!!!"

"Roxanne Freedman, is that any way to behave when there are guests in this house?" Gramma whispered. "Now if you can't behave right, I suggest you get yourself to a friend's."

"But—"

"Did you hear me, young lady? Did I make myself clear?"

"Gram—"

"Did I?"

"Yes...yes, you did. And you'll be sorry you did," Roxanne said, running out the front door, wiping the tears away from her face. If Gramma was going to talk to her that way, why let her find out about Gus on her own.

Roxanne started to run, even though she really didn't know where she was heading. She kept her eye out for Gus, but she couldn't find him anywhere.

Boy, had he disappeared fast. He must have had this whole thing planned for weeks. Maybe even months. Roxanne had to admit to herself that Gus could be smart when he wanted to be.

She knew she couldn't bear to go to Vicki's house. She was too absorbed in makeup and boys to listen to Roxanne's problems. The only place she could think of going was to Rick Templeton's house. Even though she didn't know him or his folks well, she figured that they might be sympathetic. And didn't Rick say that his dad was a shrink? By the time she had run over there, she had become so upset and humiliated by the circumstances of her life that she couldn't force herself to walk up to his front door. She had always assumed that if she behaved correctly, God or someone like that would make sure her family changed. They would simply become what she had always wanted them to be. Perfect. A family on a cereal box. Now she knew there was nothing she could do about her family's behavior; she had never had any control over them, and she never would. Her body shook so hard that her knees gave way, and she wrapped her arms around a newly-planted peach tree and cried into the trunk.

Joan Templeton happened to look out the kitchen window and saw Roxanne all hunched over in her front yard. The girl looked familiar, but she couldn't place where she had seen her before. Probably some little friend of Rick's who had a crush on him. It wasn't the first time that a young girl had come over all moonie-eyed, asking for Rick. But this girl looked upset. Really distraught. She'd better let her husband handle this one. And she was prepared to call an ambulance in case, God forbid, the poor thing was on drugs. Joan wrapped a cardigan around her shoulders and went outside.

"Are you okay?" she asked Roxanne, trying to pull her to her feet.

"Noooooo," Roxanne wailed, holding on to the tree trunk and refusing to stand.

"Come on, dear. Now let's be sensible. I've got some fruit, and I can make some hot cocoa. Now, let's go inside...."

"Is Rick home?"

"Uh, no, he's out with some friends, I believe...."

"I never should have come here," Roxanne blurted out, still hanging onto the tree.

"Don't be silly. This was the right place to come. But the person to talk to who'll really listen and know just what to say is my husband. How would you like to wait for him? He'll be home very soon."

"Really?"

"Really."

"You don't mind?"

"Of course not."

"If Rick comes home, I don't want to see him. He'll

146

think...he'll think," Roxanne said, crying against the tree again.

Joan still could not remember where she had seen this girl, but she felt sorry for her anyway. "Let's not worry about Rick. Let's just go inside, and we'll fix something to eat. That is, if it's okay with you."

"Sure, yeah, I guess," Roxanne said, trying to gain some of her composure. Joan put half of her sweater around Roxanne's shoulder and guided her into the house.

Joan mixed some hot chocolate for herself and Roxanne and put a bowl full of fruit on the breakfast table. Roxanne took two sips of cocoa and stirred it around with her spoon.

"Darling, tell me your name again," Joan said, running hot water into the sauce pan.

"It's Roxanne...Roxanne Freedman."

"You were just over here, right?"

"Yes, Mrs. Templeton. After the carnival."

"Oh, do call me Joan. Now I remember...I think Rick just mentioned your name the other night...something about your father...."

"He just died...."

"Oh, yes, that's right, oh, I'm *so* sorry. How could I be *so* thick?"

"That's okay, Mrs. Templeton, I mean Joan."

"My husband's really the one to talk to about these sort of things. He's a wonderful listener. As for me, well, if it has to do with theatre, I can gab all night. And listen, too, of course."

"I like theatre," Roxanne said, wiping her nose.

"You do? How wonderful!"

"I went to see *Flower Drum Song* at Starlight a few summers ago with Gramma and Gus, and it started raining and blowing so hard that the scenery was flying around the stage. The rest of the show was cancelled, but we didn't get our money back. Gramma sure was sore. And then before that, Gramma took us to see *How to Succeed in Business without Really Trying*..."

"Well, that's a very good start, Roxanne, but there's much, much more to theatre than just musicals—why there's Shakespeare, of course, and Tennessee Williams. Have you ever seen *The Glass Menagerie?*"

147

Roxanne shook her head.

"Now, that's what I call theatre. You remind me just a little bitty bit of the character, Laura, in that play. You've got the same vulnerable qualities. You would do a marvelous job of playing her."

"Really? Me?"

"Yes, you. Wait, I think I hear my husband's car. Yes, that's him. Now you just sit here and let me go talk to him. Will you be all right by yourself?"

"Yeah, but what if Rick comes home? What do I do then?"

"Why, look him straight in the eye and give him a big hello. Don't worry so much, all right? Repeat after me. 'Joan, I won't be a worry wart.'"

"Joan, I won't be a worry wart," Roxanne said, starting to laugh. She wished that Joan Templeton or someone just like her would let her crash on her couch indefinitely.

After a few minutes, Dan Templeton walked into the kitchen, rubbing his hands. "Well, well, well, what do we have here?" he said in a jovial voice.

"I don't know. You tell me," Roxanne said, starting to cry. "I shouldn't even be here."

"Yes, you should. You came to the right place. Now, if you'll come into my office, you can tell me why you're so upset. I'm a pretty good listener."

"That's what she said," Roxanne said, nodding toward Joan. "Is it okay, I mean, I'm not taking up your time, if I do talk...just for a while...."

"You can talk to me as long as it takes. After today, if you want to keep talking to me, we'll figure something else out," Dan said, putting his arm around her shoulder.

They went into a long, narrow room that had one wall lined with books and the other full of pretty, French windows that faced the neighbor's house. There were two captain's chairs that were turned toward each other, and a small couch with an afghan draped across the top. Roxanne debated between the couch and the captain's chair but finally chose the latter. It seemed more grown-up to be sitting up straight, looking at him eye-to-eye. But the minute she started talking about Gramma and Gus and her mom and dad, she felt weak and had to lie down. And then the sobs rose from her chest to her throat in uncontrollable hiccups.

Dan did not say much, just leaned back in his chair and lit his pipe a few times. He asked her how old she was and if she were the younger or older child.

What a fascinating family, from what he could gather in their three-hour talk—dead father, who was suspected of having an affair, mad mother, runaway brother, a strong-willed grandmother, and Roxanne, probably a perfectly normal child, trying to cope with her surroundings. And she certainly had a lot to cope with.

Dan knew that she needed professional help, but there was the matter of money. The girl might not be able to afford the weekly fees; and the grandmother would have enough financial burdens keeping the mother in a hospital. Perhaps he could give her some kind of loan that she could pay back with interest. But then again—wouldn't she make an intriguing case study for a paper? Perhaps they could work out some sort of sliding scale if she agreed to be a subject for a book about adolescence, something he had always wanted to write.

Part II
1972

14

Road Atlas

Roxanne couldn't believe that everything had come to this. Here she was in the middle of Bennett Schneider at a book signing party—a book that was all about her, for chrissakes. Of course, Dan had changed her name in *A Portrait of Adolescence* from Roxanne to Rachel (actually Roxanne liked the name Rachel more than her own), and he had changed her physical description (for the better, Roxanne thought), so no one at the book signing even had a clue who she was and why she was even there. She *did* feel out of place in this crowd of academic shrinks and their intellectual chitchat. The women were all dressed in flowing skirts and blouses that made them look pregnant, and the men wore tweedy clothes similar to Dan's. Perhaps shrinks were so busy trying to figure other people out that they didn't pay attention to what they themselves wore; they simply bought the same clothes as their colleagues so that they wouldn't have to bother with such trivial matters.

Roxanne wondered if anyone thought her new knit dress from Macys was at all cute. As she sipped her watery Coke, she felt self-conscious about not having anyone to talk to. She found it difficult to relax out in public, and she hardly ever went to parties. Since she was too shy to approach anyone or strike up a conversation, she stood in front of a long bookshelf and pretended to be concentrating on the ice in her plastic cup. Yes, it was true that Dan had helped her be more confident about her appearance in general and especially about her nose. She was almost starting to like her nose, especially after Rick said that it resembled the ones on Botticelli's women.

153

And speaking of Rick, where in the hell was he? He was supposed to come after his painting class at the Art Institute. And he was the one, after all, who had convinced Roxanne to attend the book signing, that it would mean a lot to Dan if she were there. That goddamn jerk was probably trying to impress another little Foundations student into bed. Sometimes Roxanne thought that Rick's brain was divided into four places on his body: his hands (she would, at least, give him credit for his painting abilities) and his balls.

Sure enough, in walked Rick with some chick in a black leather jacket and heavy eye makeup. Dan spotted him and Roxanne at the same time and ran over to them, embracing them both in a bear hug.

"You must come meet some people," Dan said, leading Rick and Roxanne to the center of the room. The girl in the leather jacket gave Rick a spiteful look and nervously lit a cigarette.

"You promised you wouldn't say who I am," Roxanne said to Dan.

"Of course he won't, Roxanne. You should trust him by now."

"As far as I'm concerned, you are a close friend of the family's. That and nothing else," Dan said.

"So, who did you bring to this thing?" Roxanne asked Rick.

"Oh, some girl I met at lunch. She's interested in art for mental patients."

"Great. Maybe *you* can be her first client."

"Knock it off, you two. Lyle, I would like you to meet two very special people. My son, Rick, and Roxanne Freedman, a very close friend of the family's."

As Dan was talking to Lyle, a child psychologist whose practice was in Overland Park, he did something to his hair that Roxanne had never noticed before. He started fussing with it— combing it over to the side with his fingers, smoothing it down over his ears like a fledgling actor would do at his first movie premiere.

After she got home from the book signing, Roxanne kept reading Dan's inscription over and over again:

> *Without you, Roxanne, I could not have written*
> *this book. You are like a daughter to me. I love*
> *you very much.*
> > Dan

154

She had shown the book to Gramma, who was as unimpressed with it as she had been when she was first told about the project. Gramma did not like the idea of airing the family's dirty laundry to the public, even if no one knew that it was about her own family. Something about this book made her feel uneasy, as if this Dan Templeton had used Roxanne for his own career boost. And there was something about him that was a little too nice. She didn't trust people who seemed to care about others right off the bat. As far as she was concerned, these peace-and-loveniks were all a bunch of con artists. But at least this Dan Templeton had shown Gramma enough respect to come over to the house and ask her personally if it were all right to use Roxanne as a subject for his book. At least he hadn't tried any funny business behind her back. And even if Templeton *had* used Roxanne, he was someone whom Roxanne could really talk to. Strange, how the world had become a place where people had to pay someone else to listen and respond to them.

"Honey, I've got something to show you, too. Come over and read this. It's from Gus. Rather it's from Gus's house mate or friend or whoever he is," Gramma said to Roxanne who had settled into a chair in the kitchen.

"From Gus. To us?"

"Yes, and this man, this Mr. Goldfarb, is inviting us to stay with him and Gus in his Bel Air home. And he'll pay for our plane fare. Isn't that something?"

"Yes. It's something. I can hardly believe it."

"What's not to believe? This guy thought it was terrible that Gus had barely spoken to us in four years. I mean, imagine receiving one measly postcard from him after being missing for an entire year."

Gramma was grateful for even that scrap of communication because at that point in time, she could no longer afford to pay the detectives she had hired to look for Gus. The jerks could never locate him anyway—all they came up with were a lot of dead ends and Gus look-alikes carrying surfboards on Laguna Beach. And there were so many of Emma's bills to pay, even with the good insurance coverage that Stern Brothers provided that year.

"He did call Emma at Menninger once, I think on her birthday. That was mighty big of him," Roxanne said sarcastically. Lately Roxanne had gotten in the habit of calling her mother by her first name. Dan thought Roxanne did this because it distanced her from all the grief she still felt about losing Emma as a mother figure.

"Now, don't give me any of that, I'm just not in the mood. You know, I've been looking through my old issues of the *Enquirer*, and I've never seen this Goldfarb's name or picture anywhere."

"Why would his name be mentioned in any magazine? He isn't supposed to be famous, is he?"

"Well, a lot of famous, glamorous people along with just rich people like dentists and plastic surgeons live in Bel Air. And they all tend to marry each other and go to the same parties."

"Hold it, hold it, I just thought of something. We can't pick up and leave. What about Emma? We can't just leave her."

"Both Mr. Greene and Dr. Melrose say she's doing all right. And she's got that new friend. A man friend at that. Isn't that something? My daughter might have gone completely mad, but I swear she hasn't lost her looks."

"I thought you didn't like this guy, that you didn't want her to have anything to do with him."

"I don't, but that's not to say I'm not proud of her ability to catch a man. If anything, this ordeal has made her look even prettier. Her skin has gotten so clear and pale, she sometimes just glows like a deranged angel."

"Yeah, all she has to do is stand still and stare, and she looks great."

"Now, now, Roxanne. I don't like that jealous way of talking about your own mother. Just because you don't—or won't—go out with boys."

"Come on, Gramma, that's not fair. What does one thing have to do with the other? Anyway, what about my job?"

"You'd give up a free trip to California to keep your empty-headed job at Smak's?"

"Hey, I was just promoted to assistant manager. I want you to know I worked hard for that promotion."

"Please, I don't want to hear anymore. If you had just decided to go to the community college, you could have done a lot better for yourself—wait a minute, wait a minute, I think I'm beginning to understand. I know what the problem is. It has nothing to do with not wanting to leave your mother or your job. It has to do with seeing Gus."

"Come on!"

"I'm serious. Admit you're nervous. Admit that...that, maybe you don't like the idea of seeing him living in Bel Air with movie star neighbors."

"Gramma, first you say I'm jealous of Emma and then you say I'm jealous of Gus. Next you're gonna say I'm jealous of you."

"Hmmmm, I never even considered that."

"And how can I possibly be jealous of Gus after all that's happened to him. I mean, we're fortunate we even know where he is. We can thank this Mr. Goldfarb person for convincing Gus to invite us."

"You're right, sweetie. I'm sorry. There I go again, being too hard on you."

"You've always been, so what's the difference. And you know something? If you weren't so quick to judge people all the time, you would have made a damn good shrink."

"Really? Why do you say that?"

"Well, you know what's going on in people's heads, even before they know what's going on...."

"Oh. And I guess that's good."

"Sure, it's good. Why do you think shrinks are paid so much an hour. Because they have that extra insight into people."

"Hmmmmm. Too bad I was never interested in school. But that doesn't mean *you* shouldn't be enrolled at the community college. You could meet more people your own age. Maybe you wouldn't be so afraid...."

"Can't we just drop this conversation. I mean, really."

"So the book signing was fun?" Gramma asked, starting to make an iceberg lettuce salad for dinner.

"Sort of. That is, no one had any idea that the book was about me. It was as if I knew about something that only a few of us knew about."

"Like Rick."

"Of course, like Rick. God, you wouldn't believe who he brought to this thing. Practically someone off the street."

"I still think that—"

"Don't even say it 'cause it's not true. We would not make the greatest couple this side of State Line. We are friends and that's it. It just upsets me to see him be so rude to his father, bringing someone like that girl to such a special thing like this book signing. It shows such a lack of respect. But that kind of stuff doesn't make Joan and Dan blink. They just let him do what he wants, and he mooches off them and lives in the apartment above the garage and does his art and brings home girls whenever he wants. He told me once that sometimes he invites one of them into the house for breakfast. I can just see it—Joan and Dan and Rick and some strange girl sitting around eating pancakes as if it were the most natural thing in the world."

"Well, it seems to me that it's the parents' fault that he's the way he is. I think he'd stop if they raised a fuss about his behavior."

"Oh, I'm not so sure it even bothers them. I think they're too open-minded for their own good. Or rather for Rick's own good."

"Hah, that's a new one. Come on, let's put the rest of these leftovers on the table. Remember we're seeing your mother tomorrow afternoon after you get off work."

"Oh, God, I almost forgot."

"Well, you can go, right?"

"Of course I can go. She's my mother, so I guess I have to go."

"Don't give me any trouble about going. You know I don't like it."

"I'm not giving you any trouble. God damn you, sometimes."

"ROXANNE, I'M GETTING TOO OLD TO FIGHT WITH YOU, AND YOU'RE GETTING TOO OLD TO BE AS INSOLENT AS YOU ARE."

"Jesus, is Gus gonna laugh. He'll see us bickering and fighting with palm trees in the background instead of elms and oaks, and he'll realize that in four whole years, not a thing has changed."

The next day, on their way to Menninger, Roxanne kept thinking about what John Oakley, the manager of Smak's, had said about her intended vacation to Los Angeles. He said that it would be okay for her to go, but when she came back she better be prepared to work her can off. He wasn't used to giving his employees any slack, especially those who showed such promise. Why he couldn't remember the last time he promoted someone as fast as Roxanne.

"Maybe if they kick me upstairs, you know, where the big boys are in the Smak's operation, you could be the one running this place," he said, twisting his mustache and then sticking the end of it in his mouth. Roxanne found this habit particularly annoying to watch. She knew that John Oakley didn't have a prayer of getting "kicked upstairs." He was far too repulsive to make it even in a small, local company like Smak's.

"Remember the three keys to success in this kind of business," John Oakley had said as she was getting ready to leave work that day. "Be friendly no matter what. Wash your face at least four times a day so you don't look greasy and turn a customer off. And always look busy, even if there isn't a single soul in the place. You never know who might just pop in for a Smaky burger. Maybe someone famous like Ewing Kauffman or Henry Bloch. You just never know...."

Maybe what Gramma said about the job being empty-headed wasn't so far off the mark.

As soon as they passed Lawrence on I-70, Roxanne started feeling queasy. Her old stomach problems always recurred when she knew she had to face her mother all over again. She still resented the fact that her life had taken such severe emotional turns. All the therapy in the world couldn't change or soften that resentment, and Dan told her frequently that his role was merely to help her deal with it.

She resented the way she felt while she finished high school; it was as though she had been stuffed into a cardboard box and surrounded by swatches of cotton. She felt cut off from the day-to-day swirl of classes, activities, sports, gossip, applying to college, all those components that are supposedly a part of teen-age life. Some of the teachers tried to be helpful and consoling, but after Roxanne ignored their overtures, even they backed off. And Roxanne continually had to fight off the feelings of sadness that threatened to overwhelm her and cause her to go into a depression that would paralyze her for days.

Everything that went wrong in her family had frightened her

to such an extent that she had a difficult time trusting anyone—especially boys. Dan felt that the reason Roxanne was so withdrawn socially was because she was afraid boys would desert her as her father and brother had.

She and Vicki eventually drifted apart, since Vicki had trouble understanding what Roxanne was going through. (Vicki was always too selfish to be a sympathetic friend over the long run.) The only peer that Roxanne could rely on was Rick, and during his senior year, he took a painting class over at the Communiversity which started his transformation from a well-liked, well-rounded kid into an artsy Don Juan who tried to seduce every girl within reach. At one point during a therapy session, Dan let down his professional guard. He said that Rick was going through an interesting phase, but he hoped, for his sake, that this behavior would not be a life-long pattern, since he would be setting himself up for years of unhappiness and confusion.

Gramma and Roxanne never talked much during their drives to Topeka. It was as if there were an unspoken rule that each should be left alone during this time. Roxanne remembered that Dan had even commented on this fact in his book.

> *While Rachel is driving to Topeka to see her mother, she needs to have plenty of quiet time in order to sort out her feelings. Just an innocent remark by her grandmother about the weather is likely to set off an outburst of temper.*

Roxanne sometimes saw her life not only as something she experienced, but as something that had been written about and analyzed. Sometimes she was so conscious of this fact that she objectified her own actions and words, as though she could remove herself from her own body and watch herself function in the world. In her thoughts, she often referred to herself in the third person—"she does this, she does that." But what was even worse was that she often called herself Rachel instead of Roxanne. Luckily, Dan had not made any predictions about how Rachel/Roxanne's life would turn out. Roxanne could almost see herself shaping her life around his words, so that the book literally became a self-fulfilling prophesy. Sometimes, Roxanne longed for the days when she could be spontaneous and did not have to consider how a certain incident in her life sounded on paper. But she was proud of *A Portrait of Adolescence*, and she was especially proud that she had helped type and edit the lengthy transcript and even proofread some of the galleys.

"Well, here we are, finally," Gramma said, making a sharp turn into Menninger. "I don't know if it's me but this drive just doesn't get any shorter. Why, do you suppose?"

"Don't ask me," Roxanne sighed.

"Oh, you're no help at all," Gramma said, stepping suddenly on the brake at a stop sign. "And get your fingers out of your mouth. It's unbecoming for a girl your age."

Roxanne actually enjoyed the layout of the Menninger Foundation. It resembled a college campus with its old brick buildings and rolling lawn. Sometimes she fantasized that she was not really visiting her mother at a mental institution, but that she was being driven to her first day of college. Maybe she really did want to enroll at the community college, but something in her resisted that notion because, once again, Gramma would be right about what Roxanne should do with her life.

They drove up to the clinic and parked the car. Inside, Roxanne asked the receptionist to speak to Mr. Greene and Dr. Melrose. Both Gramma and Roxanne knew the routine of their visits well. They first discussed Emma's progress with her psychiatrist, Dr. Melrose, and then with Mr. Greene, her social worker. Usually Mr. Greene sat in on the discussion with Dr. Melrose, and then Dr. Melrose would leave when it was Mr. Greene's turn to speak. After that, they ate with Emma in the dining room; recently, Jerome, Emma's "man friend," as Gramma called him, would join them at the table. Jerome was from Salina, Kansas, and had been a bachelor farmer for many years before his nervous breakdown. Roxanne liked Jerome because he was a kind man, but Gramma thought that he wasn't good enough for her daughter.

"Look at who she married," Gramma would tell Roxanne. "Your father might have been an oddball, but at least the man had class. And he knew how to make a decent living. Now, look at farmers; they have to struggle with chores and be around smelly animals, and they're still so poor and wear those awful overalls. I guarantee you, your mother would not be happy as a farmer's wife. I grew up in a community of farmers in Louisiana, I know what I'm talking about."

Roxanne dreaded it when Gramma would go into one of her tirades about Jerome, and she started to bite her nails again, a habit she found impossible to break over the years. She figured there was little chance that either Emma or Jerome would be well enough to ever make a go of their relationship outside of Menninger. They were good companions for each other, and that was probably all there was to it. So, what was wrong with that?

"Good to see you, Roxanne, Mrs. Sendall," Gordon Greene said, shaking hands with them in his small office. He had papers scattered all over his desk and had floor-to-ceiling bookshelves stuffed randomly with books and worn, yellowing envelopes and folders. Mr. Greene was a dark, well-built man from Baltimore who, when he spoke, would frequently pat the few strands of his hair over his bald spot. If something irked him, or he was especially worried about Emma, the top of his head turned a shiny pink. Both Roxanne and Gramma preferred him to Dr. Melrose. At least he seemed to care about Emma and his patients in general. In contrast, Dr. Melrose was chillier and far more condescending. For a while, Gramma was convinced that Emma would be better off if she switched doctors, but when she asked Emma if she were happy talking to Dr. Melrose, she said that she was, and that sometimes Dr. Melrose reminded her of James.

"Dr. Melrose is in a meeting right now, so I thought I would talk to you first and then you can see him in his office," Mr. Greene said, jotting something down on his calendar. "Now about Emma. She seems to be gaining a sense of who she is and expressing her likes and dislikes more. I feel she's gradually developing into an individual with her own tastes. She's interacting more with people and with the world at large. She especially enjoys her work in the greenhouse. And believe it or not, she's taken up bowling."

"Bowling? You've got to be kidding?" Gramma said, fiddling around in her purse for a Tums. "I mean, she's always liked flowers. But bowling?"

"Well, her friend, Jerome..."

"Oh, him," Gramma said, rolling her eyes.

"Jerome seems to like to bowl."

"Really? How terribly sweet," Gramma said.

"Mrs. Sendall, your daughter has made tremendous strides in the last few months. I'm sure you remember her silence that lasted for months. Her staring off into space. Her refusal to eat. Do you realize the breakthrough she has made, socially, allowing someone else to enter her life. We at Menninger are very proud of—"

"Enter her life? What do you mean by *that?*"

"Nothing, Mrs. Sendall," Mr. Greene said, wiping his mouth with a handkerchief. "They are friends in every sense of the word. Nothing else, as far as we know."

"What do you mean, 'as far as we know'? She is forty and forty-year-olds have been known to get pregnant."

"Mrs. Sendall, Emma is doing very well under our care."

"Gramma, listen to the man. I apologize for her, really," Roxanne said in a half whisper.

"No, no, no, Mrs. Sendall has every right to be concerned. Remember that your mother is still very vulnerable and probably will be for a while. We'll keep an eye on Emma and Jerome, make sure they don't get into anything over their heads."

"I'd appreciate that, Mr. Greene," Gramma said, folding her arms triumphantly.

"Oh, and another thing," Mr. Greene said. "Emma and Jerome have been fantasizing about traveling out west these last few weeks. They're not about to jump into a car, mind you. They seem to just enjoy looking at a road atlas and discussing various tourist spots and which roads and highways to take. Of course, we would never allow them to do such a thing. They're hardly ready to go into Topeka unsupervised. But I wanted to prepare you two because they will probably be discussing their so-called trips in great detail at dinner tonight."

"Are you sure there is nothing to worry about, Mr. Greene? Is this Jerome to be totally trusted?"

"Absolutely, positively. He is the most gentle of men. He would never dream of breaking any rules. Mrs. Sendall, if you continue to feel uneasy about this situation and about their relationship in general, please give me a call tomorrow morning.

Now, do either one of you have any questions? If not, Dr. Melrose can probably see you now. Sorry to have to rush off like this, but I also have a meeting to attend."

"Quite all right, quite all right," Gramma said. "You see, if you don't make a fuss about things, nothing will get done," Gramma whispered to Roxanne as they walked down the hall to Dr. Melrose's office.

The door was ajar, but he had apparently not returned from his meeting. Gramma and Roxanne settled into the wingback chairs across from his desk. His office was certainly larger and neater than Mr. Greene's. He had a handsome display of all of his degrees. Harvard undergraduate. A master's and Ph.D. from the University of Michigan. A certificate from the Psychoanalytic Institute in New York City. Licenses from the states of New York and Kansas. He had once shown Gramma and Roxanne his most prized possession that was framed on his wall—a letter written by Sigmund Freud dated 1914 that he had bid on at an auction at Sotheby's.

Gramma couldn't stand his arrogance and his impeccable manners. He spoke through clenched teeth, and his vowels had a slight British inflection. She didn't think a real man was supposed to act so haughty and upright—especially a man who was so knowledgeable about the human mind. There were too many twists and corners in the human psyche. How could he honestly keep himself so prim and clean, so far above the riffraff?

"Let's get out of here," Gramma said, jumping up from her chair. "I can't stand it any longer. I'm having trouble breathing."

"Oh my God. Should I call someone?"

"No, I mean it's this place. This office. It's closing in on me."

"You mean, we're going to ditch our appointment with Dr. Melrose," Roxanne said, starting to smile.

"Sure, why not. Let's just look around for your mother in the dining hall. It's around dinner time, anyway. She should be coming around soon with her boyfriend in tow."

Gramma and Roxanne stood in the cafeteria line and looked at the display of desserts. Roxanne often wondered why the desserts were usually at the beginning of cafeteria lines. Was it because desserts looked so much more appetizing than most cafeteria fare? Her hunch seemed right, at least that night, since the entrees were meat loaf and some kind of chicken smothered in a runny butter sauce. Roxanne chose to eat a small salad with shaved carrots and thin slices of cucumber.

Sometimes Roxanne felt funny about being seen in the dining room at Menninger, as though people would look at her and think she belonged there on a permanent basis. After all, many of the patients at Menninger *did* look like anyone else off the street. Of course, there were those with the deep circles under their eyes standing in doorways or walking aimlessly on the sidewalks, wearing shabby clothes, mumbling something about big business and politics. Those were the basket cases—basket cases with money, of course, since Menninger was a private institution that cost plenty. But who was Roxanne to talk? Her own mother had been considered one of those "basket cases" until just recently.

Roxanne still wondered how her mother got so sick. Dr. Melrose had at times suggested that Emma's role was to be sick, that for many years the family—and especially Gramma—had a need for Emma to remain child-like and dependent. Every once in a while—especially after a difficult therapy session with Dan or at Menninger—Roxanne still had fantasies about being rescued or just disappearing from Kansas City altogether.

Gramma and Roxanne paid for their meals and looked for Emma and Jerome. Apparently they had not arrived yet, so they found a table fairly close to the cafeteria line in order to flag them down easily.

"You know something," Gramma said, trying to cut the chicken which had the consistency of a deflated beach ball.

"What?" Roxanne asked.

"These doctors. Even that Mr. Greene who's a decent sort. They never come right out and say what's *really* wrong with Emma."

"What do you mean?"

"I mean about the fact that Emma's schizy. They never come right out and say she's schizy, but I know she is because I've been reading about it and she acts like she is."

"Gramma, *please* lower your voice!"

"And another thing those experts say is that it's inherited. I remember my mother talking about her daddy and all the peculiar things he used to do like spending all day sitting on the porch with a bowl of peas, and he was supposed to have shucked those peas, but all he would do is stare and talk about things crawling around like bugs or something. And as I recall, my grandmother tried to keep him fed and happy because he was getting on in years, and she didn't want to be alone because no woman ever wants to be alone, especially a Southern woman."

"Why a Southern woman?" Roxanne asked. "A lonely person is a lonely person. What's the difference, really, if it's a Southern woman or a Northern man who's lonesome?"

"I'll tell you the difference. There's nothing quite like the suffering of a woman, there's nothing deeper, nothing worse, and there's a lot you don't know about when it comes to the South and Southern women, and I don't have the patience right now to go into a lot of explanation that you might not even understand or appreciate. Just watch Blanche Dubois on TV sometime visiting her sister in New Orleans. She understands what it's like to be a woman in the South suffering. Why, here comes Miss Emma with her beau. She really looks like she's queen of the kooks. Look at that—head held high, back straight. It's all that good training I gave her as a teen-ager. She really was a Mardi Gras vision... you've seen the pictures."

"A million times, Gramma."

"It just goes to show you when a person has all the potential that your mother has and then doesn't use it. I'm telling you, it's beyond a shame. It's a downright, wasteful sin. Well, will you look at that. They really are serious about all this traveling nonsense."

Underneath his arm, Jerome was carrying a bulky road atlas. He was wearing his good, Sunday clothes—black slacks, slightly tattered on the bottom, and a white dress shirt. His dark hair was slicked back with something greasy like Vitalis or Brylcream. He was an unassuming man, with a large nose and gawky hands, the kind of man you might see sitting in small town diners, nursing a cool cup of coffee, discussing the weather and bits of local gossip. Emma was wearing blue stretch pants and a blue work shirt that was embroidered with daisies and tied together at the bottom. Her blonde hair was pulled back with a plaid scarf babushka-style. She reminded Roxanne of pictures of country western singers relaxing on their tour buses between concerts, or perhaps of Tuesday Weld trying to dress down so that she could go to a Hollywood grocery store without being noticed.

As soon as Emma saw Gramma and Roxanne, she gave them a slight wave of her hand and then started whispering to Jerome and pointing to the array of desserts. He put his arm around her shoulder and whispered back to her, and Emma hesitantly reached for the apple crisp and then moved her hand toward the vanilla cake and then back to the apple crisp.

"Still as indecisive as ever," Gramma said to Roxanne with disgust. "I wonder how much good this place has done for her, I mean, really. Have I been throwing my money away? Have I?"

"Oh, leave her alone."

"I mean, is it going to take her all night to get through the goddamn line? We haven't got all the time in the world."

"Emma's always moved like a low tide."

Gramma let out a sigh. "Oh my, how right you are. How right you are. Hush up now, here they come."

"Look who needs hushing up."

"Good evening, ma'am," Jerome said to Gramma. "Good evening, Roxanne."

"Oh, good evening, Jerome," Gramma said in a perturbed manner. His excruciatingly good manners never failed to set her nerves on edge.

"Mama, you'll never guess where we're going."

"You're right. I give up. Tell me."

"We're heading west to the Painted Desert. Jerome, show Roxanne and Mama where it is on the map."

"Well, ma'am, Roxanne, it's right here in Arizona just off Highway 40, between Gallup and Flagstaff," Jerome said, setting his tray on the table and opening up the atlas. "Now, I would just assume hit Albuquerque some time in the evening and maybe rest up somewhere there—that is, if that was fine with Emma."

"Oh, yes, Jerome, that would be fine with me," she said as she spread her napkin on her lap.

"And then maybe head out for the Painted Desert bright and early in the morning, when the ground is still a little damp, and there ain't much dust in the air. And we could just bypass Gallup because it's a low-down, mean town, if you'll excuse my saying so. But if Emma wanted to stop for a sandwich or a pop, I certainly wouldn't deprive her of nothing, we could stop in Gallup—but I've seen some cruel things there that's made me ashamed to be an American."

"Oh, you're talking about the treatment of the Indians."

"Yes, ma'am, I mean Roxanne. I've seen some ugliness that I wouldn't want your mother to see. Then again, we could skip over Gallup altogether and take a more southern route," he said, pointing to the map and moving his finger downward. "After Albuquerque we could go on Highway 25, through Truth or Consequences—it was darn smart of those people to name a town after a game show. At least people remembered they'd visited the place. If it was all right with Emma, I'd like to pass a few hours there just because I used to watch Truth or Consequences with mother, and she was a big fan of Bob Barker's. She used to say he had the whitest teeth on television."

"Is your mother still alive, Jerome?" Gramma asked, pointing her fork in his direction.

"Ma'am, that's an entirely different story altogether... then at Las Cruces we could head west on 10 and then at Lordsburg, catch 70 north, and I know of a clean, back road restaurant that serves tamales and chicken fried steak and the tables have checked table cloths that mother always liked, and if you don't mind, ma'am and Roxanne, I need to be excused for a spell."

"Why, Jerome, you didn't touch your plate...."

"I'll be back soon, ma'am, and I promise you, as sure as my name is Jerome, I'll eat it all." He pushed himself away from the table and walked out of the cafeteria into the night air. Emma was sawing at her chicken as if nothing unusual had happened.

"What's with your friend, Emma? Were we not supposed to mention his mother?"

"Oh, Jerome does that all the time. It's hard for him to sit still."

"Well, he's never done that to us before. And can you imagine taking a car trip with a man who can't sit still? So, tell me... is his mother still alive?"

"Uhhh, let me think. No, I don't think she is."

"Alive?" Roxanne asked as she spilled a few drops of water on her blouse and blotted them with her napkin.

"Right. I don't think she's alive."

"Well, did something strange happen to her that would upset Jerome and make him want to leave the table?" Roxanne asked.

"I'm not sure. He might have found her. They lived alone in the country. The neighbors lived quite a distance away."

"That must have been a shock. Finding her dead, that is."

"Yes, it might have been, I'm not sure."

"You're not sure about what," Gramma said.

"About finding her. . . . "

"I thought you said she was dead."

"Yes . . . but I'm not sure if he found her. Someone else might have."

"A neighbor? Or the town doctor?" Roxanne asked.

"Yes . . . maybe one of them."

"Let's cut this conversation before I have to leave the table," Gramma said, rummaging through her purse. "And where in chrissakes are my Tums?"

"Aren't they right there, Gramma. In your little silver box."

"Oh gracious, what would I do without my granddaughter? Probably sink into utter senility," Gramma said, zipping up her purse.

"Stop that poor-pitiful-me talk. So, uh, Mother, Mr. Greene told us you've taken up bowling."

"Yes. . . . "

"So . . . tell us about it."

"Well, I've just started and Jerome said he's never seen anything like it."

"Is that supposed to be good?" Gramma asked.

"Good? I don't know about good."

"Are you knocking down any pins?" Roxanne asked.

"Sometimes . . . but last Thursday, I bowled a zero and Jerome said he's never seen anything like it."

"Now I get it," Gramma said with a snort. "And here comes our wandering dinner partner now."

Jerome's face was flushed with the fall cold and after he took off his jacket and pulled up his chair to the table, he proceeded to eat the food on his plate which had congealed into an unappetizing mass.

"You'll never guess who we're going to visit," Gramma said to Emma.

"Who?" she said between bites of apple crisp.

"Gus."

"Gus?"

"You know... your only son, Gus."

"I know who you're talking about, Mother. He did call me on my birthday one year."

"You can borrow my road atlas if you're gonna drive out there," Jerome said with his mouth still full.

"I don't think so, Jerome, but thanks all the same." Gramma said. She thought this man said the most inane things. It was little wonder that he was locked up. "Anyway, we're leaving for Los Angeles next week and this Fred Goldfarb, who's a friend of Gus's, is paying for our plane tickets. Imagine that. Is there anything you want to tell Gus in particular, Emma?"

"Yes," Emma said. There was a long pause.

"So, what is it, Mother? What do you want to tell him?"

"He sent a postcard once...."

"Should we tell him to send you a postcard?"

"Yes... but I liked the one he sent. If he could send that same one, I'd like that. You see, I lost it somehow. I had it on my dresser, but it fell on the floor."

"Mother, are you sure you don't want a different postcard?"

"No, I liked that one."

"It sure was pretty. A sunset and the ocean, and a shadow of a man and woman drinkin' something out of tall glasses," Jerome said, nodding his head. "Hey, don't this Goldstein fellow have a lot of money?"

"Probably. Why do you ask?"

"I don't know. Just wondering. Does he like takin' car trips?"

"I've only spoken to the man a few times, Jerome, I really wouldn't know. But somehow I doubt it."

"Oh. Well, it always helps to go on car trips with a fellow who's got money. Then if you run out, you can, say, offer to do all the drivin' or... do some minor repairs on the car if it belongs to him. There's always a way to swap favors."

"Yes.... Roxanne, what do you say about heading for home?"

"You sure you don't want to stay the night at the Holiday Inn West?"

"Oh yes, I'm quite, quite sure."

"Don't be a stranger," Jerome said, mopping the rest of his food with the heel of his roll.

"You take care of yourself," Gramma said to Emma, shooting one of her looks at Jerome. "It's starting to get cold outside. Is your coat holding up all right?"

"I like it fine," Emma said.

"Maybe when I get back, we'll go shopping in Topeka for a new one. Would you like that?"

"Uh huh," Emma said. "Mama, sometimes . . . sometimes I miss you. And you, Roxanne . . . I miss you, too. Do you miss me?"

"Of course, sugar pea. And we'll be back from Los Angeles in no time."

"Will Gus ever come visit? We can take him shopping, too."

"We'll see. Maybe we can talk him into coming home for a visit."

"I'd like to meet that young fellow. He'd probably like another man to have a little heart-to-heart with."

God forbid, Gramma thought as she was putting on her coat and heading toward the car. She figured that Gus had enough problems as it was.

15

Damaged Goods

The next day before she had to be at work, Roxanne went to see Dan Templeton for her weekly appointment. She had gone through so many topics with him these last few years, and it wasn't as if she were running out of things to talk about; she had a never-ending litany of insecurities.

When she first started going to him, she focused primarily on her family and how to maintain her sanity among such craziness. It was a topic that she always returned to when a crisis arose with Emma or Gus or when Gramma would get particularly hostile or when something reminded Roxanne of her father. She still did not understand the circumstances surrounding his death, but she and Gramma were almost certain that there was another woman involved, even though they had no specific proof to back this idea up.

Eventually, Roxanne started discussing her feelings about her body. She hated her nose, she hated her small breasts; and then when she developed bigger breasts at seventeen, she hated them, too. They ached, she was always bumping into furniture with them, boys seemed to talk to her breasts rather than to her. But Dan did manage to help her develop a better self-image, just by getting her to understand the reasons why she felt so bad about herself. Growing up, she had gotten so little positive reinforcement at home, except, of course, from Gramma. And her type of compliment always had an edge to it. With every kind word, Gramma always managed to slip in a criticism. Or when Gramma was unduly harsh with Roxanne, she always felt the need to apologize. These confusing messages would sometimes overwhelm Roxanne, and she wondered whether she was the most fantastic or loathsome of creatures (usually it was the latter).

Lately they had been discussing how Roxanne could change her life. Dan felt she needed to get into a more action-oriented frame of mind as opposed to just analyzing the problems of her past. They were trying to concentrate on two things—her shyness with men (or why she had hardly dated at the age of nineteen) and why she was still living at home with her grandmother.

But today she did not want to concentrate on either one of those two topics. She wanted to talk about seeing Gus.

"Gramma thinks I might be jealous of Gus, especially since he's living in Bel Air with some rich guy, " Roxanne said, settling deeper into the couch cushions.

"Now, Roxanne, we've been through this before," Dan said. "Your grandmother has a unique perspective on things, especially in the way she sees her family and how they interact with each other."

"I know she's real negative and all that, but... the idea of him having it more together does get to me."

"Well, let's look at it this way," Dan said, leaning back into his chair and fumbling with his pipe and lighter. "Your visit to California might be an opportunity to make some progress in your relationship with Gus. You have not seen each other since you were practically children. Whether you like it or not, your relationship with him is still stuck in that time frame. He's an adult. You're an adult. Now, what is it about Gus that you've complained about most these last four years?"

"That he hasn't been around to help with all the problems. That he has left me and Gramma alone with all of it."

"Now how would you like the outcome of your trip to be?"

"Uh, I guess I'd like more contact with Gus in the future."

"Yes."

"I'd like for him to come back to Kansas City and be a support. And visit Emma in the hospital."

"Uh huh," Dan said, holding the pipe in his mouth and then lighting it.

"I guess that's it. I can't think of anything else. Maybe be able to talk to him without fighting."

"Good. Now, when you see Gus, I want you to keep a couple of things in mind. First of all, you need to concentrate on moving your relationship forward to the present. The dynamics between you and Gus are based on past patterns, patterns that are no longer viable or workable now that you are adults. When you find yourself getting bitter about Gus not putting in his fair share of time into the family, I want you to stop yourself from saying or doing anything that's going to alienate Gus even more. You won't accomplish anything by doing that. Right?"

"Right."

"Now, what are you going to do when you start feeling angry toward Gus?"

"I guess, uh, stop myself."

"And what else?"

"I don't know. What do you suggest?"

"That's for you to decide."

Roxanne pulled at a cuticle and tried to think of what else to do with Gus. "Try to be open?" she finally said.

"By all means," Dan said, tapping his pipe into the ashtray on his desk and standing up. He held Roxanne by the shoulders and gave them a squeeze. "I just want to let you know how pleased I am with all your growth and hard work, especially during these last few months. You are so much more willing to accept and understand things as they really are. You no longer get so caught up in destructive and wishful thinking about your family. And you've done it all on your own, without the guidance of a mother or a father. Do you know how difficult that is? And do you know how brave you've been these last few years? You should be as proud of yourself as I am of you. You'll do just fine in Los Angeles. Have a good time and see you in two weeks."

Roxanne reached out and gave Dan a long hug; she was so moved by what he had just said that she felt her eyes welling up. As Dan walked Roxanne out of his office with his arm around her shoulder, she saw him do something that bothered her, something she had seen him do for the first time at the book signing. She caught him pausing for a moment in front of his reflection in a small, hand-painted mirror on the wall, smoothing down his hair. Roxanne figured that it must be the book that was causing this new-found vanity. Had he been honest about what he had just told her or was he merely thanking her for contributing material to *A Portrait of Adolescence?*

Outside, Rick was leaning against the front end of her car lighting a cigarette. He was wearing an olive-green army jacket, a purple scarf wrapped several times around his neck and tan Wrangler boots. His hands had speckles of black and red paint all over them, and his long, brown bangs hung in his eyes.

They had an implicit agreement that her counseling was separate from their friendship, and she was peeved that he would intrude upon her time of being alone and trying to figure out what she had just gotten out of her session with Dan.

"Your tires need air," Rick said, kicking the front one. "Nah, that isn't why I'm ... listen, I want you to come by after work."

"Rick, I don't know if I ... "

"No ifs, ands, or buts, Miss Roxanne," Rick said, pretending to block her from getting into her car. "I haven't been waiting for you out in the cold for nothin'.... I want you to ... you are coming by ... just say 'yes.' Say it."

"Why?"

"Why? Don't ask why. Just say 'yes.' Come on," he said, clasping his hands together.

"Yes, yes, I'll come by," she said, pretending to be fed up with his pleading while she elbowed past him and opened her car door. It was hard for her to refuse Rick anything, and she had to admit she enjoyed the attention. "But just for a minute," she said, just before she slammed the door and drove away.

"All right," Rick said, flicking his cigarette between his forefinger and thumb into the neighbor's front yard.

When Roxanne arrived at Smak's, she found out that Valerie, a seventeen-year-old who was the head pompom girl of the Shawnee Mission East High School drill team, had called in sick.

Alex, a hippie with stringy, blonde hair who worked on the grill, was swatting with a spatula at invisible gnats that were flying around his head; Roxanne liked Alex, and she had covered for him on other occasions when he had come to work stoned. But this was going to be the last time. Seeing all this chaos would put John Oakley in one of his famous black moods, and he would go sit in the back, close his eyes, massage his forehead, and sulk for an hour, leaving Roxanne alone to run the franchise. They were dangerously short on Smaky burgers, and John needed to change the oil in the fry machine—and where was he, anyway?

She was just about to call him at home when he came breezing in with a grin on his face. Maybe he was stoned, too. Maybe Valerie the pompom girl was actually getting stoned before drill team practice, or she was in bed with a thermometer in one hand, a joint in the other. Maybe Roxanne should ask Alex to give her some of whatever he was high on, even though she did not like the idea of feeling out of control, especially at work. Roxanne grabbed John by the shirt sleeve and pulled him into the kitchen to observe Alex, who was now hitting the wall over the grill with his spatula and leaving a neat row of long cleat marks.

"That boy is a strange and clever one," John said, rubbing his chin and shaking his head. Strange, yes, Roxanne thought. But clever? Now she was convinced that John was high on something. She was probably the only person within throwing distance who was straight.

John then wrapped his arm around Roxanne's waist and started spinning her around the kitchen area, ballroom-style. Roxanne was amazed he was so light on his feet.

"She said yes," John said with his eyes closed, dipping Roxanne to one side and humming the Irving Berlin tune, "Cheek to Cheek." "Heaven, I'm in heeeeaaaaven," he crooned as he spun Roxanne away from him and then back into his arms. Being in such close contact with him made her stomach churn.

"Who said yes?" Roxanne asked, trying to politely wiggle away from his grasp.

"Michelle. Michelle said yes." Then he started to sing the words to the Beatles song, "Michelle." He had a hideous baritone voice. Roxanne prayed that he would not attempt the French lyrics. Even Alex had stopped swatting the wall and was staring at John with unfocused curiosity.

"Who's Michelle?" Roxanne asked, getting more and more nauseous and impatient with John singing into her hair.

"His old lady," Alex said, throwing the spatula up into the air and missing it. It fell on the floor with a clatter.

"You better wash that before you start grilling any more burgers," John said, not breaking his stride for an instant. "By the way, have you grilled any burgers?"

"I was just gettin' around to that," Alex said, pushing his hair out of his face. "I had some other business to take care of."

Roxanne saw this as an opportunity to pull away from John. "So, you're getting hitched. Congratulations. Have you set a date?"

"No...she wants to go to Vegas when the mood hits her—wait a minute, where are all the fries?"

"John, you need to put the oil in the fryer."

"Oh, right. Who's supposed to be here today?"

"Carolyn, Nancy, Valerie called in sick, Michael, David and of course Alex..."

"Did the shake machine get cleaned last night? Did anyone sweep the floor yet? The counter...I bet the counter needs to be scrubbed." John stuck his moustache into his mouth and then sucked on it.

John was back to his old, persnickety self. Roxanne was glad, since she wanted to know as little about his personal life as possible. She figured that if he were a real human being to her, she might feel bad about despising him so much.

The lunch business was slow, but then again it always was. McDonald's was such stiff competition; the ones on State Line and Metcalf were always packed. And if people wanted a slightly higher quality burger—and a little more atmosphere—they went to Winstead's on the Plaza. Roxanne wondered if an operation like Smak's could survive for many more years.

While Roxanne was bussing the tables and taking the garbage out back, Carolyn—who was supposed to be waiting on people—was flirting with some football star from her high school, ignoring two old women who were on their way to a movie at the Ranchmart Theatre. Carolyn was twirling her hair around her finger and giggling and sticking her chest in the football star's face while the old women were shaking their heads and checking their watches. Finally Roxanne went back behind the counter and waited on them herself. If she caught Carolyn doing that again, she was out of the Smak's operation. OUT! Hell, there was a thick folder of applications from eager high school students who were dying for money and employment. Why not get the best she and John could find? Why not? And speaking of John, he could have been waiting on those old women.

In back, Alex was frying burgers in slow motion while David was quickly preparing, wrapping and sliding them into their correct slots. John was straddling a stool and talking on the phone. All that Roxanne could hear over the sizzling was that John was promising to send something in the mail right away. When he hung up he shrugged and looked at Roxanne sheepishly. Again, he was not acting like his usual obnoxious self.

"Michelle thinks I ought to be making more money. Things change when there are two of you to think about," he said as he cleared his voice and smoothed down the creases of his polyester pants.

"You don't need to explain," Roxanne said, turning around and going back out to the counter. Roxanne vowed to herself that she would not give her time off from work another thought. And that, yes, she would look for another job as soon as she returned from Los Angeles. Damn it—once again, Gramma, in her own inimitable way, was right.

When she knocked on Rick's door after work, she felt winded from climbing up the narrow staircase from the garage. She could hear Traffic's *Low Spark of High Heel Boys* playing softly on the stereo. Such sexy music. Roxanne hoped that some young girl had not decided to drop over, and the two of them were going at it. But when Rick answered the door, and it was obvious that he was alone, Roxanne was relieved. And as much as she hated to admit it, as she observed his mussed-up hair and his rumpled khaki pants and flannel shirt, she still felt a certain pull towards him.

Rick's paintings hung on the walls in his bedroom/studio. Most of them were what Rick referred to as creative portraits or his reinterpretation of historical figures. There was one of Carrie Nation, wearing a Royals baseball cap, swinging at a pyramid of beer cans with a baseball bat. Another one was of Adolph Hitler strapped into a strait jacket and being lead into the back of an ambulance. The one he was working on was a psychedelic Jesus pushing a shopping cart through Kmart, looking lost. The entire room smelled of turpentine. Roxanne could not understand how he slept at night with the strong smells and the eyes of all of his painted figures staring into the dark.

"Come over here," Rick said sleepily, as he patted the rumpled space on the bed next to him. "Want some wine? I know you don't smoke...."

"I'll have some wine," Roxanne said, defiantly sitting in a rickety chair across from the bed. Rick was always teasing her about how straitlaced she was.

"So," Rick said, as he handed her some sour red wine in a coffee mug and settled back on his disheveled bed, "I've given this some thought for a while, and I think it's about time."

"Time for what?"

"You know... time. This is not fly-by-night thinking. I've thought about this for a good three weeks. Do you know what I mean?"

"No... I don't know what you mean."

"Come on, Roxanne...."

"You're stoned."

"Maybe... but that's not the point. What I want to say is that it's time for you to unburden yourself of, of..."

"Of what?"

"Your uptightness, your inhibitions, your..."

"Oh, I get it, I get it now. You're offering yourself to me."

Rick nodded. "Why not? It's better to have a friendly screw the first time around than to have some stranger pokin' at you and then feeling like trash later on."

"Aren't you forgetting something?"

"Probably."

"What about waiting for someone who you have something with... like a relationship."

"Yeah, but that could be forever. What I'm trying to say is we've been friends for a long time, and I know I'm not dependable, I can't promise you anything, I see a lot of women, and I'm not faithful and I don't pretend to be. But when I see a friend in pain—"

"In pain? Oh, come on, Rick."

"I want to be there for them."

"If it isn't Florence Nightingale with an erection."

"Now, just cool out for a minute. I also thought this would be good timing, since you're seeing Gus for the first time in four years, and I know your relationship is somewhat, I don't know..."

"Combative, competitive," Roxanne said, as she drank the remains of her wine. "At least that's what it used to be."

"I thought this would give you an edge. You know, confidence."

"What you're trying to say is that if I'm not a virgin, I would be able to stand up to Gus better."

"Yeah, I mean that's not the only reason. You would just feel better about yourself. Now, I want you to be straight with me. Have you ever really, you know, gotten it on with anybody? Not necessarily gone all the way but..."

"That's really none of your business."

"Yeah," Rick said with a grin. "I thought not."

"So what if I'm inexperienced."

"You're nineteen years old, you haven't even made it with a guy, you slop shit at Smak's, and you live with your grandmother. That's no way for anybody to be. You're shuttin' yourself off from the world, you'll turn around one day, and you'll be old before you're ready."

"Stop it, stop it, STOP IT!" Roxanne said, holding her mug as if she were ready to throw it at him. "Has your father been talking about me? Has he? Has he?"

"Of course not. You don't have to be a therapist to see things, Roxanne. Now, come over here," he said again, patting the area next to him.

"Huh uh," Roxanne said, sinking back into her chair and gripping the sides.

"Come on."

Roxanne shook her head.

"You're a baby. A chicken," Rick taunted jokingly.

"I don't care," she said, trying not to smile. She could feel her resistance giving way.

"Want some more wine."

"NO!"

After staring down at her lap for a few minutes, she finally mumbled, "So, what now?"

"Well...we could try to uh..."

"I feel so uncomfortable, Rick. I mean, it seems so calculated. Aren't people supposed to be swept away when this sort of thing happens?"

"Not necessarily..."

"I mean, here we are having this very adult, rational conversation about you screwing me... I mean, why are we even talking about it? The fact that it needs to be discussed makes it seem unnatural."

"Roxanne, I know what you're doing."

"What do you think I'm doing?"

"You're talking yourself out of it. For a moment, you were going along with the idea, but now you're trying your hardest to talk yourself out of it."

"Says who?" Roxanne said, getting up from her chair and snuggling close to Rick, touching his cheek with the tips of her fingers.

"Says no one," he said, turning her hand over and kissing each fingertip. Rick slowly unbuttoned Roxanne's blouse, kissing her shoulders as he slid it off, and then kissed her mouth hard, sticking his tongue deep into it. Roxanne made a slight gagging noise and pushed his lips away.

"No offense, Rick, but do you have to kiss so hard," Roxanne said.

"Sorry, sorry," Rick said, unhooking her bra with one hand while stroking her thigh with the other. Roxanne's mind was going in so many directions that she couldn't tell whether she was excited or not.

"Oh my God," Roxanne said, pushing him away and sitting up straight.

"Oh my God, what?"

"What about birth control?"

"What about it?"

"What are we planning to do?"

"I was going to pull out."

"RICK, that isn't very safe!"

"Come on, Roxanne, I haven't gotten anyone pregnant and you're just using that as an excuse to stall," Rick said, gently pushing her back down on the bed and unzipping her pants. "Just relax and let's enjoy each other. Come on... why don't you at least put your arms around my waist."

"Oh...I didn't realize," Roxanne said. She had been lying there the entire time with her arms rigid at her side. She reached up and laced her fingers around the back of his neck.

"That's a girl," Rick said while pushing down his pants and underwear around his ankles. He then reached up and placed his hands on Roxanne's nipples. "Why don't you touch my penis now."

"Oh...okay," Roxanne said, brushing her fingers up and down the length of it.

"Hold on to it as if you were holding a baseball bat," Rick said. "And go up and down with your hand."

"Like this?" Roxanne asked.

"Yeah, fine. Now let's not talk anymore." Rick started to touch Roxanne's pubic area, but he felt her pull away. He figured maybe it would be a good idea just to stick his penis in her, before she fully realized what was happening to her. He gently spread her legs and tried to push himself inside her, but she was so dry and tight, it was like trying to penetrate the surface of a trampoline.

"Ow, Rick," Roxanne said, twisting her body away from his.

"Sorry, sorry. I'll be more gentle this time." But the next attempt was even worse than before.

"I thought this was supposed to feel good," Roxanne said as she pushed his hips away from hers.

"Wait a minute, let me try and make it easier." He kissed her stomach and then the inside of her thighs and worked his way down to her clitoris.

"Do you have to do that?" Roxanne asked.

Rick looked up at her in disbelief and continued to stick his tongue inside her. Most chicks begged him to go down on them.

"I don't know if I like this," Roxanne said, arching her back and trying to catch her breath.

You like it, don't worry, Rick thought. It's only your fear that keeps you from liking it.

"I think I've had enough, okay?"

"Roxanne, honey, give it a chance, please. Now, we'll try one more time, all right? And no talking. Good sex doesn't need good conversation," Rick said, trying to make light of the situation to put her a little more at ease.

Roxanne knew that this was not good sex. And she doubted the quality of the conversation.

Rick couldn't believe it. When he tried again, he wasn't able to stick half of the tip of his penis inside her. What happened to all that lubrication? This situation reminded him of a joke he had heard as a kid of a king who put a guillotine in the promiscuous queen's vagina and of the one knight who got his tongue cut off. Or of one of those Chinese finger traps in which the more you struggle to remove your fingers from the bamboo tube, the more stuck they become.

"Okay, Roxanne, you win," Rick said, rolling off her.

"What's that supposed to mean? I wanted it, I really did."

"Sure you did."

"You don't believe me. You're being sarcastic."

"No, I'm not."

"Yes, you are. I thought you were supposed to help me."

"This isn't sex therapy time. Don't project your feelings about my father onto me."

"What do you know about projection?"

"Let's just say it's part of the family business."

"I have never, ever, ever—"

"Never what?" he said, buttoning his shirt.

"—ever been so embarrassed or humiliated."

"Oh, come on Roxanne. We're buddies, let's just forget it."

"Forget! forget!" Roxanne said as she pulled on her pants and, realizing that she had forgotten to put on her underpants, stuffed them into her front pants pocket. "I can't do anything right. I can't have a normal mother. I can't have a normal brother. I can't have a normal grandmother. And my father...he obviously wasn't normal. Now I can't even lose my virginity normally."

"This has nothing to do with your family."

"Oh, yes it does—everything that's important has to do with my family."

"Oh, bullshit. I've heard this sort of thing happens to a lot of different people."

"But not to you."

"Well, I don't go to bed with a lot of virgins."

"Oh, excuse me, Mr. Stud-of-the-Year," Roxanne said, throwing on her blouse and buttoning it quickly. She had forgotten to put on her bra so she stuffed it in her other front pants pocket.

"Listen, I should be the one who's upset. Don't you think this hurts my ego, too?"

"Ego, shmego, I'm the one who's damaged goods. You'll have girls panting at your doorstep at any—"

"DAMAGED GOODS? Whatever gave you that idea?"

"You did, treating me like some charity case."

"I was just trying to be, uh...Roxanne, your blouse...it's buttoned crooked."

"OH, GO TO HELL," she said as she grabbed her purse and stuck her hand in it, fumbling around for her car keys.

"Your keys are on the table."

"FUCK YOU!"

"Maybe some other time...sorry, sorry, I couldn't resist," Rick said, holding up his hands as if trying to deflect invisible blows. Much to his amazement, Roxanne started to laugh. Then she dropped her purse and was doubled over, holding her stomach.

"Oh my God, it's too much," Roxanne gasped, between giggles. "This could only happen to me...."

"It was a big goof," Rick said with a puzzled look on his face, putting his arm around her. "A great, big goof."

"Let's just say it didn't happen."

"All right. It didn't happen."

"And we'll never mention it again."

"Right."

"And let's shake on it," Roxanne said, sticking out her hand.

Rick grasped her hand, tickling her palm with his middle finger.

"Rick, be serious," Roxanne said, pulling her hand away. "No one will ever know?"

"No one."

"Not one single girlfriend. Not your parents."

"I told you, no one," Rick said, picking up her purse for her and walking her to the door. "Relax your gray matter, man, and have a groovy time in California. Remember your shades and sandals and as the natives say, surf's up."

"Oh, shut up."

"See you when you get back. Until then, peace," Rick said, blowing her a kiss from the palm of his hand and closing the door behind her. He shook his head and ran his fingers through his hair. That girl was temperamental as hell. But he cared about that girl. Sometimes he wondered why. Sometimes he wondered whether she was worth all the hassle. But he cared. He cared a lot. He bent over his record collection that he kept in an orange crate by his stereo and pulled out *Workingman's Dead*. Something to relax to after all that weirdness. Rick then got the roach that was balancing on the edge of his ashtray, lay back on his pillow and lit it up, careful not to burn his lips.

16

Bel Air

When Roxanne stepped off the plane in Los Angeles, she couldn't believe how warm and strong the wind was, whipping her hair all around her face. The sun was shining overhead, yet she wondered why the sky was so murky. Then she remembered about the rotten air in Los Angeles, and that the sun and the sky often looked that way.

As Roxanne walked toward the terminal, she tried to picture Fred Goldfarb's appearance. She imagined him short. Fat. Wearing a shirt with screaming, swirling colors, bell-bottom slacks held up by a thick, white belt, and white patent leather shoes to top it all off. A lounge lizard from Long Island who had worked hard, made it big in something like real estate, and had decided to move to a sunnier climate to make deals on desert property and strip shopping centers. But she couldn't imagine what Gus looked like after all this time. It was as though she had a mental block about what it would be like to be with him again. Therefore, she was devoting her energy to making Fred Goldfarb as grotesque a human being as possible in order to distract herself from some questions she had about Gus. Like what was Gus doing with this guy in the first place. Maybe she wasn't being fair. Maybe this Fred Goldfarb wasn't as disastrous as she was making him out to be. And she was trying not to think about the other evening with Rick so she wouldn't feel humiliated all over again.

She remembered how she went through a phase when she was eight years old, when every doll in her room had to be in its own particular place, or she would throw a tantrum and refuse to eat. Perhaps it had something to do with witnessing her fami-

ly's slow collapse and needing to have control over her immedi-
ate surroundings. But sex wasn't about maintaining control; it
was about letting go and giving yourself over to another person.

"Look over there," Gramma said, tugging at Roxanne's
sleeve.

There was Gus with an attractive man in his forties who was
dressed in neatly-pressed jeans, a red and black plaid shirt and
lots of necklaces, bracelets and rings—beautiful silver Indian
jewelry with chunks of turquoise as big as a baby's fist. The tan
on his face was glazed and smooth as though he had been
dipped in a vat of honey and left out to bake. Gus on the other
hand was wearing a baggy T-shirt—gray from too many wash-
ings—that advertised Yamaha motorcycles, and cut-off blue
jeans that revealed spindly, white legs and sunburned knees. He
had tufts of hair on his chin and cheeks, and his straight blonde
hair hung in his eyes and down his shoulders. Around his neck
was a strand of minuscule, multi-colored beads. Gus pointed in
Roxanne and Gramma's direction, and Fred came rushing over,
his arms outstretched.

"Welcome, welcome, WELCOME, Gramma," he said to her,
bending over and giving her a great big hug and a kiss on each
cheek. "And Roxanne," he said, taking both of her hands in his.
"Why, you're so much prettier than I ever imagined." Roxanne
couldn't help giving Gus a dirty look for having described her as
looking like a *Glamour* magazine "don't." Then she remembered
what Dan Templeton had said about keeping an open mind, and
she quickly transformed her expression into a smile. Roxanne
also noticed that Gus was now towering over her; he was a lot
taller than their father had been.

There was an awkward moment when Gus and Roxanne and
Gramma hung back, each afraid to make the first move.

"So, what are you waiting for, silly," Fred said, ruffling up
Gus's hair. "Hug your family, for goodness sakes."

Gus put one arm around Gramma and the other around
Roxanne and kissed them both on the cheek. Not just one kiss
but two kisses each. And much to Roxanne's surprise he kept
his arms around their shoulders. Roxanne looked over at
Gramma, and she was wiping her eyes. Roxanne was feeling
somewhat misty-eyed herself.

"I can't believe this boy sometimes. Here he hasn't seen his family in four years, and he just stands there like a nincompoop. And such a nice family, too. Sometimes I really wonder."

"Yeah, they're pretty neat," Gus said, hugging them both against his side.

"Sure, sure, real neat," Fred said, rolling his eyes and taking a Player's cigarette out of a flat, silver box and lighting it with a silver lighter. "What ever happened to the word 'neat' as meaning tidy. I mean really... now you two girls must have luggage, right?"

After Gus pulled the suitcases off the airport carousel, he lugged them over to the exit doors, walking five steps behind Gramma, Fred and Roxanne. Gramma started to wonder what the relationship was between these two. Fred seemed to treat Gus like a man servant. And another thing about this Goldfarb man. His gestures, his voice, everything about him seemed, well, girly. There was no other way to put it.

"Here we are," Fred said in a sing-song voice as they walked up to a black Mercedes parked illegally in a loading zone with its emergency lights blinking. "My humble carriage."

"Hardly humble," Gramma mumbled.

"What did you say, Gramma dear?" Fred said, unlocking the passenger door.

"Nothing, nothing," Gramma said while Roxanne nudged her and gave her a stern look.

"Oh, Gus, be sure not to squish the shopping bags in the trunk. Just lay them on top of the suitcases."

"Sure, Fred," Gus grunted while lifting the suitcases into the back of the car.

"I got these shirts yesterday at a fabulous little shop on Rodeo Drive. I once saw Warren Beatty there, and I almost passed out on the spot, I adored him in *Splendor in the Grass* with Natalie Wood. But once I got the shirts home and tried them on I knew they were wrong, wrong, wrong. So I've just got to take them back."

"You say you saw Warren Beatty?" Gramma asked, trying to sound nonchalant.

"Honey, he is gorgeous... oh, that's right. Gus told me you're crazy for movie stars."

"Well...."

"We're just going to have to go out and find some, right? Right?"

"If you want—"

"Sure, I want. I always love seeing the stars. That's half the fun of living here. Gus, we don't have all day. Come on, you're not supposed to be arranging flowers back there."

"Right," Gus said as he slammed down the trunk of the car and slid into the driver's seat.

"I taught this boy everything he knows. Isn't that right, Gus?" he said, ruffling up Gus's hair again.

"Sure," Gus said, pulling away slightly from Fred's hand.

"I've always said that most women would kill for his hair. Whose hair did he inherit anyway?"

"Emma's I suppose," Gramma said. "She's a blonde." Gramma paused for a moment and stared intently in front of her. "When did you learn to drive, Gus?" she finally asked.

"Fred taught me."

"In this very car, I might add. And I'm making him get his high school degree through the mail. I will not have an uneducated boy living in my home. He's quite smart when he puts his mind to it. Sometimes the things that come out of his mouth absolutely astonish me, they're so fantastic. And he's starting to cook like a restaurant chef. His coq au vin is as good as Ma Maison's."

"Yeah, I like cooking," Gus said.

"When I found Gussy, he was a little nothing, a boy from the streets," Fred said, lighting another cigarette. "But I saw his potential and vowed to make something out of him. My friends accuse me of being a Pygmalion when it comes to Gus, but I think they're simply green, that's all there is to it. And when he told me about his relationship with you all, I simply couldn't tolerate the idea. I'm very, very close with my family, and I consider it one of my primary joys in life."

"And that's why we're here. Simply on your invitation," Roxanne said with some scorn in her voice.

"Well, no, not exactly. You see, after spending some time with my family, Gus started talking about how he would like to see his again. But it took him a while to admit it. I think he was scared."

"Scared?" Gramma asked.

"That so much time had passed and you might not be interested anymore."

"Why, that's silly," Gramma said. "We had sort of given up seeing him again, I do have to admit, since he had managed to hide from us until recently, that is...."

"I told you that Gus of yours is a bright one," Fred said, stubbing out his cigarette.

It started to bother Roxanne that they were all talking about Gus as if he weren't even there. "So what do you think about all this, Gus?" she asked him.

"All of what?" Gus asked. The way he responded reminded Roxanne of Emma.

"Your life with me, living in my home, eating my food, wearing the clothes I bought you. And speaking of clothes. I've gotten him the most exquisite things, but he absolutely refuses to wear them. Everyday he puts on those awful shorts and T-shirts. I mean, he's not a baby, I can't dress him myself. So, what do you think of everything I've done for you?"

After a short pause, Gus said, "I, uh, guess I owe you."

With a satisfied expression on his face, Fred leaned back into the leather passenger seat and was quiet the entire way to his house.

Roxanne suddenly understood Gus and Fred's relationship. She had always suspected that Gus was a homosexual and here was Fred, the knight in a Mercedes, who had saved him from the streets; Fred, the swishy sugar daddy to the rescue. Tah-dah. But the question was, did they care for each other or were they just using each other—Gus for Fred's money, Fred for Gus's youth and, perhaps, for his sexual prowess and the cheap labor he provided.

Gramma was fidgeting in the back seat, she had so many conflicting feelings. She was grateful to this Fred person for saving Gus from God-knows-what. She had read about runaways and had talked to enough people to know what elements these kids got into. And she remembered the first year Gus was missing. Waiting by the phone, talking to the police and detectives every day, spending thousands of dollars trying to track him down, trying to get through the nights with no news or clues concerning

Gus's whereabouts, expecting to hear that his body had turned up by the side of some dirt road in Utah or Wyoming. And Emma—being as sick as she was during that first year—hardly spoke five words at Menninger. Fortunately, the doctors kept her on Thorazine for a while so she wouldn't be immobile anymore. Gramma's heart must have aged a decade during that time, she grieved so for her daughter and her grandson. And for her dead son-in-law, for that matter.

The second year was better. They received the postcard from Gus in Los Angeles. Emma seemed to be responding to therapy or whatever it was at Menninger that helped her so much. She wasn't just responding, she was thriving; the doctors had switched her over to Stelazine and were considering taking her off medication all together. But Gramma had to make a decision. Her savings from her husband's estate, the money James had from his savings account, his life insurance policy and the dividends from James's stocks were dipping to an all-time low. And her new health insurance—the one she got when James's Stern Brothers policy expired—still did not cover all of Emma's expenses at Menninger. It was either take Emma out of Menninger or stop the expensive search for Gus. She decided to stop the search. Emma was so close by, desperately needing care. In Gramma's mind, there was really no choice in the matter. She continued to keep in touch with the Los Angeles police to be on the look-out for Gus, but she called it quits with the detectives (who hadn't come up with a whole heck of a lot anyway). To this day, Gramma still felt guilty about the choice she made.

After a while, Gus started seeming vague to Gramma. (Sometimes she had to look at a photograph to remember what he looked like.) He was frequently in the back of her mind, but his being gone was no longer so gut-wrenching. Gramma figured that she and Roxanne would never be in direct contact with Gus again. Until he hooked up with Fred Goldfarb. And here was Gus now—once so confused and angry about his family that he simply left home—here he was, driving them on a day filled with sun to some fancy suburb in Los Angeles as calm as he could be. She was grateful to this Fred Goldfarb. Yet, she sensed something else going on between those two, and it made her uncomfortable.

Fred's house was Spanish-style stucco with picture windows and sliding glass doors in the back, overlooking a huge, clean swimming pool. The living room was immaculate with white couches, a white, fluffy carpet, and the overstuffed chairs had a splashy chintz material of green tropical plants. Fred had quite a collection of landscape paintings on his walls, all in varying shades of greens and pastels to blend with the rest of the colors in the house. Off the dining room was what Fred referred to as the pool room, with a full-service bar and plastic furniture with plastic cushions so that people could sit in wet suits and chat and drink. Roxanne liked the airiness of the home, but at the same time, it made her feel exposed to the outside. She was used to the more conventional homes in Kansas City that had walls instead of glass to keep one enclosed.

Roxanne and Gramma were put in a guest bedroom that had twin beds with lace canopies, a Queen Anne chest of drawers, and a marble and iron wash stand with a Waterford vase full of zinnias set on top of it. The wallpaper had a pattern of tiny yellow and violet flowers. The room was strikingly different from the contemporary feel of the rest of the house.

"My, how pretty," Gramma remarked as Gus placed her suitcase down on the bed.

"Gus and I had it redone with you two in mind. With the help of Fernando, my decorator, of course. The three of us had a ball scouring estate sales. Do you like it, Roxanne?"

"I feel right at home."

"I was hoping you would say that," Fred said, practically jumping up and down. "I can't wait to tell Fernando.... Oh, Gussy, it really is time to get those leaves out of the pool, don't you think?"

"Sure, Fred," Gus said, leaving the room without saying another word.

"I can't tell you how much that boy of yours has grown up," Fred said to Gramma. "When he first came here, he was, I mean, angry, hostile, bitter, you name it. But I could smell quality in that boy, I knew he was from a good background, not trash. It's been two-and-a-half years now that he's been living here. Sometimes I feel like his father, and I know that may sound odd. My only regret is not getting you two out here sooner, but Gussy had to come to that realization himself."

"Mr. Goldfarb," Gramma said.

"Please call me Fred."

"Fred...may I be so bold...may I ask you what kind of relationship...how you met my grandson? We're grateful to you—Lord knows what would have happened to him if you hadn't come along...."

"I figured this would come up. Gus always said you were a straight shooter, that you don't like to mess around," Fred said, tucking his shirt into his pants.

"You can say anything you want about me, mister, but Gus isn't that much older than a child, and a child can be taken by the toys of the rich. And can be used as a toy, if you get my drift."

"GRAMMA, how can you say such a thing. We're Mr. Goldfarb's guests."

"Honey, if she weren't suspicious, I would probably think a little less of her. Gussy and I would laugh later over beef Bourguignonne and say, 'See, she's not such a mind reader, she's not as fantastically perceptive as we thought.' Let me tell you, I saved your grandson from some terrible things out there, and yes, you could say that our relationship was a little like you think—in the beginning, that is. But it's changed, believe me, it's changed. What I said about being a father, I know it sounds peculiar, but it's more like that than...than...what you suspect. Sometimes I would like it to be the way it used to be. And, yes, he does work for me, and sometimes I can be a demanding bitch and I know it will eventually drive Gus away. I can feel his anger drilling through me sometimes."

"Then why treat him that way?" Gramma demanded.

"Honey, I've always been like this, and I'm too old to change. It's like my line of work, the wholesale jewelry business. You meet a lot of insane people in my business—the Hasidics in New York, and their plotting, clannish ways and how they're always trying to outsmart and gyp you. Good Lord, they even smell bad. Not that I'm anti-Semitic, I'm Jewish myself, and I know Gus is half. And the Chinese in Hong Kong, they're sneaky and secretive, you don't know whether you're coming or going with them. Listen, it all comes down to not only believing in yourself but embracing your own negative qualities. Because when you move in and out of situations that threaten to blow up in your face, you have to be stable among the chaos, even if some people don't like what they see. So, you ask about changing. Hell no, I'm not about to change for anybody, and if I'm a bitch, so be it." As if on cue, Fred got up and flounced out of the room in a dramatic huff. Both Gramma and Roxanne looked at each other and managed to stifle their laughter.

"He's a manipulative son of a gun. Nobody's fool," Gramma finally said, clearing her throat and starting to unpack her suitcase. "I wonder if he sells jewelry to the stars."

While Gramma took a nap, Roxanne put on her swim suit and a T-shirt and went outside to try to talk to Gus. It had been so long that she was concerned that they would have nothing to say. And it wasn't as though they were able to communicate with each other before he ran away. He was absorbed in skimming the surface of the water with a net attached to a long, metal pole. A small radio on a white wrought iron table played Led Zeppelin. The bushes were immaculately trimmed into round balls, and bougainvillaea bordered the concrete area surrounding the pool. Roxanne sat down on one of the lounge chairs near Gus and applied sun tan lotion to her arms and legs. She opened a *Time* magazine but could not concentrate on any of the sentences.

"Hard work?" she finally said.

"Not really," he said, continuing to fish leaves out of the water.

"It must be nice working outdoors," she said.

"It's okay." There was a long pause. "Wanna go for a ride?" Gus asked her. "The only way to see this town is on wheels."

"Sure," Roxanne said. Maybe they would have more to talk about in Fred's Mercedes.

Roxanne felt as though they had been climbing up a winding road for hours, but she knew it had only been a few minutes. Their conversation was not only lagging—it was as limp as some of the half-dead palm trees on Wilshire Boulevard. They came to an abrupt stop in front of a large stone house on a secluded cul-de-sac.

"Take a guess who lived here," Gus said. Roxanne raised her eyebrows. "Come on. Guess." Roxanne felt as though they were playing the same guessing games they had played as children.

"I don't know. You tell me."

"Maybe if I told you the address, it'd ring a bell."

"Maybe..."

"10050 Cielo Drive..."

"Gus, it doesn't ring a bell. I give up."

"I'll give you a hint. She was one of the most beautiful starlets of the 1960s. She was married to a man from eastern Europe, a director."

"Gus, I still don't know..."

"Now, I'm gonna give you a really big hint. *Valley of the Dolls.* Now, if you don't guess it, you've been livin' in the Dark Ages."

"I've been living in the Dark Ages."

"Dummy, it's Sharon Tate's house. Sharon Tate and Roman Polanski. This is where it all took place. With Tex and the Manson girls and Charlie giving orders to—"

"You mean—"

"To kill. You know. Helter Skelter."

"I'm a little creeped out. Let's go," Roxanne said, hugging her bare arms and looking at the house again.

"This is just the beginning of my tour," Gus said, putting the car into drive as they wound back down Benedict Canyon Road. "Lots of bodies have been found in these woods. Prostitutes. Drug addicts. Hippies. Supposedly, there are more psychopaths in L A than anywhere else in the world, including Amsterdam and Bangkok. You see, they're drawn to the climate and the general wildness of the area...."

Roxanne had a feeling he was making this information up, but she wasn't going to say anything. Twenty minutes later they pulled up to a one-story stucco house on Waverly Drive.

"Now, where are we?" Roxanne demanded. "Aren't you going to show me, like, where Fred Astaire or Lucille Ball live?"

"This is night two—"

"Night two? I don't get it."

"I'll give you a hint—LaBianca...."

"Come on, Gus, I've had enough. Let's go on a studio tour or something."

"If you look real close through the windows, you can still see the outline of the words, 'Death to Pigs,' written in blood on the living room wall."

"You know something. You haven't changed at all since you were making those coffins in your bedroom. You're sick."

"No sicker than anyone else."

"SICK."

"You should feel honored I'm taking you on this tour. I only take the out-of-towners I really like on this tour." Roxanne was stunned, since Gus had never been preferential towards her before. She decided that she'd better sit tight and keep her mouth shut.

Roxanne was frightened while they were speeding down the freeway. Six lanes across and cars whizzing around her and Gus. She had read somewhere that people in LA played a homicidal game of highway chicken with those that they didn't like on sight. Finally they were in downtown LA with the office buildings awash in white smog. Gus pulled up in front of a hotel.

"Nice," Roxanne said, trying to be polite.

"Not just nice. This is the Ambassador Hotel."

"Oh?"

"The very hotel where Robert Kennedy was assassinated. We could even try to sneak into the kitchen where—"

"Let's just drive someplace scenic."

"On the very highway where Jayne Mansfield was decapitated?"

"Gus?"

"Yes."

"Enough of this."

"Enough? What about Marilyn Monroe's bungalow?"

"You heard what I said."

"All right, okay."

Gus headed west and ended up on the Pacific Coast Highway which had enough scenic overlooks of waves and cliffs to satisfy Roxanne. But Gus kept on driving north as if he had no intention of stopping. Since they were spending time doing something he was not particularly interested in, he had become quiet. Finally Roxanne insisted that he pull over, and he did so—grudgingly. They had passed other areas that had much prettier views—this one overlooked a rocky area cluttered with tree limbs, milk cartons, and soup cans—but Roxanne felt that at this point, she could not be particular. Gus got out of the Mercedes, took a couple of deep breaths, lit up a cigarette and threw the match down into the brush below.

"You know, you are getting more and more like Gramma, with your talk of dead celebrities and murder and mayhem," Roxanne said.

"No way. I've seen things...too many things...."

"Like what, for instance?"

"Like trying to break into the music business at the age of fourteen," Gus said, kicking a couple of stones off the cliff onto the beach. "I don't know, I thought maybe I was this prodigy or somethin'...that I was a Stevie Winwood or a Jackson Five. I went around to a lot of the studios, auditioned to be a studio musician. Little did I know that I was a talentless nothin'."

"Who says?" Roxanne demanded.

"I say...where was I...oh, yeah, as I was sayin', money was tight. After a while I started workin' evenings at an Alpha Beta on Santa Monica Boulevard and Fairfax, sacking groceries and making the rounds during the day, tryin' to find people to jam with or start a band with, crashin' with strangers or whoever would take me. I started with the major studios—Warner Brothers, MCA Records, Capitol—and then worked my way down to the smaller labels. One guy by the name of Mr. Lobella had an operation on the side specializin' in young guys—"

"Young guys?"

"Don't get stupid on me, Roxanne. There were lots of hard-up guys like me, hangin' out on Santa Monica Boulevard, waitin' for johns to cruise by in their Lincolns. These same guys would come into the Alpha Beta and buy gum and cigarettes to pass the time between tricks. I soon realized I could make more money on the street corner than sacking groceries."

"And that's how you met Fred...."

"Yup. I guess you could say...I wasn't out there too long."

"You could have ended up at the bottom of that canyon."

"Nah, not me. I was careful. I wouldn't get into just anybody's car. He had to be clean."

"But how do you know who's safe?"

"You know, believe me, you learn real fast. But now..." Gus paused and lit another cigarette.

"But now what?"

"I want out of Fred's house... away from his friends... away from his mother... her lectures. She makes Dad look cool."

"Come on, really?"

"Really."

There was a lag in the conversation, but Roxanne felt as though they were making progress, like Dan Templeton said they would, if only she would act understanding. She realized that Rick's idea for her to lose her virginity was ridiculous. There was no need to prove herself to Gus anymore.

"How 'bout coming back to Kansas City... with us?"

Gus frowned and stubbed out his cigarette with the toe of his sneaker. "Thanks, but—"

"But what?"

"No, thanks."

"Wait a minute, don't—"

"Too much shit under the bridge."

"So? It's the same with us. Only we've had to live with it."

"But it's, I don't know, it's... different with you. And Mom... how's she?"

"She's the same, too... maybe a little different."

"She got that postcard, right?"

"Yeah, we sent it to her."

"Do you... do you think she was always, you know, totally out of it? Like, all her life? Even while we were babies?"

"Yeah, I do. I think Daddy and Gramma covered up for her a lot. And when she lost it in New York, she lost it for good." Roxanne paused for a moment and decided she didn't want to talk about Emma right now. "But back to what we were talking about before... if you really want to get away from this Fred guy, he wouldn't stop you from going off with your family."

"Wait a minute... I know I've put you and Gramma through a lot and I owe you... I guess at this point I owe everybody... but I just can't deal with the scene in Kansas City right now."

"What do you mean?"

"It's hard to explain."

"Try," Roxanne said.

Gus paused before he started speaking. "Okay, okay...you know, when you've been away from a place for a while and feel like you've changed some. But when you go back and look around, everyone and everything is still the same...that's the way I feel about me and Kansas City. Like I've come this far and Kansas City will never change, it will always be the way it is, and everyone will look at me as the same old me because they haven't changed, and they won't see that I've changed.... But LA...LA is always changin' and movin'. You can think you know somebody, and then two weeks later, boom, that person has a totally new house, a new hair style, plastic surgery, and even a different way of talkin', only it would be the same person."

"Come on, Gus..."

"I swear to God, I've seen it happen more than once."

"Emma...Mother would like to see you."

"She said something?"

"Sure, uh, she said she'd like to go shopping with you."

"Shopping? With me? For what?"

"I don't know. She just said she would." Roxanne thought that she'd better change the subject before she got herself in trouble and said something that wasn't true.

"When did she say this?"

"Just this week, when Gramma and I went to see her. Oh, she'd like a postcard just like the one you sent her."

"The same postcard?"

"Well, you know Emma...she likes what she likes."

"Yeah, I guess," he said, grimacing. "Uh, why do you call Mom 'Emma' now?"

"I don't know. It happened in therapy."

"You've been in therapy?"

"Yeah. As a matter of fact, my shrink has written a book about me and my problems called *A Portrait of Adolescence*."

"You're kidding...that's pretty cool. You have a copy with you?"

"Nah."

"Fred's been making me go to a psychiatrist. I'll go as long as he pays."

"You like him?"

"He's okay...actually, he picks his nose when he thinks I'm not lookin'.... He specializes in guys like me."

"Like you?"

"Yeah, like me. You know..."

"Runaways?"

"Uh, no...like fags."

"Oh." There was a lull in the conversation; Roxanne couldn't think of how to respond to what he just said. She figured it was hearing him confess his homosexuality that made it seem more real—and surprising—to her.

"Well, now you know," Gus said, lighting up another cigarette.

"I knew before this," Roxanne said. "It's been obvious for a while."

"Since when?"

"Since the time I caught you putting on my makeup."

"Oh, yeah, that...I forgot all about that...I don't do that kind of stuff anymore."

"Let me say one more thing about why it wouldn't be so bad to come back to Kansas City with us, and then I'll drop it and I won't bring it up again. Sometimes it's true—you get the feeling that you live in a fishbowl in a town the size of Kansas City. You go to King Louie bowling alley, and you see the folks who live two doors down; you go to the Safeway in Prairie Village, and you see a couple of geeks from high school; you go to Putsch's Coffee Shop and see people you worked with at your first job. You start feeling real self-conscious and claustrophobic, like you can't go anywhere without running into someone you know. You think that everyone is talking about you, that maybe you want to be more anonymous living in a larger city. Well, let me fill you in on a little something. People may talk in a town like Kansas City, but essentially people are too busy and preoccupied with their own lives to really care about what's going on in yours. So, what I'm trying to say is that if people find out about you and your new identity or whatever, I say big deal. At the very most, they'll discuss you for fifteen minutes."

"Fifteen minutes. Jeez, that's a long time."

"No, it isn't when you consider how much people talk in a

single day. Do you see what I'm gettin' at?"

"Sorta," Gus said, eyeing her skeptically.

"And remember how old you were when you left. You were *fourteen*. I mean, how many people did you know at the age of fourteen?"

"Plenty."

"Like who?"

"Like . . . plenty. I don't know."

"See what I'm saying. You were too young to make a real impression on anybody. So, what I'm saying is . . . why don't you give your hometown a little time?"

"You sound just like Gramma."

"I do?"

"Speaking of Gramma, don't you think we ought to be getting back?" Gus said, opening the passenger door and bowing to Roxanne as if he were her chauffeur.

In the car, Roxanne had one more question to ask Gus. "Do you ever think about him?"

"Him?" Gus asked.

"You know, him. Dad."

"Oh, that him. I wasn't sure . . . yeah, I think about him all the time. Sometimes I feel so, so . . . "

"Guilty?" Roxanne asked.

"And mad. Sometimes when I think about him, I want to, to . . . do something terrible. Like tear up furniture or shoot a gun at a house. Or wreck a car," Gus said, swerving the car toward the ocean.

"DON'T," Roxanne said, bracing herself against the dashboard. "Have you talked to your shrink about him?"

"All the time. I talk about him all the time. Sometimes I wish Dad would just leave me alone. I hear his voice tellin' me what to do. How to wear my hair, what jobs to get, to please finish high school. He lectures me more as a dead person than he did alive. After he died, I couldn't stand it. It's what I wanted and when it happened . . . well, that's when I knew I had to leave . . . I guess I had been thinkin' about leavin' anyway, you know, to be a musician and all—but no matter how much I talk to Dr. Polsky about it, and try to sort it out in my head, I still feel like I caused it."

"Caused what?" Roxanne asked.

"His death. I caused it."

"Don't be crazy. He died. It had nothing to do with you. It still makes me crazy, too…maybe you should try another psychiatrist. Have you ever thought of that?"

Gus did not answer her question, nor did he say another word the rest of the drive home.

In the car, Roxanne was thinking about everything she and Gus had been through and how each had reacted to their family's troubles. Roxanne had chosen to cling to what she knew, to her home and to Gramma, even though Gramma was not always the healthiest influence; with her outspokenness and her constant criticisms, Gramma was probably the emotional architect of her family's neuroses. Gus at least had broken away from home and formed a new commitment, even though she had doubts about the depth of his feelings toward Fred. But who was she to doubt their relationship? She could hardly maintain her one friendship with Rick. Dammit, that Gramma. She was the one who said Roxanne was jealous of Gus. And she was. She was jealous of his independence, of his rich boyfriend who bought him things; even though he didn't seem interested in those things, at least he had the chance to reject them. She was jealous of Gus preparing fancy meals and watching television with Fred, simple every day things that Roxanne shared only with Gramma. She was jealous of Gus having someone to wake up next to in the morning. Were Roxanne's feelings so transparent that Gramma was always able to read them, even before Roxanne was aware of them?

When they walked into Fred's house, they heard music and counting. The couch and chairs had been moved, leaving a large space in the center of the living room. In front of the piano, Fred was trying to teach Gramma how to cha-cha. Gramma kept stepping on Fred's feet and breaking into a synchronized box step.

"One two, one-two-three. One two, one-two-three. One two, one-two-three. One two, dah-dah-dah. Thatta girl, that's better," Fred said, pausing a second to brush a wisp of hair out of his eyes. "Dahling, you dance divinely," he said, teasing her.

"Oh kids, oh kids," Gramma said, waving while Fred spun

her around. "We had the most divine day. Why, I don't think I've ever used the word, 'divine,' before."

"Everything's divine according to the stars," Fred said, winking at Gus.

"We had daiquiris in the Beverly Hills Hotel lobby and who walked in but—"

"Gramma, *you* had a daiquiri?" Roxanne asked.

"—George Hamilton!"

"And what a tan that man had," Fred said. "Puts the rest of us to shame. Of course, he had a gorgeous blonde on his arm...."

"Man or woman?" Gus asked.

"Freddy, are all the gals in Beverly Hills gorgeous blondes?" Gramma asked.

"Some are gorgeous brunettes, some are gorgeous red heads. And some...some have gorgeous bank accounts," Fred said, pausing to laugh at his own joke.

Gramma started feeling woozy from the daiquiris and dancing, and she held the side of her head with her hand and stumbled over her feet. "Wait a minute, honey," she said, grasping Fred's hand. "I've just got to sit."

As soon as Gramma lowered herself down onto the couch, she patted the spaces next to her. "Come here, kids. You aren't gonna believe what I've got to tell you."

"What?" Gus and Roxanne asked at the same time.

"Well, as you probably know, I think there are only two performers in the world worth seeing. Do you know who I'm talking about?"

"I think I can guess," Roxanne said.

"Then who?" Gramma asked.

"Elvis..." Gus said.

"...and Frank Sinatra," Roxanne said.

"How right you two are. See, I've taught you well. Anyway, I was telling this very thing to Fred in the Beverly Hills Hotel lobby, that before I die I would like to see at least one of them sing in the flesh. In person, that is. Have you ever had a peach daiquiri, Roxanne?" Roxanne shook her head. "Well, honey, you should try one. They're good, but they make my head hurt."

"Go on, Gramma," Roxanne said.

203

"Well, that Fred of yours marched right over to the man behind the desk and he made a few phone calls, and do you know what he found out?"

"What?" Gus and Roxanne asked.

"Elvis Presley is playing at the International Hotel in Las Vegas. Tonight. Imagine that. Well, your Fred asked to use the phone, and he booked two reservations on a plane and at the hotel, and we're leaving to go to the concert..."

"Tonight?" Roxanne asked.

"It's Elvis's last night. It's tonight or never. Now, you kids aren't interested, are you? 'Cause if you are, we could easily book two more."

"Nah. Me and Fred go see him whenever he's in Las Vegas. You two go on ahead."

"How 'bout you, Roxanne."

"I think...I think I'll pass. I'll probably hit myself for not going."

"Then go, for chrissakes. There aren't many times when something like this is possible. You've got to take advantage."

"I guess I'll keep Gus company," Roxanne said, reaching over Gramma's head and giving him a pinch on the shoulder. "Besides, seeing Elvis is not what I've always dreamed about."

"You liked him fine as a child."

"But things aren't..."

"Hey, Gramma, don't worry about Roxanne and me, we'll have a really great dinner. There's this Mexican place in Pasadena where the Hell's Angels like to hang out."

After arguing about where to eat and driving around for more than an hour, Gus and Roxanne ended up splitting egg rolls, Crab Rangoon, and an order of Moo Shu Pork at a Chinese restaurant in Westwood. While they drank tea and picked at their fortune cookies, Roxanne felt that she had made some headway with Gus, that maybe they could learn to put up with each other. She still wasn't sure if she liked him; he was, after all, her brother, so she felt some obligation to feel something. But she wasn't sure if she actually felt "like." Perhaps a stirring of affection, a passing interest in his perverted sensibility. She really hadn't decided yet.

* * *

The day after Fred and Gramma returned from Las Vegas, Gus, Roxanne and Gramma spent the afternoon at Forest Lawn Cemetery in Glendale where many celebrities were buried. They had a contest to see who could find the most celebrity tombstones and, naturally, Gramma won. She found Errol Flynn, Walt Disney, Humphrey Bogart, Irving Thalberg, and David O. Selznick; Roxanne found Clark Gable and Gus found Spencer Tracy and W.C. Fields. They picnicked near the private garden surrounding Walt Disney's tomb, and Gramma said if she weren't so attached to Kansas City, that this was where she would like to be buried. Then, while they ate apples and brownies for dessert, she told them about seeing Elvis live.

"He was truly something. He was all in white, as pretty as a bride. Now, you may wonder why I say 'pretty.' That boy has the prettiest profile I have ever seen. And after every number, he posed like a statue, except, of course, he was sweating. And pearls. Everywhere on his body were pearls—around his waist, his neck, I've never in my born days seen anything like it. And diamonds."

"What about the music, Gramma. Did you like the music?" Gus asked impatiently.

"My goodness, he had the most extravagant, I mean the biggest number of musicians and singers. He had an entire symphony orchestra and some girl singers and electric guitars and drums, to boot. And after songs like "Suspicious Minds"—one of my favorites—he would kick and chop with his hands—"

"Elvis is into karate," Gus told Roxanne, acting as a translator for Gramma.

"He wiped his forehead with his scarf and threw it out to the audience. I would have loved to have caught it. He sang "Love Me Tender" and kissed all kinds of women. He shook the microphone while singing "All Shook Up—"

"Funny, how different people will notice different things," Gus said, looking at Roxanne and making a face. Roxanne nodded and could not stop grinning the rest of the afternoon. She couldn't put her finger on it, but somehow that one comment made things between her and Gus better.

* * *

The rest of the week was right out of the guidebook that Gramma had picked up at B. Dalton. (Fred gave Gus time off from work so that he could do some of the things that he had always wanted to do in California.) They went to the dog races in San Diego, and none of them picked a winning greyhound. They went to Grauman's Chinese Theatre and perused the hand and footprints of movie stars such as Shirley Temple, John Wayne, and Charlie Chaplin. At one point, Gramma got on her knees and placed her hands inside Joan Crawford's cement hand prints. She had a problem standing up, and both Fred and Gus had to lift her up by the elbows. They took a drive up the coast to San Simeon and took Tour A of the Hearst Castle. Roxanne tried to imagine what it would be like to live with marble everywhere she stepped and a zoo in her front lawn. They went to Venice Beach and walked down the boardwalk, watching shirtless weight lifters straining and sweating, and the street people playing their guitars, taking bites of alfalfa sprout sandwiches between songs. Gus, Roxanne, and Gramma took a tour of Universal studios and saw Lana Turner's dressing room, a western shoot-out and unemployed actors and actresses dressed up as cartoon characters. Roxanne and Gus laid out by Fred's swimming pool on a day that had a smog alert. Gus declared it was the best time he had had in years. Gramma declared that she had never been so relaxed, and made Fred and Gus swear that they would start collecting celebrity autographs for her. Roxanne declared that since she had come to Los Angeles she had never felt closer to anybody than she did to Gramma and Fred and even to Gus.

Part III
1977

17

Without Her

Roxanne couldn't believe what was happening to Gramma. It was true that she was acting peculiar, but something else worried Roxanne. It was the look that Gramma had in her eyes, similar to the one that Roxanne's hamster had just before she found him that one fall morning before school, his legs pointing to the top of the exercise wheel. It was a shaky look, as though Gramma was losing her ability to focus and cope with things.

For the last few months, Gramma had become a recluse, transforming her bedroom into a hodgepodge celebrity shrine. She didn't leave it except to bathe and eat the food that the Broadmour Market delivered. Everyday she pored over her old magazines and cut out and taped to her wallpaper anything pertaining to a particular movie star or scandal. Recently, she had seen *Singing in the Rain* on late night television and had become interested in Debbie Reynolds. She was looking through her magazines from 1958-1959 for articles on the break-up of Debbie's marriage to Eddie Fisher, who had fallen for Elizabeth Taylor. To Gramma, Fisher was no catch, but Elizabeth Taylor was a hussy, and worst of all, a homewrecker. Gramma used to like Liz because her life made such good headlines in the tabloids, but she stopped respecting Liz after she had the gall to remarry that rummy, Richard Burton. Gramma's theory about the Liz-and-Dick affair was that they should have left well enough alone. They had divorced once already. Why did they have to do it a second time? But Debbie Reynolds was a different kettle of fish. She was a vivacious girl, a cute girl. Too bad she had to be a victim of that piranha, Liz Taylor.

One of Gramma's most prized possessions was still the program from the Elvis Presley concert. She kept it by her bed like other people would keep the scriptures. The edges were creased, and the pages flimsy from being turned so often. Over her bed was a poster from the movie, *Viva Las Vegas*, that had Elvis and Ann-Margret in a variety of dance poses and a large picture of them embracing in the middle. Gramma also admired Ann-Margret in *Bye Bye Birdie*. What a great little dancer she was in that movie, even though she wasn't wearing a bra under her red dress. In real life Ann-Margret was married to Roger Smith who seemed like a nice, yet boring sort. When Elvis and Priscilla got divorced, Gramma secretly hoped that Ann-Margret and Elvis would start dating again as they had during *Viva Las Vegas*.

Even though Gramma was still fascinated by the stars, she was unable to put forth the energy that was required of a true celebrity watcher. Just the other day at four in the afternoon, she was reading an article about Steve McQueen and Ali Macgraw, and she put it on her lap to rest her eyes and didn't wake up until the following morning. She had never done that before. Gramma blamed the heart pills that her doctor had prescribed; they were what was whittling away at her strength.

She had always resisted any form of medication due to her overall distrust of doctors. They were nothing but a bunch of over-educated, money-mad fools. But she had to admit she was afraid to stop taking her pills. One morning she was so disgusted with them that she poured them all into the toilet. Panicked by what she had done, she managed to scoop them out with a tea strainer.

Everyday, Roxanne kept telling her boyfriend, Willie, how worried she was about Gramma. She couldn't stop thinking or talking about anything else. Maybe she should move back into Gramma's house for a while, take care of her and run her errands, she told him one day at work while he was carrying dirty plates back into the kitchen. It wasn't like Gramma to stay put in her room for so long.

Willie didn't want to alarm Roxanne, but he had seen similar behavior in his own grandmother before she died. What Gramma was going through was a natural part of life. It was a giving up of sorts, a pronouncement that a person was at an age when she was ready to leave her life and loved ones behind. So it was just a matter of waiting, and different people waited in different ways. If they had the strength, they tried to keep busy. Toward the end of her life, Willie's grandmother cooked compulsively—especially desserts—but she frequently substituted or forgot certain ingredients. One time she baked a pecan pie with salt instead of sugar. Another time she forgot flour in a lemon cake. She would serve her creations to Willie, and he would have to brace himself for whatever had gone awry in the kitchen.

Willie promised Roxanne they would both move in with Gramma if she became too frail to take care of herself. At the age of eighty, Gramma did not want anyone helping her. She only wanted her independence and especially her privacy. When Roxanne told her she was moving in with Willie, Gramma practically helped her pack her bags. All along, Gramma had said that it was unhealthy for a young girl to live with her grandmother. But what she really wanted, underneath it all, was the house to herself.

Roxanne and Willie had met almost two years earlier while they were both waiting tables at Harry Starker's. After they dated for five months, she moved into his house at Thirty-ninth and Harrison, which he had inherited from his grandmother. At first Roxanne didn't care for his neighborhood, but she gradually started to like the mix of people—college students, black families, policemen, construction workers, widows, store clerks, architects, hair dressers, Hallmark artists, and insurance adjusters—and she no longer felt so frightened when she drove home alone at night and walked up to the house from her car parked on the street.

Roxanne also felt that they had enough experiences in common to get along; both were virgins when they met. Like her, Willie was close with his grandmother and was emotionally distant from his parents. His father had been an alcoholic all his life. Eventually, he wandered the streets of downtown Kansas City, stopping to drink quarts of beer in front of the ABC supermarket on West 12th Street. His mother had divorced his father at a young age, remarried, and started a new family of her own; she only saw Willie during the holidays.

He was the first guy Roxanne had been attracted to who was a realistic choice for her. He was cute—tall, string-bean thin with straight, black hair—but he didn't make girls' heads turn. As a result, Roxanne didn't feel jealous or insecure when she was out in public with him.

He was a kind person, perhaps a little too kind at times. Once she came home from work and saw him in the front yard trying to coax an injured squirrel to its feet with a stick. He also had a habit of throwing bugs out of windows instead of smashing them with a rolled-up newspaper. Roxanne sometimes complained to Gramma that he was a bit too soft to be a real man, but Gramma reminded Roxanne that her own father had been soft. And wasn't her brother a homosexual? Naturally she would be attracted to that kind of man. Besides, who else could understand her family difficulties the way he did? Gramma had approved of Willie from the very beginning, and Willie adored Gramma, since his own grandmother had also been strong and outspoken.

During the entire time that Roxanne and Willie had known each other, they had dreams which revolved around fast food. Not junk fast food but something delicious and, according to Willie, something foreign. They had both been in the restaurant business for years, and they wanted a franchise of their own. (A real, sit-down restaurant was too much money and responsibility.) They knew what made a franchise successful. First, a catchy concept. Pleasant decor. Consistency. Good service. Word of mouth.

A few years back, before Willie thought about having a franchise, he had been admitted to Gilbert and Robinson's management training program so he could become an assistant manager and be sent out to one of their restaurants. He was guaranteed that if he worked hard and fit in well with the corporation, he would eventually become manager of the restaurant. He lasted in the training program all of two weeks. He discovered he was not a company man. All of those suits made him nervous. But what he did have was ideas about franchises. What about a fast food Chinese restaurant called Hot Woks. Or an Indian one called Hurry Up Curry? Or an Italian one called Fasta Pasta? Willie liked exotic food and was convinced that people in the Midwest needed excitement for their taste buds. He had a theory. Since there were no scenic highpoints in the Midwest—namely an ocean or mountains—that people needed to find this sort of stimulation through food. Willie had a feeling that 'fast food with a foreign flair' would work. That would be the concept he would present to the financial backers. He and Roxanne were not going to be waiters at Harry Starker's forever, he was certain of that. But being a waiter gave him the flexibility to work on his franchise ideas.

Roxanne believed they should go in the direction of health food. People in Kansas City were conservative and probably not open to fast foreign food. And who didn't crave sprouts, avocado, whole wheat bread, organic lettuce and tomatoes, especially in the smothering summer heat when hamburger meat felt like shrapnel in one's stomach. The only health food restaurant in Kansas City was the Golden Temple run by Missouri-born Sikhs who wore white turbans and white pajamas and never spoke above a whisper. Only the most open-minded could go in there and not be put off by those religious cultists. Forget bringing the kids into the Golden Temple—still damp from running through a lawn sprinkler, screaming to see *Star Wars* for the seventh time. Health food for middle America would be Roxanne's marketing strategy. Perhaps they could throw in organic french fries as a compromise. It would work, she was convinced of it. All she had to do was convince Willie.

She also believed that if Gus could have his new business—financially backed by Fred, of course—so could she and Willie. (Roxanne was surprised that Gus and Fred were still together after all these years. She suspected that Gus stayed with him because he was afraid of being poor and alone.) Just a few months back, Gus and his business partner, Ronald, had opened up a card shop on Sunset Boulevard that catered to the Los Angeles gay community. Lots of greeting cards of men wearing black leather jackets and Brando-style leather caps, kissing on the mouth and grabbing each other's buttocks; plastic pens in the shape of penises; fake handcuffs; oriental paper umbrellas with Japanese erotica painted on them; dildoes; gardenia-scented massage cream; notepaper of two men performing fellatio on each other; life-size blow-up nude men with huge genitals. Roxanne and Willie flew into Los Angeles for the opening of the store, and both of them were taken aback by its contents. Fred was especially friendly but tipsy during the opening and kept asking the same questions about Gramma. What was wrong with her? Was she physically ill or was it just psychological? Did Roxanne trust Gramma's doctor? Were they getting the best treatment for her? Toward the end of the opening, Roxanne found Ronald and Gus in the back room, dancing and caressing to taped Donna Summer music. She knew that Fred accepted Gus's dalliances as a matter of course. He probably figured it was the only way to keep Gus content and living in his home.

Gus and Roxanne's relationship had improved over the years. They still fought over the phone about his avocation—at one point he wrote fan letters to the Zodiac killer through the *San Francisco Examiner* and nominated himself as the president of the Richard Speck fan club (in his eyes, 'the pioneer of mass murderers'). But at least they spoke on a regular basis.

Gus and Fred had visited Kansas City four times in the last five years and had always stayed at the Alameda Plaza hotel. (For some reason, they would not stay with Gramma or with Roxanne and Willie. Roxanne figured they wanted their freedom to cruise the gay bars on Main Street.) They also enjoyed being close to the Plaza, since Fred loved to shop and usually ended up spending too much money on sweaters and crystal at Halls.

When Gus and Fred visited Emma at Menninger for the first time in 1973, Fred could not get over how beautiful she was. He swore that she could be in movies playing worried mothers of sex kittens and ingenues. "I've seen so many stars in LA, and she's still so dewy and gorgeous compared to those cheap girls. She looks straight out of a Dove commercial," Fred exclaimed to Gus, Roxanne, and Gramma at the dinner table. "Your mother would do fine in Los Angeles. Besides, most movie stars are crazier than she is."

Gramma smiled at the thought of her daughter being a movie star, but quickly pooh-poohed it. Roxanne had smiled, too. It was remarkable how fresh Emma still looked, and how helpless she actually was. Since Roxanne and Gramma had been around Emma so much, they could deal with Emma's condition with a sense of humor. But Gus saw nothing funny about his mother's illness, and he scowled at Fred for making light of it. Every time he saw his mother after that, he would be in a depression for a few days. He also complained about a recurring nightmare of his father turning into a German Shepherd and gnawing on his arms. Roxanne, too, had been having disturbing dreams about her father dying in a huge bed in the middle of a highway. She went back to Dan Templeton for a brief period of time to figure out why she was having them.

After Emma had been in Menninger seven years, the doctors felt that her schizophrenia was under control as long as she continued with her medication. (At one time the doctors tried taking her off of it, but she had had a violent outburst and pulled the heads off all the geraniums she had planted in the greenhouse.) In May of 1975, she moved into a family care home and worked as a receptionist at the Women's Resource Center a few days a week. Mr. Greene and Dr. Melrose eventually wanted Emma to be an out-patient at Menninger, living in her own apartment and leading her own life. She was still seeing Jerome who was also living in a nearby family care home. They took chaperoned car trips into Topeka and Lawrence and went on group camping trips to Lake Perry under the supervision of therapists.

By late July, Gramma's health had grown worse. She slept most of the day, and her breathing seemed labored. The doctor said her heart was simply giving out. Roxanne wanted to have her moved to a hospital, but Gramma refused. She compromised by having a full-time nurse take care of her at home.

Roxanne no longer just talked about moving in, she did—and so did Willie. They both took shorter hours at Harry Starker's to help take care of Gramma. They each had responsibilities. Willie answered the phone, ran errands, went grocery shopping, and Roxanne paid bills, gave the nurse instructions from the doctor and started a file system for Gramma's celebrity clippings.

Gus flew in from California to be with them and spent most of his time reading *People* magazine out loud to Gramma. She was eager for any news about John Travolta whom she considered very sexy. Gus went to Time To Read newsstand and looked for magazines that had articles about him. Fred promised he would come to Kansas City as soon as he could get away from his jewelry business. For the next couple of weeks, Gramma continued to have problems breathing, and she had to keep a tank of oxygen in her bedroom. Whenever she couldn't catch her breath, which was becoming more frequent, the nurse would cover her mouth with a mask.

When Roxanne drove down to Topeka to tell Emma about Gramma, she was frightened by the mournful sounds that came out of Emma's mouth. "What am I going to do?" she kept saying over and over between sobs.

"You'll have me and Gus. You'll have Jerome," Roxanne said, trying to reassure her, but knowing how she felt. She too wanted to just cry and cry—from fatigue and from imagining the future without Gramma—but there was too much to do and think about.

"I'll be…there'll be…there'll be no one to talk to," Emma cried.

"You'll have us," Roxanne said again. It was all she could think of to say. But she knew that she and her brother were poor substitutes for Gramma's counsel.

18

Death in the News

On August 14, Fred arrived in town and gave Gramma a glossy 8x10 photograph of Fabian in a silver-plated frame, which she hugged like a child would hug a favorite stuffed toy and then dropped it on the bed from exhaustion. Gus was furious at Fred for giving her a picture of Fabian instead of one of Elvis. Fred claimed that he was in a hurry to buy the gift and get to the airport and couldn't find one of Elvis in time.

"And besides," Fred sniffed. "She's fairly out of it. She won't know the difference between Elvis and Fabian. As long as the hair is somewhat the same, she'll be happy."

"You're such an asshole. You can only think of what's convenient for you. How...how can you deceive an Elvis fan on her death bed." With this comment, Gus ran into his old bedroom and slammed the door behind him, only to come running out a few minutes later to check on Gramma's progress.

Emma was crying in the hallway outside Gramma's bedroom while Willie gave her shoulders a massage. Emma did not have the courage to see Gramma while she was dying. Dr. Melrose also felt that it wouldn't be wise to push Emma emotionally. The staff at Menninger did not want to undo all the progress they had made with her. But Gus did tell Gramma that Emma was in the house and that the reason she had not been in to see her was that she had a touch of the stomach flu and thought it might be contagious. Gus knew this excuse sounded flimsy, but he didn't want to risk hurting Gramma's feelings.

Roxanne sat next to Gramma and squeezed her hand while Gramma stared at her granddaughter and then at the picture of

Fabian by her bed. She was too weak to speak and had been put into an oxygen tent and was being fed through IV tubes. The nurse was sponging her forehead to make her more comfortable. Roxanne tried to keep up a brave front, but her lips shook and the tears dripped onto her jeans. How could she function in the world without Gramma? Who would be around to tell her about the way things worked? She was well aware of Gramma's faults and weaknesses, yet there was still no one else whom she loved more—or better.

Another thing she was depressed about was Willie. Everything he did and said was starting to get to her. He just acted too nice sometimes. Not just sometimes—all the time. The way he took her hand at the dinner table for no reason. The way he modulated his voice as if he were always apologizing. The way he brought sweet rolls and coffee to everyone. The way he made everyone's bed and joked with the nurse. All of a sudden it occurred to her. How could he be anything else but nice while her grandmother was dying? She wondered why these bad feelings were surfacing during the time when she needed him the most.

When they first started seeing each other, she had been so grateful for his love, his undivided attention—and for sex on a regular basis. Even though she suspected that he was not a great lover—there was no one else to compare Willie to (not counting Rick Templeton, of course)—she was grateful for having someone to snuggle up to at night. Now, she wasn't so sure. Recently, while lying in bed, Willie had reached out for her, and she had turned her back to him—as she had done the previous five nights. She asked if he were okay, and said that she was sorry, she just wasn't in the mood because of Gramma. Roxanne could tell he was upset, but he refused to talk about it. Instead he got up and sulked for an hour in the kitchen.

Gus sat on the other side of the bed holding Gramma's hand and wishing it was Fred who was dying instead. It was a horrible thought, but he was angry about the Fabian picture. This wasn't the first time he had wished Fred dead. In his mind, he compared the two. Gramma had an unusual angle on life. She was unique. She deserved to live. Fred, on the other hand, was just another rich fag in a long succession of rich fags he knew in Los

Angeles. He was more dispensable, but Gramma... Gramma was not. Gus was ashamed of the way he thought about Fred, but sometimes he couldn't help it. He knew he was undeserving of all that Fred had done, especially all the money he had lavished on him. But Fred made him feel like one of those white-collar prisoners in a minimum security unit—the surroundings were elegant, but he was still behind bars. Trapped. He had always felt that way. Yet Gus chose to stay with him, and in his own ungrateful way, he loved him. And he probably would for a good, long time.

"I, I..." Gramma gasped. Both Roxanne and Gus bent down to the opening of the oxygen tent to savor her words. Fred was in the corner of the room, blowing his nose into a silk handkerchief. He couldn't stand to watch Gramma struggle so, but he knew he wouldn't be able to live with himself if he left the room.

"I guess..." she said faintly.

Roxanne and Gus bent down even closer.

"I guess... I guess... I guess I've had it pretty good." With that, she squeezed Gus and Roxanne's hands, and they heard a soft wheeze in her throat.

"She's peaceful now," the nurse said, pulling aside the oxygen tent and covering her face with a sheet.

"Huh?" Roxanne and Gus said. Neither one was aware that she had just died. They were both waiting to hear what else she had to say.

It was a good thing that Fred and Willie were around to make the funeral arrangements, since Roxanne and Gus were totally incapacitated by Gramma's death. They did not emerge from their bedrooms for two days except to go to the bathroom. At one point, Fred considered hiring a Judy Garland impersonator from the Pink Garter to sing "Over the Rainbow" at the funeral, but Willie convinced him to drop the idea. "It would have been the most memorable funeral ever," Fred said, smoking cigarette after cigarette. "Gramma would have loved it."

Just before Gramma died, Willie had called Dr. Melrose to ask him what would be the best way to deal with Emma. Dr. Melrose felt that she should have as normal a schedule as possible, that as soon as Gramma died, someone should drive Emma home, and she should remain in Topeka until just a few hours before the funeral. Then after the funeral, she should return to Topeka right away and get back into her routine. People with her condition did best when they led highly structured lives.

Like Gus and Roxanne, Emma cried into her bedroom pillow and felt as though everything had come crashing down on her. Gramma used to talk about the time when she would go 'bye bye.' But Emma never believed it would come. Never. She remembered what it was like losing James. She felt as though she had been chopped into pieces. Her skin had fallen from the bone. She no longer felt human. She had become something else. A building. The Empire State. It had happened in a big, strange city. With big, strange noises. But here she was protected. Here she was with family. Gus. Roxanne. Jerome. Willie. Fred. She felt her skin beginning to tear like before. First on her forehead. Then on the bridge of her nose. Then on her neck. But this time she could stop it from splitting. This time she was determined to stay whole.

Roxanne was touched by the turnout at Gramma's funeral. So many people she knew showed up. Dan and Joan Templeton. Rick came in from New York with his beautiful, emaciated girlfriend who was a model. Willie's mother. Jerome. A couple of the psychiatric nurses at Menninger. Mr. Greene. Betty and Susan from Harry Starker's. The Langworthys. The delivery man from the Broadmour Market. Vicki—whom she hadn't seen in years and who happened to read about Gramma's death in the paper—showed up, looking plump and dowdy in a plaid skirt and a cardigan sweater. She was working as a legal secretary at Stinson Mag law firm and going to law school at night. Roxanne couldn't believe how this girl—who for years had only sex on the brain—had changed into a plain, serious woman. She was pleased that her old friend had decided to attend.

The funeral was held at Stine and McClure funeral home where James's service had been. Roxanne could not help sensing the contrast between the two funerals. James's death had been so sudden that nothing about it made sense to Gus and Roxanne. It had taken years for them to unravel some of the questions they had about his death, to make peace with their own misgivings toward him, and to feel strong and secure enough within themselves to mourn.

But there was more of a feeling of community at Gramma's service. Here was a woman whom they all had admired, not only for her point of view on things, but for her eccentricities as well. They could mourn with a clarity of purpose that was missing at James's funeral.

Roxanne felt something else at this funeral. It was a sense of ease. (Her nails—always an emotional barometer for Roxanne—had never been longer or in better condition.) For the first time in her life, she felt relaxed with the idea of her family (or what was left of it), that there was no need to cover up or make excuses for them anymore. If they were going to come apart, it was okay. Fine. She no longer had to make things look good. She no longer needed the lies or the illusions. If her mother was going to flip out again, she could handle it. If her brother was going to take off for Katmandu for four years and not give anyone a mailing address, she'd miss him, but she could handle it. Because she realized she wanted her family to be just what they were. She wasn't sure why—but she did. Maybe it was maturity. Maybe it was the commitment of having to take care of Gramma up until the time she died. Maybe it was her relationship with Willie. There was fulfillment in it, something she could look at and be proud of. And if she and Willie were to break up, she could handle it. At least she thought she could.

There was no priest overseeing the service; the closed casket covered with white roses was in front of the podium. A string quartet from the Conservatory played Bach. Gus and Roxanne thought it was appropriate for Fred to deliver the eulogy, he was the most eloquent person they knew and spoke well in front of a crowd. And they invited any guests to stand up and speak about Gramma after Fred had finished. (Willie had been brought up in the Quaker church, and Gus and Roxanne liked this particular tradition.)

"First of all, let me explain who I am," Fred said, straightening his tie and pulling from his jacket a thin pile of notecards. "I am a special friend of Gus's. And I was a special friend of Gramma's, too. Her full name was Edna Sendall, but everyone always knew her as Gramma, even when she was a much younger woman. After her husband, Edgar, died, she moved here from New Orleans in 1950 with her daughter, Emma. Since she left the South, she considered Kansas City her home. Emma then married James Freedman and had two children, Gus and Roxanne, whom Gramma loved very much.

"Now, Gramma and I first met in 1972 during a difficult time in young Gus's life. He hadn't seen his family for a long while, but he had started to dream about Gramma. Gramma talked to him in his sleep and told him how she wanted to be with him again. I encouraged him to follow through with this unconscious message because I understood its importance, since I come from a very tight-knit family. And I also knew that Gramma was the mechanism that made this family operate. She was the glue, the unifying force. Without Gramma, this family didn't have a chance.

"But enough background information—let's talk about the woman herself. She was resilient. I don't think I need to go into any detail about what this woman experienced—most of you in this room already know. All I can say is that she was unbelievably strong, and every adverse situation seemed to add to her strength.

"She was unusually perceptive about people. She could cut through all the veils that people use to disguise themselves and their actions, and see the truth of the matter. The real person. The real motives. Gus and I believe that she had psychic powers, but she was too much of a pragmatist to believe in what she considered hocus pocus.

"Gramma had a roughness about her, but it was always tinged with affection. She was especially rough with people when they were acting foolish or self-destructive so that she could help them get back on track. Beneath it all, she had a wellspring of good intentions. Anyone who knew her for very long could see that.

"She had a passion for movie stars. She loved reading about their marriages and subsequent divorces, the ups and downs of their careers, their public spats and private times. She was completely and totally absorbed by them. It was almost a scholarly obsession for her. Perhaps she was a frustrated anthropologist. Perhaps she learned so much about human nature by observing the pampered and famous ones in our society. Some of us didn't quite understand her passion, but we all respected it. One day I would like to establish a scholarship in Gramma's name for young men and women to attend acting school in Hollywood."

There was a brief pause. Gus started to stand up, but when Fred didn't acknowledge him right away, he quickly sat down. Roxanne was taken aback by Gus's boldness and asked him for his handkerchief, since she had run out of tissues.

"Gus, is there anything you want to say?" Fred finally asked.

"Uh, yes, there is," Gus said, standing up again, his reddened eyes focused on the casket in front of him. "Roxanne and I were, uh, talking earlier today about, uh, you know, what it would be like without Gramma and that we were both feeling kinda, you know, scared and stuff like that. But I, uh well, like, uh, I really, you know, loved her a lot. Yeah, I really did . . . "

"Yes," Emma said, standing up while Jerome held her by the elbow.

"Yes, you loved her, too, Emma dear?" Fred asked.

"Yes," Emma said, looking at Jerome and then at Fred. "Yes."

"And you'll miss her?" Fred said, feeling like a grade school drama teacher coaching a child with stage fright.

"Yes. Just yes," Emma said, shrugging and laughing nervously.

"I agree with Emma," Willie said, jumping up to his feet and turning to face the rest of the people. "I think we should all say, yes. I think that's what Gramma would've wanted. She wouldn't want us to mourn. Not now, not at any time. She would have wanted us to say yes. So everyone, join me in saying YES, YES, YES, YES, YES, YES," he said, clapping his hands and chanting as if he were at a football game. Soon everyone in the room was chanting along with Willie.

Fred looked around puzzled but then joined in with the rest of the crowd. After everyone finished chanting, he raised his hands to hush them up. Then he deadpanned, "If only Norman Vincent Peale would walk in right now. Wouldn't *that* be fabulous?"

After the funeral and Roxanne's teary recitation of the Lord's Prayer at the grave site, everyone went to Gramma's to eat the cake that Roxanne bought at McClain's Bakery and to drink orange and cranberry juice punch that Gus spiked with champagne. Everyone was quiet and solemn, just as people are while paying condolences, when Rick and his girlfriend Meg pushed their way through the front door all out of breath.

"Turn on the television, turn on the television," Rick said.

"Rick, we can't. Not now," Roxanne said.

"Elvis is dead," Rick said. "It's on the news."

They stood around the small color TV in the den and saw for themselves. Crowds were already starting to gather outside of Graceland. Fans were weeping to the TV reporters. No one could believe it. No one on television could say anything except that they would miss him and would someday meet up with him in heaven. Elvis's fiancee, Ginger Alden, was interviewed. She was the one who found him dead in his bathroom. One black woman wearing a tank top compared the news to Martin Luther King's assassination.

"Maybe Gramma will finally get to meet him," Gus said.

"I did," Rick's girlfriend, Meg, said. "In New York. A bunch of girls from my agency attended a party in his hotel suite after his concert at Madison Square Garden."

"What was he like?" Roxanne asked.

"He didn't say much. He wore sunglasses the entire time and didn't move from the couch. He was surrounded by these flabby bodyguards, and whenever he wanted to talk to a girl he would tell one of them to bring her over. He acted like he was a plantation owner, and we were the slaves. You can't act like that, even if you are Elvis Presley. Not in New York, at least. We left early, we were so turned off. Plus he was messed up on something."

"It's appropriate that he and Gramma died around the same time. There's something karmic about it," Rick said, giving Roxanne's shoulder a quick squeeze. Roxanne looked at him and wondered if she still felt something for him. She decided that he was still attractive enough and that she would probably go to bed with him if the opportunity ever arose, perhaps to prove that she was more sexually adept than she used to be. But then again, Roxanne was no competition for gorgeous Meg. Yet sometimes a shared past provided that necessary extra edge.

Rick had moved to New York to paint, and his work was currently in a group show at the Vorpel Gallery in Soho. Just think. If Roxanne went to bed with Rick, she might be sleeping with someone who was going to be famous. Gramma would not have disapproved of that.

"I think it's time that we pay tribute," Fred said, raising his glass of punch to the television set.

"Tribute? Tribute to what? To whom?" Gus asked Fred in disgust. He was getting tired of Fred's high-minded attitude and wanted to go get drunk at the Dover Fox, meet an out-of-town salesman and get lucky.

"To Gramma. And to the man himself. We need to dedicate ourselves, gather our collective strength, change thought into action, follow through with our feelings," Fred said, pointing his finger in the air.

"You wouldn't, I mean, you couldn't be thinking," Roxanne said, worried for a moment that Fred had suddenly freaked out and was suggesting that they all commit mass suicide in order to join Elvis and Gramma in the great beyond.

"Yes, I was thinking a trip to Memphis would do us a lot of good. It would be, uh, what's the word. Cathartic. Yes, it would be cathartic."

"We have to go now," the Langworthys said, their smiles strained as they walked toward the front door. "It's been a lovely funeral." The others who had been over had left long before.

"It'll take you some time to drive to Memphis," Jerome said, checking his pants pockets. "Darn, I don't have my atlas with me." Emma leaned over and whispered something to Jerome, and they both began to laugh.

"What is it, you two?" Roxanne asked.

"Oh, nothing, nothing. It's just that...that...that your momma is sure a peach," Jerome said. Emma blushed.

"I think it's serious between them," Fred whispered to Gus. "You better watch out. I hear wedding bells."

"I think it's a terrific idea," Willie said, jumping to his feet. "What a better way to honor Gramma. By going to Elvis's funeral, that is."

"She would have wanted to go," Roxanne said, her eyes getting watery.

"So, we should go in her place," Willie said.

"You think?" Roxanne asked. "Really?"

"I had a chance to go to Altamont and turned it down," Fred

said firmly. "I've always regretted it. I would have liked to have seen Mick Jagger singing "Sympathy for the Devil" while the crowd flinched during the stabbing. Mass hysteria is so interesting, isn't it, Gus?"

"You turned down Altamont? Man, you weren't thinking," Gus said, tapping Fred's forehead with his finger.

"I love this boy's dark side," Fred said, turning to Gus. "It makes him seem almost dangerous."

19

Graceland

Jerome and Emma begged to go to Memphis, but Gus and Roxanne refused to be responsible for them. What would happen if one of them had a mental relapse while buying peanut brittle at Stuckey's outside of Columbia, Missouri? Willie ended up driving them back to Topeka that evening. The entire way back, Emma whined that she was so disappointed that she didn't want to go back to work for an entire month. Jerome talked non-stop about the car trips he used to take with his mother, and how she couldn't have backed out of her driveway without him telling her where to go.

While Willie was gone, Roxanne, Meg, and Rick went to the grocery store and stocked up on Pepperidge Farm cookies, grapes, plums, oranges, Cokes, apple cider, and Coors beer. Rick decided he would do a series of paintings on Elvis's funeral and bought a new instamatic camera to capture images and ideas. Meg wanted to go for what she called the media/pop culture funeral of the seventies. After all, she wasn't working on a degree in sociology from NYU for nothing. Gus and Fred picked up new styrofoam coolers and went to a gas station for maps.

The next morning the six of them woke up at 4:30 A.M. and were on the road to Memphis in Roxanne's Cutlass by six. Gus kept switching radio stations to see what was going on at Graceland. Many of the rock stations had sent reporters there to provide listeners with an hourly update. The crowd was growing by the thousands. Some reporters were predicting that close to a 100,000 fans would cram outside the gates of Graceland. At ten-thirty they picked up Whoppers at a Burger King outside of St. Louis. They didn't want to stop; from what the reporters were saying, Elvis's body was going to be brought from the funeral home to Graceland around noon for a two o'clock open-coffin service for family and friends.

Thirty miles outside of Memphis on Highway 55, cars were bumper to bumper, inching their way towards Elvis's home. At three-thirty, the six of them pulled up to a Best Western motel on the outskirts of town and rented two rooms. They then drove toward Graceland and managed to find a parking spot in a shopping center a mile from the mansion. They got out of the car and walked, keeping track of the events on a transistor. They overheard two local men bragging about their association with Elvis. One said that several years ago Elvis had stopped him on the street and given him a Cadillac for no good reason; the other said that one night around midnight he had accompanied Elvis's entourage to a nearby amusement park. "He was never true to his wife," he remarked. "He always had gals hangin' all over him, even on the ferris wheel."

Outside of the mansion, people were hawking crude buttons and T-shirts out of the trunks of their cars. Fans were lined up for miles in order to get inside Graceland to view the body. The temperature had climbed into the nineties, and people were fainting in heaps on the sidewalk.

The six of them slithered toward the front of the line and made their way into the Southern colonial mansion. No one spoke out of respect for the deceased. Roxanne felt as if she were entering a holy shrine. Two National Guards stood in the foyer. Under a crystal chandelier lay Elvis in a copper-lined casket. He was wearing a white suit, a blue shirt, and a white tie. The mortician had covered his face with dark makeup, and his hair was sprayed stiff. One woman tried to lean over and kiss him, but her husband pulled her away. Gus had never seen so many people crying at once.

When they stepped outside, they were overwhelmed by the smell of flowers made thick by the strong afternoon sun. There were over a thousand flower arrangements on the lawn in the shape of teddy bears, hound dogs, guitars and crowns. Behind the walls of the grounds, the press had set up tables; they were typing and shouting into telephones as if they were reporting on a war in the Middle East.

Fred suggested that they go somewhere for coffee and then
return to Graceland later that evening to observe the crowd.
Fred was keeping a journal about the funeral. He knew a lot of
people in the movie and television industry, and he was toying
with the idea of putting together a treatment based on his experiences in Memphis. The six of them passed by a trailer parked
on the street that had its door open, and Rick stopped to look
inside. An older, heavy-set woman, wearing a flowered print
dress and thick-soled shoes, put her finger to her lips and
motioned them all to come in. They stared in amazement. She
had created an altar to Elvis with at least forty candles burning
and a dozen photos in picture frames set up on a card table covered with a heavily embroidered shawl. A string of rosary beads
was draped over the largest photograph of Elvis in the middle of
the table; it was a publicity shot of him taken in the fifties. A
stick of incense burned from a pewter holder. "How Great Thou
Art" played from a record player in the corner.

"All pilgrims are welcome," she said, wiping her hands on her
dress. "We are all brothers and sisters in our sufferin'." She knelt
down in front of the altar and crossed herself. Rick snapped a
picture of her with his camera, but put it away when Meg shot
him a disapproving look. "Please join me in my prayers." They
all got down on their knees, and Gus bit the insides of his mouth
to keep from laughing. Willie reached out for Roxanne's hand,
but she slid it away from him. She noticed there were actual
tears in Willie's eyes. Fred got out his note pad and scribbled a
few words.

"Lord Jesus Christ, help deliver our dear Elvis Presley to our
heavenly Father. He made millions happy with his inspirational
music, he made me happy, he made these kind folks happy. Give
me the strength, O Lord, to keep the flames burning, to keep his
memory alive for the coming generations. For it is the children,
born and unborn, who are what truly count in this world, O Lord.
Let them, too, be touched by Elvis's greatness, and although we as
his fans will never be blessed again with his physical greatness, we
will keep his spirit alive. Help us to gather the means to do this.
Help us be the guardians of the flame. Amen."

The record was over, and the woman got up to place the nee-
dle back at the beginning. She then fetched a coffee can from

under the altar with the Elvis Presley Fan Club stenciled on its side and passed it around. They each dug up a quarter to con- tribute to the cause and then got out of the trailer as quickly as they could. One woman who was waiting outside said to a few people standing around that she would be able to hear Elvis sing again once he was buried. All she would have to do was put a drinking glass upside down on top of his grave and listen. "I did it with Patsy Cline, and I did it with Buddy Holly, and I swear to God it works."

"This is simply unbelievable," Meg exclaimed, twirling around. "It's the real America. And wasn't that woman in there something, Rick? She was, I mean, totally off the wall treating Elvis Presley like he was some sort of god. . . . "

"Oh, shut up," Willie said, turning to Meg. "You and your. . . your New York bullshit looking at people as if they're a strange, new breed. Can't you see that that's what people are like? And they should be appreciated, not ridiculed. This *is* the real America! You and Rick are the ones who are freaks. Just fuck you. Fuck you all, for that matter," he said, storming off.

"Willie, wait," Roxanne said, running after him and grabbing his arm.

"Go 'way," Willie said, pulling her hand off. Roxanne had never seen Willie so angry.

"Let him cool out," Rick said, holding her back. She looked up at him. She had way too many questions going around in her head. Everything seemed so tenuous. Would she and Willie last? Would she ever sleep with Rick? Would he and Meg last? What about Gus and Fred? Or Gus and his business partner, Ronald, for that matter? Or Jerome and Emma? Could they stay in Memphis long enough for Elvis's funeral and still be on speaking terms? She almost felt dizzy from all these questions concerning people and love and the uncertainty of it all. It was as if she were part of a nighttime TV drama that was suffering from low rat- ings. But when a car passed by blasting "Thunder Road" on the radio, she somehow, for a moment, felt better.

A Note about the Author

Ann Slegman's poems, stories, articles, and book reviews have appeared in numerous magazines, including *New Letters, Helicon Nine, Reader's Digest, New Letters Book Reviewer,* and *McCall's;* and in the anthologies *Kansas City Out Loud II (BkMk Press)* and the *Helicon Nine Reader.* She has served as an editor for *McCall's* and *Helicon Nine* magazines; and as director of The Writing Center at Park College, where she was an assistant professor. She is currently the resource development director of The Writers Place in Kansas City. She received a B.A. from the University of Colorado and a M.A. from Brown University in creative writing. *Return to Sender* is her first novel. She lives in Kansas City with her husband Tom Isenberg and their two children.